D0953387

THICKER THAN WATER

THICKER

THAN

WATER

KELLY FIORE

WITHDRAWN

HARPER TEEN
An Imprint of HarperCollinsPublishers

HarperTeen is an imprint of HarperCollins Publishers.

Library of Congress Control Number: 2015947626
ISBN 978-0-06-232473-3

Typography by Ray Shappell
15 16 17 18 19   CG/RRDH   10 9 8 7 6 5 4 3 2 1

First Edition

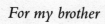

For my brother

THE BEGINNING IS THE WORD AND THE END IS SILENCE.
AND IN BETWEEN ARE ALL THE STORIES.

—Kate Atkinson, *Human Croquet*

APRIL

THIS IS THE TRUTH. THE WHOLE TRUTH. NOTHING BUT THE TRUTH.

I was seventeen, it was weeks from graduation, and I was crouched behind a foldout couch, crushing a pile of pizza boxes and trying not to gag from the smell. The footfalls on the basement floor were close; they stuttered to a stop, then moved in the other direction. For a moment, it was just me, the rotting pizza, and a busted-up beanbag chair leaking tiny Styrofoam beads onto the trash. Like snow, they made my surroundings feel almost clean and a little less desperate. But desperate was a state of mind I had started to get used to.

I tried to remember something beautiful.

I tried to remember something real.

Like how I used to hear my brother's name and picture a strong, healthy boy. Always bigger, always faster—like a hurricane or a tornado. I was just the breeze that followed.

Back when we were kids, the only time Cyrus and I were

ever equal was on the backyard swing set's glider. With our weight evenly distributed, our bodies aligned, we moved as one person. I'd felt delirious with the momentum, the up and down of it. Those were the times when I was just as good, just as steady as my sure-footed older brother. My arms and legs and hands were, like his, considered assets.

When Mom would call us in for lunch, it was a contest to see who'd jump off first. Whoever was left on the glider would have to slow to a wobbly stop before safely getting down. When I was my smallest self, Cyrus used to let me win. When we got older, though, he'd stick out his tongue and tumble off, leaving me airborne and stranded like someone he barely knew at all.

And lately?

Well, lately I just stared at Cyrus as though he might disappear, as though his flesh would fizzle and fade away. There were days when I wished he would.

And now he had.

Still squatting behind the couch, I waited through another minute of uncertain silence before moving to stand up. As I gripped the edge of a nearby trash can, I felt something ooze between my fingers. I think it was what was left of my heart.

"FREEZE!"

And I did, half of my body still concealed behind the couch and ankle-deep in garbage.

"Down on the ground! Now! Now!"

I fell to my knees like it was time to pray, but it was way

too late for that. Somehow the officer's handcuffs felt far less painful than the ache deep in my body.

"You have the right to remain silent. Anything you say can and will be used against you in a court of law."

Anything I said *should* be used against me in a court of law.

My brother was dead.

My brother *is* dead.

And I'm the one who killed him.

SIX WEEKS LATER

JUNE
PRESENT DAY
1

"YOU HAVE TO TALK TO ME, CECELIA."

Jennifer, my public defender, stares at me like I'm the laundry—an undesirable task that's never really finished, but keeps needing to be done. Over and over and over again.

I know she wants to start "prepping me" for my hearing. That's what she calls it—prepping. I've asked her not to use that word, that *prepping* reminds me of pom-poms and Lady Speed Stick. She doesn't laugh. Jennifer never laughs at what I say. That's why I trust her.

Lately, when I'm unsuccessfully trying to fall asleep, I imagine I'm online. I miss computers. I can practically feel the keyboard under my fingertips. I open a search engine. I type in my name.

The same word pops up first every time.

MURDERER.

I swallow. Jennifer is staring at me, her pen pressed hard against her legal pad. I look away and start grinding my teeth.

"I *am* talking to you," I finally mumble. I just knew there wasn't anything to say—nothing that meant anything.

She sighs, leaning back in the metal folding chair. Jennifer's tired. Tired of me, probably, but also tired of her job. I don't think she really likes being a public defender. When she caps her pen and shoves back her chair, I know she's pissed. She stands up and walks over to the wall, looking at it like it's an exit.

"There's someone I want you to meet," she says to the wall. "She's a therapist."

"*Another* shrink?"

I'm tempted to slam my head against the metal edge of the table. Instead, I tug on the ends of my hair. Frayed black strands fall out painlessly, and I'm sort of disappointed.

"*Shrink* is a verb, not a noun," Jennifer says. "Besides, you've only spoken to the court-appointed psychologist. The prosecution and the defense can have you evaluated by their own experts."

I'm not really against the idea of being evaluated. I'm *used* to being evaluated. I was a straight-A student. I scored a 5 on the AP Calc exam. I got the most strikes when I went bowling. I had the fewest strokes when I miniature-golfed.

I stare at Jennifer's back, at the place where a discreet seam runs down the center of her navy suit jacket. If bodies were divided in half, I wonder what would hold us together. I look down at my hands.

"Look, CeCe . . ." Jennifer's voice is closer, and I see she's moved back to her chair. Her right hand is resting on the table between us. "I know that this isn't easy for you, but I have a job to do here, and that job is to prove that the decisions you made weren't decisions at all—that they were involuntary reactions of a traumatized girl. It's the difference between acquittal and incarceration."

I don't want to think about that. Instead, I look around at the pale walls, calm and creamy like after-dinner mints.

Jennifer was the one who came up with the Brilliant Plan that got me here. This place, the Behavioral Therapy unit, is like a hospital, but it's inside Piedmont Juvenile Correctional Facility. A group of us are housed here together with twenty-four-hour suicide surveillance and mandatory therapy. By getting me enrolled in their ninety-day program, Jennifer said she could prove to the judge that I was "seeking and receiving treatment for my dissociative tendencies and destructive behaviors." She said I should be grateful—that I could be stuck in the general population. Here, there's less likelihood of me getting my ass kicked or my bed pissed in.

"So, then, why am I seeing this . . . therapist?" I ask her.

"Because she's different."

For the first time in—well, ever, actually—I see the hint of a smile on Jennifer's face. It's empty, though—all mouth, no eyes.

"Trina specializes in trauma therapy. She works with kids from troubled homes—orphans, teen prostitutes, the homeless."

"Is she a talk-show host?"

Jennifer gives me a dirty look and ignores my snarkiness. I don't know why I said it. She's just trying to help. "She uses unique methods with her patients. I think you should try some different interventions before we face a judge."

"I'm not big on hypnosis."

"Good, because you'll need to be awake and focused when you work with Trina."

"Fantastic. There's nothing I like better than being conscious."

Jennifer stands again and tucks her pen into her inside jacket pocket. I watch her scan the table, making sure she didn't leave any stray staples or paper clips that I could stab myself with.

"Just give her a chance, CeCe. Can you do that?"

I shrug. I was bluffing about the hypnosis. I'd do just about anything to escape reality. I used to be able to Etch A Sketch my life away—give myself a good shake, fall asleep at night, and the next morning things felt blank and bright, open to possibility.

Now my nights are full of anything *but* sleeping. It's like the only thing my brain knows how to do is remember.

"When is she coming?" I ask as Jennifer heads for the door. She juggles her briefcase and keys in one hand while she slides her ID card over the electronic sensor. The lock clicks and she pushes the door open with her foot before turning to look at me.

"Tomorrow, maybe? The day after? She'll come by before our next appointment."

I nod and mumble, "Okay."

I stand up as Tom, the security guard, comes in to get me. He's wearing Uniform #2. Tom has three uniforms that he washes and wears in rotation. You can tell which day it is by which stain is on his shirt—today it's the ketchup, still pale orange and embedded in the fibers like a scar.

"See you later, CeCe."

Jennifer always says good-bye with her back turned, already in the process of walking away. If I were more sentimental, I'd say it's because she hates leaving me here. In reality, I know she thinks I'm exactly where I should be.

"Okay, Tom," I grumble, "take me back to my cell."

Everything about Tom is dark and thick—his neck, his torso, his legs. A chip right off the Mr. T block.

"We don't call them cells, CeCe. Consider this a hospital— a place to get well."

"Sure, whatever you say."

I have years of lockup to look forward to. Might as well start "prepping" myself for the future.

I've learned that when you squint, everything looks the same no matter where you are. You can pretend you're going blind or popping muscle relaxers—anything that blurs your vision enough to make things seem hazy and acceptable. So that's what I've been doing since I got to Piedmont—longer than that, if I'm being honest. It also explains some of my bruises; I keep running into door jambs and shelving units. I'm peering down at a tender purple splotch on my arm when Aarti gets back from therapy.

Aarti is a lot of things. She's my roommate. She's Indian. She's beautiful. She was married to a hippie psychology professor she met in Calcutta when she was seventeen. But when she moved with him to the States, she learned what being married to him really entailed.

First, her husband demanded that she pose naked for one of his Human Sexuality classes. After that, he started "lending her out" to friends, like a movie everyone has to see. Like a carpet steamer. Like a whore. Which is probably why she shot him. It's too bad he survived, if you ask me.

I know this for the same reason everyone else does—because of group therapy. If it's your first time, you have to talk. At least, you're supposed to. Aarti was surprisingly forthcoming. It took me a few sessions to be honest, and even then I said only what I had to.

"Yes, I'm here until my hearing."

"Yes, I'm facing serious charges."

"No, I'm not ready to talk about it."

Aarti's hair isn't as black as mine, but it must have been once. Now it's almost burgundy—the color of someone's lipstick or nail polish. I wonder if that's something she wanted to do or if it was her husband's idea.

"Do you want lunch?" she asks me, unfolding a cardigan sweater and pulling it on over her blouse and slacks. We get to keep our street clothes in Behavioral Therapy, but that isn't doing Aarti any favors. She dresses like someone's mom—librarian chic.

"I'm not hungry."

She nods, pushing up her sleeves. The material bunches around her elbows.

"Do you want me to sneak something back for you?"

I shake my head and watch her tie her shoes, one sleeve of her sweater beginning to slip back down her arm. I bet she pushes it back up again. I'll bet she does it a dozen times before giving up, before letting the sweater win. I want to stop her, to tell her everything comes undone eventually. Sometimes it takes only a matter of seconds for your whole life to unravel.

Then I remember why she's here and I figure it's a lesson she's already learned.

"Actually . . ." I trail off when Aarti turns back around to look at me. Then I look down at my hands. "Maybe you could bring me an apple or a banana or something? For later?"

She shrugs. "Sure—no problem."

Her amenable nature feels like a gift. I wish I could let myself get closer to her. We've been sharing this space for weeks and I've barely been able to hold a normal conversation with my own roommate. Then again, it's not like this shit is college. And it's not like she owes me gossip sessions or lecture notes. We're both here as a means to an end. I wonder if her potential end feels as impossibly empty as mine.

Once the door shuts behind her, I lie back on the twin

bed and look at the textured ceiling. I've spent hundreds of hours looking at every different surface in this room: above me where the plaster swirls in cake-icing peaks, minus the sugary sweetness; below my feet at the linoleum peel-n-stick tile that I'm pretty sure is covering another, even uglier layer of flooring; and the walls, evenly coated in a pale green color that I assume is supposed to be calming.

I like the walls best; the surface ripples and flattens at points where fists or feet or foreheads slammed into the drywall, then were filled back in with plaster. All those spots are strangely smooth, like a useless, obvious cover-up, just a Band-Aid over a bullet hole.

For a long moment, I consider following Aarti, going to eat and being social and not "isolating myself within the confines of my thoughts," or whatever Dr. Barnes likes to accuse me of doing when I stay in my room for too long. I just don't want to sit there at dinner and listen to everyone chatter on like there's real hope in their future. I don't want to watch them bite and chew and swallow their food like they're fueling something when my only impulse is to abstain. The truth is that I'm never hungry anymore and I don't miss the sensation. I don't miss a lot of things, considering what's waiting for me out in the world. Or what isn't waiting for me, really. In fact, the only things I wish I had more of were books. Like a hotel room, our nightstand is stocked with a paperback King James edition of the Bible. I've yet to figure out the ethics of this; I can't imagine the Bible-thumpers look too kindly on convicts. Honestly, though, it's kind of nice to have access to words, however difficult they may be to swallow.

I've been mingling in Psalms for a few days. At first, they put me to sleep. I'd see patterns in the sentences, a rhythm that made my eyes droop. But yesterday I came across a quote I keep rehashing.

Stand in awe and sin not: commune with your own heart upon your bed, and be still.

I like it—it gives me an excuse to sit here, motionless, and consider it a part of my healing process. You can't really be doing the wrong thing when you're hardly doing anything at all. Of course, I don't think God would be too thrilled that I ripped out the page and stuffed it under my mattress. Just one more strike against me, I guess.

I pull it out now and start folding between the sections. I remember how, in Geometry, we'd make these paper triangles, isosceles and equilateral, and color them with markers. Which reminds me of another thing I miss—bright colors. Colors that commit to a hue that isn't muted or toned down or a watery, weak version of its former self.

I crease the page along the margins; the paper is almost too thin to tuck into itself without sliding back apart. Once I've finished folding, I admire the three corners, perfect and crisp. I like when things are even—equal angles, symmetrical sides. It makes me feel like there's still such a thing as order in my life, as though I still have some control in this new world I never expected to live in.

2

MOST DAYS, I'M UNIMPRESSED WITH THE SCHEDULE OF EVENTS.
There should be a maximum number of therapeutic
interventions one person should have to endure in a twenty-
four-hour period. On Monday, the day I'm scheduled to start
individual therapy, I request to speak to the social director.
Dr. Barnes doesn't think I'm funny.

"Group first. Then you'll meet with your new therapist."

"Great. You know, this is like Sunday school after
church. Back-to-back isn't always the way to go when
you're attempting to convert me."

"I'm not attempting to do anything, Cecelia. I believe
your lawyer explained the situation—you'll be seeing Dr.
Galinitus as part of your rehabilitation."

God, I *wish* this was rehab. Then I could chain-smoke
and tell stories about my fictional promiscuity and imaginary abusive ex-boyfriends. Instead, I've had to find a way

to function in my own skin.

"One of the guards will escort you from group to the E-wing. Dr. Galinitus will be waiting for you there."

Like any good doctor, Barnes wants to find an answer, a cure for my ailments. That's the only way he can really be successful. Medicine isn't about baby steps; it's about miracles.

In group, everyone has to play a role. There are those who are ready to talk and those who want to be introspective. There are the angry ones, the friendly ones, the distracted ones. The ones who are quiet fall into two categories— introspective or brooding. I like to brood. It gives me an excuse to glower at people and pretend to be surly when I'm actually just counting the pinholes in the ceiling panels in an effort to make the time pass more quickly.

Today's topic is regret. This is a shit topic. Talking about our regrets makes everyone feel worse than they did an hour ago. We're supposed to leave group every afternoon when there's nothing left to say. Topics like regret leave us with nothing left to believe in. Regret forces us to relive the moments we hate the most—the moments that drove us into spiraling downfalls, the moments where we stopped living and started surviving.

I sit next to Aarti today. Tucker is on my other side. He's seventeen, like me, and his hair and eyes are the exact same color as the carpet—industrial brown. Unlike the carpet, though, his hair looks soft and silky in a way that makes me want to touch it. When he looks up at me and smiles, his eyes crinkle like he's actually happy to see me. I grind my teeth and turn away. The last thing I need to do here is start seeing something beautiful in the disaster around me.

Cam is our group monitor—despite the fact that Dr. Barnes is technically in charge, Cam facilitates discussion and, in general, annoys the shit out of all of us. She's an "alumna"—her word—of the program, which somehow does not have the same distinction as being an alumna of Harvard or even Bumfuck Nowhere Community College. Cam seems to think that her time here should make her trustworthy or admirable or something.

Cam is an idiot.

"So, Aaron. Give us one regret. Something you wish you'd done differently."

Cam looks at Aaron. Everyone else looks at Aaron. I look at Aaron's hair. It's very distracting—white blond, the kind that only little kids have. Aaron is seventeen, and tries to look tough, but he usually just ends up looking like an angry fifth grader. I try not to watch his eyebrows as he talks. When his mouth moves, they go up and down like albino caterpillars.

"I regret being born."

"Aaron," Cam says slowly, like she's talking to a child, "you can't regret something you didn't do yourself. Your birth is someone else's decision to regret." She pauses. "Or not regret," she adds hastily.

"Yes, you can," I say.

"Ah, Cecelia," Cam says, leaning back in her chair. "Does this mean you're going to start contributing in group?"

I ignore her and look at Aaron. "You can regret the actions of others. At least, when they're responsible for your actions. When your actions are just *reactions*."

Aaron's pale hair sways as he nods. I bet he's Swedish.

"If I'd never been born, I'd never have made bad choices in the first place," he says. "I'd never have chosen to drop out or start stealing cars. I wouldn't have beaten the shit out of that guy and landed myself in here. I wouldn't have had the chance to."

Cam looks irritated.

"What about you, Cecelia?" she asks.

I shake my head. "I'm passing."

She narrows her eyes. "You've passed for the last six weeks."

"I've only *been here* for six weeks."

"So why is it that you can comment on other people's contributions but can't make some of your own?"

"I have a regret," Tucker interrupts, leaning forward and resting his hands on his knees.

My head whips around. Cam glares at me before turning to Tucker. I watch Tucker, too, unsure whether he is trying to save me or steal the spotlight. Either way, I'm grateful.

"I regret my bad decisions."

"Such as?"

Tucker shrugs. His hands are squeezing his knees methodically and I start feeling warm and nauseous.

"What decisions have you made that were bad?" Cam presses.

"I did a lot of things to my parents. To make them not

trust me, I mean. To disappoint them."

Leslie, a sixteen-year-old with curly hair, rolls her eyes.

"Please. Who here *hasn't* disappointed their parents?"

Tucker's voice sharpens. "I bet you didn't drive your mom's car through the side of the house. Or steal five grand from your sister's college fund."

Leslie shrugs. "Only 'cause my folks didn't have that kinda money."

Everyone looks at Tucker. He looks down at his hands.

"There's nothing I can do about it. It's done, it's over, and I'm here. I just have to find a way to move on."

Cam looks satisfied, nodding at Tucker like he's said the right thing.

"Good. Now *that's* a revelation. You can regret things as much as you want, but it's the acceptance of those things, the understanding that you can't or don't need to change them, that makes a regret something smaller—that makes it a memory."

How can a memory possibly be small? Mine overshadow all my thoughts.

Leslie is next on the Regret Train, but I'm distracted by Tucker's hands, still grasping his knees. His fingernails are bitten down and raging, but not actually bleeding. I watch his fingers press and release, press and release, the red rushing to the tips before fading back toward his knuckles. It's almost as though his blood is trying to get out. As though it's running for the exit and, like the rest of us, hoping somehow to escape.

I'm sitting in one of the private therapy rooms when I meet my new therapist. Dr. Trina Galinitus is a slip of a person. She's barely there. Meeting with her is almost like talking to myself. When I squint, I can't see her at all.

"Jennifer tells me you're having some trouble reconciling your role in your brother's death."

I take a deep breath. "I just don't want to talk about it."

Trina pushes her glasses farther up the bridge of her nose. Her hair is tied back tight.

"Well, one of our goals is to make you want to talk about it—or at least to make you comfortable talking about it, and about anything else you want to share with me."

I squint. Now she's bald, glasses-less, and pale as chalk dust.

"I have an idea for you," Trina says. "A strategy for you to try."

"Is it time travel?"

She reaches into her bag, pulls out a black-and-white speckled composition book and a freshly sharpened pencil. The pencil says *Parsons Cognitive Therapy Group* in white letters up the side.

"We're going to do some visualization techniques."

I frown. "Jennifer said this wasn't a hypnosis thing."

"It's not. Visualization is something you do while you're completely present. It's something your conscious mind is responsible for."

I don't need to squint this time for my vision to blur. Soon there are two Trinas, and I don't like either of them.

"I can't do this." Terror runs through my body like water or blood. It circulates, then condenses into a hard lump in my chest.

Trina looks genuinely surprised.

"Why not?"

I stand up and there's a sudden movement through the window by the door. Tom is hovering there, watching me. *No worries, Tom. I'm not going to kill her.*

I walk over to the wall, placing my hand on the cool blue surface.

"Visualization is a therapeutic way to find insight," Trina says to my back. "To find closure."

I shake my head. My eyes are almost completely closed.

"I know it won't be easy, Cecelia. All I'm asking is that you give it a shot."

I turn around and look at her. She reminds me of a guru. A yoga instructor. I bet she's one of those biodynamic, raw-food vegans who eat nothing but sprouts and grasshoppers.

"Fine," I finally say. If nothing else, it'll give me an opportunity to zone out and imagine a place completely unlike this horrible, claustrophobia-inducing room.

"Excellent." She opens the composition book and jots a few notes. "Okay, sit down and close your eyes."

"Seriously?"

"Yes, seriously."

When I sit facing the window, light floods in and my

eyelids look pink and soft from the inside. I take a deep breath at Trina's request.

"Okay," she says, her voice low and calm, "I want to start with a memory."

My body has a physical reaction to that idea—every part of me stiffens in protest.

I guess Trina notices, because she says, "Not a bad memory. A good one. A memory that makes you feel connected to your family. That makes you feel like part of a whole."

I think hard for a minute, but come up with nothing. Trina can tell.

"All you need is a moment, CeCe. A place you went together. A time you were happy and safe."

And suddenly, I do remember something—a time my dad and I went to test-drive cars a few months after my mom died. Dad wanted something new to replace his beat-up Subaru. I remember standing in the chilly reception area of the Chevy dealership while he checked out the charcoal interior of a yellow Camaro. It was summer, but cool—too cool for the air-conditioning that was blasting above our heads.

"Want to take a spin?" he'd asked me, eyebrows raised.

"Dad, you can't be serious. A Camaro?"

He shrugged, then grinned. It was the first smile I'd seen on his face in a long time.

We both slipped inside and the car sort of settled, as though our combined weight brought it down to Earth. I rested one knee against the glove compartment and folded my body in thirds: ankles to thighs, knees to chest. Dad put the car in reverse and we slid through the doors, slow and determined, as a salesman guided us out with hand signals.

What I remember now is how it felt fishlike, like we were gliding through a river. It was a time when I was sure that Dad knew where he was going, that he knew where he was taking me.

I open my eyes. Trina's watching me intently.

"Can you tell me about what you saw?"

"Um . . . it was just—just a time with my dad."

"How old were you?"

"Fourteen."

"And how did that memory make you feel?"

What does she want me to say? That thinking about my family and remembering the past feels . . . unnatural? That good memories feel like a dream and the bad far outweigh the good anyway? I shake my head.

"That memory made me feel stupid."

"Stupid?" Trina's eyebrows furrow.

"Stupid." I nod. "Stupid that I believed him when he said that everything would be okay."

It was an uphill battle through Mom's cancer—it lasted for years and it was painful and heartbreaking. But after? After she was gone, it was all downhill—quick and fast to the ditch of shit at the bottom.

"CeCe." I hear the reproach in Trina's voice. I shake my head, willing the tears away.

"Visualization isn't going to work for me—it's not going to do what it's supposed to. I'm not crazy. I know what I did, and I did it on purpose. I don't know what part of that you and Jennifer don't get."

The way my hands are shaking is almost like a shiver. I consider standing up, walking out, but the constant vibration is making me unsteady. Even if I wanted to remember the good things, it's like my body is rejecting the idea.

So, I remember all the bad things instead.

MARCH

3

IN THE BEGINNING, THERE WAS MY FAMILY. AND MOST DAYS, MY family smelled like smoke.

Dad's was from the trash he burned in the yard, a pastime acceptable only out in the sticks where we lived. My stepmom's was from dinner; she was constantly trying new recipes. They were all heavy on the Cajun seasoning, which translated to charred. And I got the hint of something else. She might have been back on her Camel Filters.

But my brother, Cyrus, had a smoke all his own. It clung to him like a shadow. If someone tells you Oxys burn clean, are odorless, they're lying. That smell is like a plastic lid melting at the bottom of the dishwasher or hair that's gotten too close to the blow-dryer. It's the unmistakable scent of ruin. Eau de Fuckup.

"Cecelia?"

I knew he was coming—not by the smell, but by the

plodding. The heavy sound of a money-grubber treading down the hall toward my last twenty bucks.

"Hey, CeCe."

He was leaning against the door jamb. I didn't look up from the computer screen. One of the few luxuries in my world was an internet connection on a twenty-acre farm in Nowheresville, Virginia.

"You got any gas in your car?"

I swallowed. He didn't want money. He wanted a ride. I'd wished he'd asked for money.

"I need a lift to Dr. Frank's," he said.

I typed another sentence of my Edenton University scholarship application essay:

> When you're little, you learn that medicines make you healthy.

The plasticky clack of the keys was almost soothing. I sighed, then pushed back my chair and turned toward Cyrus. I immediately wanted to wince. He looked like the cross between a homeless person and a cancer patient—loose dirty clothes, hollow eyes, shaved head. He reminded me of one of those actors who look like crap on purpose just to win an Oscar.

Cyrus and I were born barely two years apart and we used to look like twins—the same chestnut hair and chocolate eyes, the same lanky frame and olive skin. Now darkness was our only link—my blue-black dye job was a perfect match to the bruise-like bags beneath his eyes.

"What time is your appointment?" I grumbled.

"Thirty minutes."

"No, not how long. *When* is it?"

He scratched his nose. "It's *in* thirty minutes."

"Cy, are you kidding me? How the hell am I getting to Williamsport in thirty minutes?"

"You won't, but Dr. Frank'll fit me in."

Yeah, I'll bet he will—considering that he doesn't take medical insurance and every visit costs $250 out of pocket. Out of *Dad's* pocket.

"Fine."

I grabbed my jacket off the back of the chair. Another glance at Cyrus and I wondered if I should give it to him instead. Lately, he was perpetually cold and sort of filmy. Looking at him made me want to lather, rinse, and repeat until I felt clean enough for the both of us.

We walked out into the driveway. The Honda was the nicest thing my family owned, and that was because it was mine. Dad's truck was forever mud-caked and full of farm equipment. Jane sold her Corvette when she and Dad got married. That money went right into a down payment on the farm.

I squinted up the hill. Dad was tackling some fencing he meant to put up last fall. It was the wire kind, the mesh that bows into parentheses between two wooden stakes. I don't know what he was trying to keep in. Or out.

"Hey, Dad?"

He looked up, shaded his eyes. "Yeah?"

"I'm taking Cy to his appointment."

"Oh."

Pause. Wait for it . . .

"Hold up. I can do it."

There it was. Dad's I'll-give-up-everything-for-Cyrus voice. I shook my head.

"No. You're busy. I can take him."

"You need money for gas?"

My dad was especially adept at two things—dreaming big and bribing his kids, even when he was practically broke.

I shook my head again. "No, I'm good. We'll see you in a few hours."

He nodded. From that distance, my dad looked old—in the sun, his hair was more silver than brown. His body was hunched over like a cartoon version of a grandfather.

"You ready?"

Behind me, Cyrus was holding a large envelope with *Medavue Radiology* printed in bold black letters. He was wearing a heavy down vest over his flannel.

"Sure." I opened my door and breathed deep before Cyrus climbed into the passenger's side. It would be the last breath I took for a while that didn't reek of wasted space. When Cyrus slid in, he groaned. I looked over to see him flex his leg, then rub his knee with his right hand.

"I hate this car," he grumbled. "It's so damn low to the ground."

You'd think he would feel comfortable in something with

the potential to bottom out. I bit down hard on the inside of my cheek as Cyrus tapped a Marlboro Menthol from his soft pack and lit it. He inhaled deeply and I thought about stethoscopes. I wondered whether Dr. Frank checked if his patients were actually breathing before breaking out the prescription pad.

"So, what is it this time?" I asked him as we pulled out of the driveway.

"What's what?"

"What's the problem with your knee? I thought this doctor was supposed to be helping you."

Cyrus shrugged and looked out the side window. "He *is* helping me."

"By giving you pills?"

He didn't answer at first. Then he said, "It's degenerative."

"Huh?"

"My knee. The disc. It's breaking down as we speak."

"*You're* breaking down as we speak."

He cracked the window, spit, rolled it back up.

"I don't need a lecture, Cecelia."

"I know. What you need is rehab."

Cyrus faced forward and glared at the windshield. "I'm not an addict. It's a prescription for my pain. I don't get why you have to pull this holier-than-thou bullshit every time we talk."

"Don't you miss your friends?"

He didn't say anything.

"Don't you miss soccer?"

No answer to that either.

I watched the mile markers tick past and wondered why I agreed to do this drive again. I remembered who Cyrus used to be. My big brother, the star of the soccer team, the one headed straight for the World Cup. He was a force so fiery, he lit up the whole house. With Cyrus around, it was hard to feel anything but happy to be near him. But my brother, *that* brother, had disappeared.

In his place, he left a depressed, injured high school athlete who poor-me'd his way into Dr. Frank's office. Then the athlete and the high school parts of him went up in smoke. And what was left of my brother inhaled it.

The first time I heard of Dr. Frank Bethany was the day after Cy hurt his knee during practice. It was last year and we were all worried about the upcoming season. Coach Bryant wanted Cyrus to see a specialist. Dr. Frank came highly recommended.

"Coach says he's the best," Cyrus said that night at dinner. "Apparently, Dr. Frank treats a bunch of NFL players—I heard the Redskins quarterback has been going there for years."

Dad took a bite of his salmon. "If he's had to go there for years, this Dr. Frank doesn't sound like that great a doctor."

"C'mon, Dad. Seriously."

"Why do his patients call him Dr. Frank, anyway? Isn't that his first name?"

Cyrus shrugged. "I guess he's, like, laid-back or whatever."

"*Hmph.* I don't know if I trust a doctor who is 'laid-back or whatever.'"

It was a rare moment of clarity. It didn't last. Dad made Cy an appointment with Dr. Frank the next day. He'd been going there once a month ever since.

Bethany Pain Management was just over the state line. Different street signs. Different speed limits. Different laws. That's the only way I could figure that Wacko-Quacko still had his medical license. BPM was what people called a "pill mill": just your average, everyday strip mall, but with X-rays, an ID, and cash, you could get just about any meds you wanted. And for most people, it was Oxys they wanted.

When we pulled into the parking lot, Cyrus looked at me.

"You wanna come in or stay here?"

I raised an eyebrow. He rolled his eyes.

"I'll be out in a few minutes."

Everyone who came to see Dr. Frank was wasted in one of two ways—wasted as in high or drunk, or wasted as in they were hardly there at all. Not a single one of them was even the slightest bit athletic. If there were NFL players visiting Dr. Frank, it didn't happen on my watch. While I waited in the car, I watched a handful of people stumble through the tinted-glass double doors. They all looked the same—thin, pale, and half dead. Here's the only difference—when they walked in, they looked desperate. When they walked out, they looked relieved.

And when Cyrus came out twenty minutes later, he'd had that same relief plastered across his face. He was holding his

MRI and a prescription. I wanted to set all three of them on fire and drive away.

"You give him cash?" I asked when he opened the car door.

He looked at me blankly. "A check."

"Dad's check?"

"Jesus, Cecelia, what the fuck is your deal?"

I shook my head, anger starting to build in my throat like lava-phlegm.

"You know how tight money is right now. Why are you coming all the way out here, out of state, to give a doctor two hundred and fifty dollars when you could give someone else a fifteen-dollar co-pay?"

Cyrus sighed. He was tired. He needed a fix.

"You know why, CeCe."

He was right. I did know why. I looked down at the small white piece of paper, half crumpled in his hand.

240 OxyContin. 60 mg. I tab 4x daily.
Generics acceptable.

I read it again and I wanted to puke.

"Two-forty? What do you need that many for?"

I looked up at Cyrus, but he was staring out the window.

"Look on the bright side," he said to the glass. "Now I don't have to go back for two months."

4

WHEN MY DAD BOUGHT THE FARM, HE CALLED IT AN "INVESTMENT."
It was really the opposite.

"Look, I don't know what you want me to say," Dad said, his voice elevated just below a yell. "I'm doing the best I can."

I stood at the bottom of the stairs and listened to him on the phone. He didn't know we were back from Dr. Frank's. Cyrus had immediately slunk downstairs to smoke, despite the fact that we stopped in a rest area less than an hour before. There's nothing like watching your brother pulverize a handful of pills on top of a flyer about preventing forest fires.

Dad hung up the phone like it had feelings—a fierce clatter. That was my cue; I started up the stairs.

"Dad, we're home."

"Oh, CeCe. Hey. How's it going?"

I watched the transition, which was slower than usual. The one where Dad pulled his face up into a contorted smile, like there were strings attached to his skin that made it defy gravity and stress. Ladies and gentlemen—my father, the puppet.

"I'm okay. Who was on the phone?"

He waved a hand dismissively. "Oh, you know how telemarketers are. Always wanting your money for something."

Translation: You know how creditors are. Always wanting your money because you owe them.

"Can I make you something to eat?" he asked, heading for the pantry.

"No, thanks. I need to finish my application."

"Oh, okay. The scholarship thing, right?"

"Yeah. The scholarship thing."

He ran a hand through his hair. Like yawning, the move was contagious; I touched my ponytail. The black strands felt ratty and knotted together from having the car windows down.

"Actually, I think I'll take a shower first," I said, turning to go.

"Your brother all right? His appointment go okay?"

I stopped under the weight of the question. There was *my* answer and there was the answer Dad wanted. I closed my eyes.

"Fine, Dad. He got a script for two months instead of one."

I could almost hear his smile.

"Well, now, that's smart of him! That'll save us a bundle

in gas and a visit fee. See, Cecelia, you aren't the only one with brains in the family."

It took almost an hour for those words to stop echoing in my ears.

My hair was still damp when I sat back down at the computer to finish my essay, but I couldn't really concentrate. Instead, I stared at the screen.

Should I say something to Dad again? Should I remind him that Dr. Frank's just a quack, more interested in money than medicine? Should I convince him that Cy's crushing and smoking and snorting his pills, transforming them until they can't possibly be considered a prescription for pain and can only be considered drugs?

Yeah, right.

Let's run through my previous attempts at enlightening my father, shall we?

"Dad, I don't think it's a good idea for Cyrus to go to this doctor. I've heard some bad stuff about him—Natalie's dad said he's a total pill pusher."

"CeCe, we need to be supportive of your brother. You know how hard it's been for him. If this doctor makes the difference, it's worth it."

Fast-forward . . .

"Dad, Cyrus is skipping classes. A couple of the guys on the team talked to me today. They're worried about him."

"I'll ask your brother about it. It must be a misunderstanding."

And only weeks later . . .

"Dad, I think Cy's in trouble. Those pills he's taking—I think they're becoming a problem."

"Oh, so, what, you're a doctor now?"

"No . . . I just think he might be abusing his prescription."

"Your brother is fine. He is taking medication, prescribed by a DOCTOR, for his knee. We can't afford surgery right now, Cecelia. This is the best I can do."

So, no, I didn't think it would matter if I tried talking to Dad again. Denial isn't a river, it's a refuge. It's where you go for answers when the truth is a) too upsetting, b) too far-fetched, or c) too ugly.

I pulled up my half-complete application and watched the flashing cursor. The blinking black line was distracting, like a neon sign. *This is pointless*, it flashed. *Scholarships aren't awarded to charity cases.*

We all make choices. The college fund my parents started when I was little went into Cy's soccer training and equipment. They thought he would've gone pro by now. Things didn't quite go as planned. Mom's dead and buried, and Cyrus—well, he's on his way there, too, I guess.

When I turned fifteen, I was old enough to get a part-time job—old enough to start saving for the future. But Dad convinced me that I should load up on academics, take more AP classes instead.

"Colleges look at transcripts first and foremost," he reasoned. "Not work experience flipping pizzas."

But that was before the farm, before every cent he had went into tillers and irrigation and Leafgro. A few days ago, I'd heard him say something to Jane about foreclosure. As much as I resented the farm, it was the last bit of stability we had left.

Losing it would mean admitting how lost we really were.

I clicked until I reached the Edenton scholarship application checklist. I scanned the page. High School Transcripts—in the mail. Activities and Awards List—saved and printed. Essay—making progress. SAT scores—hopefully on their way. I sat for the test later than I wanted to; it took a while to scrape together the enrollment fee.

I scrolled back my application essay and reread my words. All my application topics had similar vague topics that had deceptively simple answers. Case in point—"Describe one life event that has shaped you as a person."

It was hard enough to narrow it down to one.

Cecelia Price
Application #: 21184

Topic Choice:
Describe one life event that has shaped you as a person.

I was barely a teenager when we found out my mom was sick. At first, it was hard to see it. She didn't stop working or cooking dinner. It wasn't until the prescription bottles started lining the kitchen window that it was really in our faces.

Those bottles were impossible to ignore. In the morning, they were like a sunny panel of stained glass—the full ones let through a smattering of gold sunlight, while the almost-empty ones allowed a wash of color to bathe the counters and sink. At night, I'd scrub the soapy dishes and pretend they were candles, a line of tea lights that caught the reflection of the setting sun or the ceiling lamp. It was easier to see them as glass or fire. It was too hard to call them what they were—vessels filled with something my mother needed, something her body found necessary to keep her alive.

When you're little, you learn that medicines are a good thing, they make you healthy. If you have an ear infection, you swallow gooey pink liquid that's kept in the fridge. If you spike a fever, a dropper of grape syrup bathes your mouth in something sweeter than candy.

The first thing I learned from my mother's cancer was that medicine doesn't really make you better. It just delays the inevitable, allowing you to hang on for dear life. But it doesn't make you stronger or brighter. It just buries your flame in something like ash. You might still smolder, but you will never flare again.

On Monday, my friend Natalie was waiting for me next to the college tour bulletin board. It had been stripped of last year's university pamphlets and it looked like a face—tan and pockmarked, with a few pushpin piercings. Our high school guidance office made a lot of promises—not the least of which was that they'd guide us toward something. The bulletin board was a halfhearted attempt.

"You look at the list yet?" I asked her. Natalie shook her head.

"I wanted to wait for you—that way we can sign up for the same ones."

I rolled my eyes, but smiled. I'd known Natalie since middle school and she'd never grown out of the bandwagon mentality. Case in point—when lacrosse became the sport du jour, she immediately began dating a series of varsity players. The most recent one, Jeremy, was actually sticking around.

I looked at the sign-up sheet on the back of the office door. Our high school started the College Tour Crawl two years before—you could hitch a ride to different nearby universities every other Saturday. It was free and it meant you didn't have to rely on your parents to take you on the weekday tours.

There were ten schools on the fall list. I'd been accepted to three of them, but I started signing my name next to every one.

"You're going to go to *all* of them?" Natalie sounded doubtful. "I thought you were, like, completely committed to Edenton."

"Edenton is expensive." I shrugged. "I just figure I need to keep my options open. Have a backup plan—isn't that what the counselors are always saying?"

"I dunno. I usually zone out when I'm in those college prep assemblies." She took the pen when I finished and jotted her name next to the first two schools. She paused with her hand hovered over the Edenton slot. "So—I mean, if you're probably going to go there, is there any reason to take an informational tour? Can't we just explore the campus in the fall when you're actually enrolled?"

I slung my book bag back on my shoulder and shook my head.

"I want to go see it."

What I don't say? That going on a college tour at my dream school might actually make my dreams still feel possible.

"I gotta go to Chem. I'll see you later."

Some classes seem fundamentally useless. Chemistry was the opposite. I liked the whole concept of substances interacting with one another, of creating something new when there was nothing there.

Dr. Schafer was our only doctor-teacher. It made kids either listen to her or try to see if they could push her buttons. Fortunately, Organic Chem was for advanced students, not assholes who threw things covered in their own spit. I was halfway to my seat when Dr. S called my name.

"CeCe? Could you come here?"

I knew what she was going to say. I could see it in her down-turned mouth, her furrowed brow. I braced myself for impact.

"CeCe," she said, her voice lowered, "I still haven't received your lab fee."

"I know. I'm sorry."

"I wouldn't bring it up, except that we're starting acidity

and alkalinity at the end of this week and, in order to supply you with your materials, I have to have —"

"My dad must have forgotten to send in the check. I'll say something to him tonight."

"Right. Okay. Well, listen"—voice even lower, eyes full of pity—"the guidance office runs a program for people who need some assistance with school fees. If you'd like, I can say something."

"No, that's okay."

"Are you sure? It's nothing to be ashamed of, CeCe—"

"No," I repeated icily. "I'll take care of it." I tried to sound a little less hostile. I liked Dr. Schafer. I was hoping she'd write me a another scholarship recommendation letter. Besides, you really shouldn't bite the hand that grades you.

When lunch rolled around, I headed for the library. I never ate in the cafeteria, not since Natalie found Jeremy and spent the whole time making out with him. Instead, I made a deal with the librarian: I could hang out for my thirty-minute lunch if I spent fifteen of it shelving returns. I liked the library. It was a good place to work through lab reports or homework.

I started with my statistics problems. There was just something about solutions—the fact that they existed, I guess—that made me feel a little more grounded. There's a reason why they're called math *problems*, so there had to be a reason why I was able to solve them without even breaking a sweat. Either that or numbers were an easier language for me to read. The beginnings and endings were much clearer and the absence of emotion was refreshing.

After I finished, I sifted through that day's returned books and started to roll my cart toward the far end of the room. The front left wheel let out a high-pitched squeak and I pushed a little faster.

"Is that her?"

I heard the whispered words, even over the protesting wheel.

I'd seen them come in a few minutes ago, before I got up to start shelving. Jason Oliver and Lucas Andrews. If everyone in high school had to wear a label, Jason's would have said "Stoner." I'd gone to school with him since elementary—I think he'd been a smoker even then. He usually reeked of BO and pot.

I didn't know much about Lucas, except that he was too blond and tan to be from around here. Someone once told me that he grew up in L.A., and that made sense. He was almost too good-looking, like a silk flower arrangement. Too pretty to be real.

I figured they were here to ditch class, and I wasn't going to be a narc about it—ignoring them was good enough for me. Apparently it wasn't good enough for them.

"Hey, Cecelia—that's your name, right?"

Jason. He had long, stringy hair that was brown, I think—it was a little too greasy for me to be sure. Sometimes he had it tucked back in a hat, but that day he'd chosen to follow the school rules—no headgear. It might be the only one he'd ever followed.

I'd reached the paranormal shelf, but I'd have to slide past him to put the books up. I grabbed one in each hand.

"Yeah. I'm Cecelia," I said, trying to sidestep him. "And you're Jason. We've gone to school together since we were five."

Despite my efforts not to, I brushed up against him. I forced myself not to shudder.

Jason smiled and leaned against my cart, and it groaned in protest.

"Your brother is Cyrus, right?"

I just nodded this time, wanting to cringe—it was the inevitable "Dude, your brother was so talented. What the hell happened?"

But these weren't fans. They'd probably never been to a game where Cyrus kicked ass and took names.

And then it dawned on me. They didn't know Cyrus the Jock. They knew Cyrus the Junkie.

"Listen." Jason came forward a few more feet, this time blocking the shelf. Lucas hung back, leaning against a poster that boasted, *Reading Is Fun-damental* with a picture of two girls jumping on a trampoline. He was watching me in a way that made my face feel hot.

"From what I hear, Cyrus has a steady supply of Oxys," Jason was saying, "and I want a piece of that action. You tell your brother, if he's ever looking to make a little cash, he knows where he can find me."

Oh? And where is that? Dumpster or ditch?

"I don't . . ." I began uncertainly. Jason didn't wait for me to finish.

"Just tell him, all right?"

He turned and headed out the double doors and Lucas followed him. I gripped the side of the cart and tried to catch my runaway breath. When I did, it felt solid, a weight pressing right on my heart. Times like that, when my brother's reputation sideswiped me, never ceased to make me wish I could just disappear, that the earth would rise up and swallow me whole.

Then I wouldn't have to face my brother at home or claim him at school. I'd be far belowground where no one could touch me and Cyrus would be up here, doing his best to join me.

"SO, HOW IS THERAPY GOING?"

I was wondering how long it would take Jennifer to mention my sessions with Touchy-Feely Trina. I've met with my new therapist three times already, but I've yet to adjust to her tofu-tasticness.

"It's going fine," I tell Jennifer.

"Did you like talking to her?"

"It was fine."

She rolls her eyes. "You don't have to tell me right now, but Trina was hired to extend your treatment. Her assessments will serve as evidence of your progress."

"Assuming I'm making progress, of course."

"Which you are." Jennifer's holding her ever-present legal pad, pen poised above a blank page. "We need to talk today. More specifically, *you* need to talk today."

"Sure. What do you want to know? I can tell you about

my trip to Six Flags when I was ten. Or how about when my class visited the National Zoo?"

"You know, you can only avoid the inevitable for so long."

"I disagree. If I distract you with harrowing childhood tales, I can potentially avoid the inevitable forever."

Jennifer shakes her head. "Except I'm not going to let that happen, no matter how exciting the story."

I cross my arms. "You haven't heard my Girl Scout camp adventures."

She smiles tightly. "I *need* to ask you some questions today, CeCe. I *need* you to answer them honestly. We have less than a month to start building your defense."

I lean back in my chair. Jennifer takes this as a good sign.

"I need to know more about Cyrus. About his lifestyle— how long he was using, when he started, the impact it had on your family . . ."

I scratch my nose. Look out the window again. Stare down at my hands.

"CeCe?"

"Okay, okay." I uncross, then recross my legs.

"How old was Cyrus when he started doing drugs?" Jennifer begins.

"Um, eighteen, I guess."

"Nothing before that? No marijuana or anything like that?"

I shrug. "I don't know. I don't think so."

"And what was his drug of choice once he started using?"

"Painkillers—Oxys."

"And those were prescribed to him?"

"Yeah."

"And did he take them as prescribed?"

"Like, was he taking more than he should or was he taking them other than directed?"

"Either. Both."

"He was always running out early, so I guess he took more than he was supposed to."

"And he took it orally?"

"He snorted them. Or smoked them. It depended on the day."

Jennifer is scribbling furiously. I bet her handwriting is terrible.

"Was he ever an IV drug user?"

I shrug again. Jennifer squints at her writing.

"You said before that he was a dropout. When did that happen?"

"It was his senior year. May of his senior year."

Jennifer stops writing and looks up at me, confused. "Cyrus dropped out one month before graduating high school?"

"He didn't technically drop out, I guess. He just stopped going and never took his final exams."

She pauses to push her glasses back up the bridge of her nose.

"So, how did your dad react to that?"

"He was fine with it."

"Fine?" She's incredulous. I rake my hair over my face

and start to examine the split ends.

"Okay, maybe not *fine*," I say, "but what was he going to do? I mean, Cy was practically an adult and it's not like he could drag him to school."

"Sounds like you're defending him."

"Who?"

"Your dad."

I roll my eyes. "I'm just saying that he could only do so much. We all could only do so much."

Jennifer cocks her head a bit, then looks back down at her notepad.

"But Cyrus never went back in the fall to finish, correct?"

"You got it."

"And by then, his drug use had escalated?"

"Uh-huh."

Jennifer takes a minute to read back over what she's written. Her lips move as though she's muttering an incantation. When she gets to the end, she looks up.

"Your mother died when Cyrus was, what? Fifteen?"

"Something like that."

"Did he struggle with that—with the loss of your mother?"

I look at Jennifer like she's stupid, which is an expression I usually save for group.

"Of course. But we all knew it was coming. We had fair warning."

"That doesn't mean it doesn't hurt when it happens."

I swallow hard. "Yeah."

Sometimes I think that kind of advance notice made it

hurt more—that dull ache of a future loss that increases methodically, rapidly, with every breath you take. I remember the night when Mom went into the hospital—the last night she was ever admitted without later being discharged. Cy and I sat with her for hours. He'd even skipped a game to stay with us, even though Mom slept most of the time we were there. We'd watched *Steel Magnolias* on full volume, hoping that she would wake up and tell us to turn it down.

She didn't.

It wasn't until she needed meds that we saw her eyelids flutter. With a groan, she writhed in her bed—a fish too long out of water and drying up from the outside in. She was just waking up at the part of the movie where Shelby, the dying daughter, admits that her mother is giving her a kidney. I considered what body part I could give my mother to save her life. At that point, the cancer was like a fast-food chain—setting up multiple franchises in the surrounding areas of her body.

The next time I'd looked over at Mom, she was gazing at my brother. She had aged from her illness, the wrinkles settled deep into her forehead and around her eyes. She smiled with lips that made more of a grimace. Her intention was "brave" but the result was "decomposing."

"You're missing your game," she'd whispered to Cyrus. He shook his head.

"I'm not missing anything, Mom. I'm right where I want to be."

Now I blink rapidly against the tears, focusing instead on Jennifer as she looks at her paper again.

"So what about this doctor? Dr. Bethany."

"Dr. Frank. What about him?"

"You said in your original police interview that this doctor prescribed your brother OxyContin for"—she looks at her notebook—"a year and a half?"

"That sounds about right."

"And you said that you would take Cyrus to his appointments?"

"Sometimes. Most of the time, Dad did it. Cyrus lost his license."

"For?"

"Speeding tickets."

"And you'd just take him to the doctor, drop him off, and wait for him?"

I pick at a hangnail. "Yeah. That's about right."

Jennifer shakes her head. She looks troubled.

"I don't understand, CeCe," she says quietly, propping both elbows on the table and leaning toward me. "This doctor was corrupt, he was a drug dealer in disguise. So why didn't you report it to the authorities?"

I look out the window. The sky is the color of paste. I feel sick.

"C'mon, Cecelia."

My whole first name. I must be in trouble.

"Please, don't clam up on me now," she urges. "It's obvious this doctor is the real villain here—he was prescribing heavy narcotics to patients who didn't require them. I need to know everything there is to know about him. *He* is your ticket to freedom."

I want to tell her that the tickets are sold out, that the train's already left.

Instead, I say, "I don't know if you'll have any luck finding him—I've heard he's moved."

Abruptly, Jennifer gathers up her things.

"Well, then I'm going to go track down this doctor." She reaches out to squeeze my arm. "Once I get his statement, we'll have a lot more to work with."

Her smile is triumphant; I almost can't bear to spoil her sense of achievement.

"Look, you don't understand. When I say he moved, I mean moved out of the *country*—like to the Dominican or something." I shrug. "I guess that's what you can expect from someone with a dead patient and a couple million dollars."

Jennifer narrows her eyes, then shakes her head.

"Well, that just means I'll have to search a little harder, that's all. It's my job, CeCe. I'm here to help you."

I sigh at that. "Okay—I just figured you should know."

In the end, she'll realize what I already know—that no matter what Dr. Frank prescribed my brother, there's only one person responsible for Cyrus's death. That, and the only place I'm moving to is a jail cell.

"Today I want to talk about your support system."

Dr. Barnes is running group today. I guess he got tired of

hearing us complain about Cam. Either that or he realized that Cam is a snotty bitch who likes to hear herself talk.

Aaron snorts. "What support system?" Barnes gives him a patronizing smile.

"Family. Friends. This group. Your individual therapists. Anyone you think helps you out or has 'got your back' or wants you to succeed."

"Count me out, Doc." Aaron rubs his nose. "I got nothing and no one but me."

"So you think we just want you to curl up in a ball and die?" Lola, a tall, willowy blonde asks. Everything about Lola is miraculously long—her hair, her legs, the vowels in her words.

Aaron looks her up and down, then shrugs. "I'm just sayin'—I mean, I can get better or I can get worse. In the end, you don't give a shit what happens to me as long as it don't change what happens to *you*."

"What about you, Tucker?" Barnes asks, attempting to redirect. "Who's in your support network?"

Tucker is across the circle from me. He's wearing a dark green sweater. Today his eyes kind of look like tree bark—rough and layered, in multiple shades of brown.

"My parents are all right," he is saying. "They hung in there with me. Honestly, they probably should have turned their backs on me a long time ago. It means a lot that they're still supportive."

"Yeah, if you stole that kind of money from me, I'd kick your ass—family or no family," Aaron pipes up.

Barnes gives him a look. "Any sisters or brothers?" he asks Tucker. He nods.

"Sister."

"Older or younger?"

"Older. She lives out of state."

"Are you close with her?"

Tucker's dark hair falls in waves across his forehead and around his ears, listing forward and back. He seems like he's thinking. Finally he shrugs.

"I was. There was a time when she was my best friend."

"Anything else you'd like to say?" Barnes asks. Tucker gives his head an almost imperceptible shake.

"Okay, who's next . . . Aarti? How about you? Who is supporting you?"

"My sister," Aarti says quietly. I have to strain to hear her even though she's only a few feet away.

"Your sister?" Dr. Barnes repeats. Aarti nods.

"She came here a year after me. She married a lawyer in Saint Louis, a friend of my husband's. I don't get to see her much, especially now. But knowing she's here, on the same continent as me, is a great relief. It gives me a purpose, a reason to heal."

Knowing Aarti's version of alone isn't as alone as *my* alone makes me feel a little bit better for her and a little bit worse for me. Dr. Barnes eyes me. It's as if he sees my self-pity etch itself across my face.

"And what about you, Cecelia? Can you tell us about your support network?"

It was easier for me to avoid answering Cam. Dr. Barnes's eyes are piercing. I cough, a hand over my mouth, praying blood will magically spew from my throat. It doesn't. You just can't rely on spontaneous hemorrhages these days.

"I, um, I guess my dad was my support system."

"You say 'was.' Why is that?"

I blink. "Well, I'm here now. So, I mean, I'm not his responsibility anymore."

Dr. Barnes leans back in his chair. It has wheels and it rolls a few inches outside the circle.

"So you think that means he doesn't support you?"

What I think: *My dad will never forgive me for Cyrus's death.*

What I say: "I think it means that he doesn't have to worry about taking care of me. I know he supported me enrolling in this program, but that wasn't my choice."

"And whose choice was it?"

Dr. Barnes is looking at me expectantly. I can tell, even though I'm still examining the ragged edges of my nails. At least I'm not squinting.

"CeCe," he says quietly, "I know that being here is challenging for you. I know that you are having a difficult time opening up to the processes that come along with treatment. You need to open up to us—it will help you. *We* can help you."

When people tell you that therapy is a stress-free environment, they're lying. There are the same pressures, the same worries you have in the "real world." You want people to like you. You don't want people to judge you. It's just as hard to be honest here as it is anywhere else.

Dr. Barnes is watching me. Aarti and Kevin and Lola are watching me. Everyone in the circle is watching me. Everyone but Tucker. He's staring out the window, his face turned away from the group. I give in and close my eyes a bit, watching the dark waves of his hair blur into a fuzzy ball.

"I'm here because I have to be."

"Why do you have to be here?"

"Because it looks good."

"Looks good to whom?"

His words saw at my patience. I squint into slits so small, I can't see anything but shadows.

"Dr. Barnes, do you always ask questions you know the answer to?"

"What do you mean?"

I stand up. No one expects it. No one leaves group without being excused. Two guards are next to me before I can take a single step.

"Those people matter because they make the decisions now. The last decision *I* made landed me in handcuffs. I'm not allowed to make decisions on my own behalf anymore, Dr. Barnes. Isn't that the point? Isn't that why I'm here?"

Dr. Barnes doesn't stop me as I head for the door; he just motions for the guards to follow me out. I bite down hard on my lower lip until I taste the coppery blood ooze between my teeth. It's the only thing that prevents me from screaming.

6

AT DINNER, I'M SITTING ALONE NEXT TO A STAPLE-LESS,
pushpin-free bulletin board in the cafeteria when I see a pair
of corduroy-clad legs approach.

"Is someone sitting here?"

I look up. Tucker is peering down at me, one eyebrow
raised. I gesture to the bench across from me. He sits and
places his tray parallel to mine. I look at what's on it. Smooth
scoop of mashed potatoes topped with mucusy-looking
gravy. The canned green beans are more brown than green.
There's an apple in one corner, a carton of juice in the other.

"Are you a vegetarian?"

He looks surprised. I'm sure he assumed we'd eat together
in silence—maybe we'd do that for a few days, a week,
before I finally broke down and said something insightful.
Whatever. I'm not that determined to continue my isolation.
It sort of sucks.

"Why do you think I'm a vegetarian?"

I point to his food. "No meat."

He looks at my BLT. The bacon—bits, not slices—spills out onto the yellow plastic tray. He shakes his head.

"No, I'm not a vegetarian. I just don't eat stuff that looks like something that used to be meat. Like your Bacos there."

"Right." I take a big bite of my sandwich. A dollop of mayonnaise smears against my cheek.

"So, is it an act?" Tucker asks. He takes a bite of his apple.

"Is what an act?"

He makes a flailing gesture, which I think is an attempt to sum me up.

"This . . . this person you're being. All tough and relentless, like you're wearing armor. Is she real?"

I shrug. "As real as anyone is, I guess."

"Is she the same person you've always been?"

I'm starting to feel a little prickly under his scrutiny. I finger my wrist, remembering how I used to wear bracelets to fiddle with when I was nervous. I wonder if they're still in my jewelry box at home. If I still *have* a jewelry box. Or a home.

"Are *you* the same person *you've* always been?" I finally counter.

It's his turn to shrug. "I've always been a fuckup, if that's what you're asking."

Tucker stares at me, then his eyes soften a little.

"So, why are you in here?" he asks.

"Did you not get the message in group? I don't want to talk about that stuff."

"Look." Tucker props an elbow on the table and rests his chin in his hand. "I think it's total crap that you know stuff about me and my life and I don't know anything about you and yours."

"I never *asked* to know about your life. You *chose* to share it."

"True, but when you agree to go to treatment, you agree to all the shit that goes along with it. That means hearing sob stories from people you don't care about. It also means you have to tell them yours. It's like an eye for an eye or something."

"Uh, I wouldn't call my being locked up here 'agreeing to go to treatment.'"

"Whatever. All I'm saying is that people are sharing their stories with you because they want to get better. I have a feeling that getting your life back—the life you *had*—might rely on you trying to get better. Right now, you aren't trying to do shit."

The last thing I want is to get my life back.

"I think you need to be less concerned about me and my progress and more concerned about your own," I mutter.

Tucker takes another bite of his apple, chews, and swallows.

"You know that whole thing Barnes was talking about—about support systems?"

"Yeah, what about them?"

"I don't know. I just think that if you actually talked to the group, then you won't feel so alone."

"I'm not alone." I say it too fast and Tucker almost smirks.

"Yeah, you are. You're just afraid to admit it."

He stands up and looks me over.

"If you ever want to talk, let me know."

It's been a long time since I've been able to talk to someone who isn't being compensated for working with me. Having a person to confide in, to trust, is a desirable prospect. Then again, it could also be a huge mistake—one I wouldn't realize I've made until it's far too late.

"No," I say, forcing myself to glare at him. "My life is none of your business."

Besides, if I let him in now, I know I'll never be able to get rid of him. His empathy will set up shop somewhere inside me, like in my chest cavity—in the space where my heart used to be.

"Let's try something else."

Trina's leaning against the wall, looking up at the ceiling. Now, when I squint at her, she looks more like a kid than an adult.

"What does 'something else' entail?"

She comes back over to the table and reaches into her bag. Out comes her trusty notebook and pencil.

"If visualization isn't your preference, then how about we do some journaling."

"Journaling?" I raise an eyebrow. She nods.

"Therapeutic journaling. I teach a psychology course here and last week we did this great activity. I thought you might want to give it a shot."

"You teach psychology *here*?"

"For the DOJ Education program. The classes are free, but you have to have a pristine record to sign up. I've actually had a few people earn their associate's degrees while they were incarcerated."

For a second, I consider the ways being locked up is like being in college:

1. You have a roommate.
2. You share a bathroom.
3. There's no privacy.
4. You're away from your parents and family.

And then, of course, there are the ways this place is NOTHING like college:

1. You're under twenty-four-hour surveillance.
2. Your roommate is a criminal and probably wants to hurt you.
3. You don't gain the freshman fifteen; you lose it.
4. Two words—*Strip. Search.*

I could go on.

"Journaling is a great way to get down your thoughts, anything that's bothering you," Trina is saying. "My students really like it."

"Of course they do. They're bored out of their minds. They need something to fill up the time."

Trina rolls her eyes. "Stop being so surly. Just give it a shot."

I reach for the notebook and open it to the first page. I narrow my eyes until the blue lines blur—then I start to write.

Once upon a time, there was a girl. She had a family
that was like a glass slipper on a stepsister—it was just
the wrong fit.

I stop writing and push the notebook back across the table.
Trina shakes her head.

"No way."

"What?"

She gestures to the page. "That's not enough. You can do
better than that."

"No, I can't."

"I see. So are you telling me you want to try visualization
again?"

I scowl. "Tell me again how this is supposed to be helping me."

"Just write, CeCe."

So I do.

The girl tried to forge her own path through the forest.
Hansel and Gretel stopped at the candy house, but the
girl wasn't much for sweets. Little Red Riding Hood was
helpful at first, but she became too worried about her
grandmother to run from the danger.

I hand it back to Trina. She peers at my chicken scratch through her glasses. I brace for the inevitable irritation—the I'm-not-taking-this-seriously talk.

"This is good, CeCe. Really good."

"Yeah, right," I scoff, crossing my arms over my chest.

"Have you ever written before? Creatively, I mean?"

"I'm not the writing type," I say, shrugging. "I mean, I never kept a diary or anything. I was more of a science nerd."

Trina pulls up the waist of her jeans. All her clothes are baggy; they swallow her like she's something delicious.

"Would you be willing to try the writing thing more consistently? Use the journal as a regular intervention?"

I shake my head.

"I don't have to be here every time you write in it," she urges. "It can be something you do on your own when the mood strikes you."

"I'm not trying to be difficult," I say, tugging at one earlobe. "I just don't need this therapy. Not to mention the fact that they won't let me keep a pen in my room. Far too many self-harming possibilities."

"I can fix that for you—anytime you request it, a pen can be provided for journaling therapy purposes."

I shrug. "I don't know."

Trina drops her chin into her hand and looks me in the eye.

"Don't you want to get out of here, CeCe?"

I huff out a breath. "I want a lot of things."

"Well, whatever those things are, none of them are going

to happen here. You have a chance at getting a lesser sentence if you can prove you're being rehabilitated. If you can prove you're getting help."

She turns the notebook back around to face me. From here, my words look like dark train tracks winding over the page.

"A written journal expressing your feelings would be evidence of improvement for Jennifer to present to the court."

Everyone around me has a strategy. A strategy to make me talk, a strategy to fix me, a strategy to win this case. I think I'm the only one with nothing invested in my own potential future.

"So, what do you think?" Trina asks me, cocking her head.

I used to know how to sugarcoat things. How to let people down easy. It's not a skill I've managed to sustain since I came here. Instead, I pick up the pencil again and scribble my response.

When the girl finally got home, the wolf was waiting.
That's the thing about fairy tales—they're rooted in magic
and dreams. And, like fairy tales, magic and dreams
don't exist.

I push it over to Trina, who scans it quickly. Then she shakes her head.

"Cecelia—this is a place where you can be honest. You know that, right?"

I want to snort or laugh. Instead I just shrug. "Like I said, I'm not a good writer."

Trina raises her eyebrows. "I beg to differ—but, regardless, this isn't about talent. It's about expression. Getting things out that are bottled inside you. Giving yourself a release."

I don't know if I deserve that. Most days, the thick, oozing regret and horror that travel my veins like rotting blood—well, most days, *that* is what I think I deserve.

"Come on—if you start writing in the journal, I won't have to ask you as many questions out loud."

I lift a brow at her, then grip the pencil a little harder. "You promise?"

She holds up her hand in an oath-like motion. "Absolutely."

I had hated everything about talking, so forcing myself to write in a spiral-bound notebook every now and then didn't feel like that bad of a trade-off. I look down at the notebook, then up at Trina.

"What should I write about?"

She thinks about that for a second. "How about you start with a memory of you and your brother?"

Since she doesn't smile when she says it, I guess that means she isn't kidding.

"I don't know if I can do that," I admit. The honesty rolls off my tongue like a kind of bitter honey.

Trina does smile then, but says only one word.

"Try."

June 14

Cyrus was always good at sports, but I was good at
playing pretend. I could create entire worlds in my head—
people and places and things and ideas. Living, breathing
nouns. Before he got too old to imagine, Cyrus would
visit the worlds I built in my bedroom. We'd pretend my
frayed rug was a raft, floating over my wood floor ocean.
We'd build forts with anything—chairs, pillows, stuffed
animals—and live within those walls, even when those
walls had Care Bear faces. Back then, it didn't matter
who was watching.

Soccer was Cyrus's calling, but it was the cancer
before Mom's cancer—it ate away at our family like it
would never be satisfied. My parents were more than
happy to feed it, and that's when things started to
change. I'd invite Cyrus to tea parties that he never
attended. I'd ask him to join me on journeys I believed so
strongly in, journeys he was quick to discount as "fake"

and "for babies." I was Cyrus's sister most of the time, but I was his baby sister when he wanted to keep me at arm's length.

Cy spent more and more time in the backyard and on the field, backed by my parents' encouragement. I spent more and more time in my room, and my raft became even more real. Out on my own ocean, I was adrift and Cy was the shore. He was where I should want to be, but I kept paddling out into the deep blue strangeness. It felt more like home than anything I already knew.

C.P.

JANE GOT HOME FROM WORK LATER THAN USUAL. SHE WORKED AS a clerk for a lawyer in town. *The* lawyer in town. It was the one-of-everything kind of town—one stoplight, one diner, one Elks lodge, one Kroger supermarket. If you blinked, you wouldn't miss it, but you'd wish you had.

"My feet are killing me."

Jane always complained about her feet. When we were moving into the farmhouse, she didn't carry anything because she couldn't put too much weight on her arches. She was constantly bitching about that place—the floorboards hurt her bunions, the land was too rocky to walk on. But when Dad first decided to buy the farm and start his organic seed business, Jane was his biggest supporter. Cyrus and I thought he was nuts. That was back in the good old days—Cyrus was the jock, I was the brain, and Dad was a somewhat normal parent.

"What about your job?" I'd asked.

Dad shrugged. "I'll quit."

"What about money?" Cyrus had asked.

"I've got some saved up. Jane's got a little, too. We'll sell the house, get a small business loan. There are all kinds of programs for green businesses."

That was the appeal at first—"going green." Dad had a tendency to succumb to trends, just like a thirteen-year-old girl would.

But a year later, Jane had buyer's remorse.

She slammed the kitchen cabinet doors as she cooked dinner and grumbled, "I'm so sick of being the only person bringing in any money around here."

She rooted around until she found the jumbo bottle of Cajun seasoning I'd stuffed behind the cereal boxes. That meant spicy, smoky air that wouldn't clear with the exhaust fan, air that made you cough like you were inhaling your first cigarette. In this house, we didn't eat comfort food— only food that somehow hurt us.

I started shoveling my shells and cheese into my mouth so that I could get out of the kitchen. Dad was sitting at one end of the table, poring over seed statements. He had a complicated chart system modeled after some successful agriculture company. I couldn't understand it and I don't think he really could, either.

"How's the seed business, Dad?"

He looked up, sniffed. "Okay. We're getting in big orders for heirloom tomato seeds."

I nodded. Dad didn't have much help during the last seed harvest. I had Academic Team and Mock Trial. Cyrus had nothing but time, but he spent his in an Oxy-coma. Tomatoes were big business, all things being relative. They were the Google of the organic seed world.

Jane slammed a drawer and Dad and I jumped.

"I don't give two shits about tomatoes if they don't pay the damn mortgage," she muttered. I scooted out of my chair and gave my dad a look. He forced a smile and rolled his eyes to heaven. I wondered if he could see Mom when he looked up there.

"'Night, guys," I said, putting my bowl in the sink. I moved into the shadows of the hallway and stopped at the stairwell, waiting for the explosion. It took only a few seconds to detonate—Dad was the one to set it off.

"Dammit, Janey, you know I'm doing the best I can!"

"No." Her tone was scathing, a blade of fury. "Your *best* would be selling off this land and getting a real fucking job."

"What happened to our dream? Living off the land? Growing a life that matters?" He lowered his voice. "Having a baby?"

That one was a punch in the gut. It was the first time I'd ever heard them talking about having kids. A kid that belonged to both of them. But Jane just laughed.

"Are you kidding? We can't pay our bills as it is, Craig! How in the hell would we pay for diapers?"

"We could use those cloth ones . . ."

"Look." Jane sounded tired. "We're not having a baby

until we can break even. Right now we're in so deep, we're lucky they haven't taken the farm already."

"I know. I'm working on it."

She didn't respond to that, but her silence said enough. A moment later, Cyrus started pounding up the basement stairs—I could feel each stomp through the floorboards. When he got to the landing, he brushed past me like a man with an agenda.

"Hey there, Cy-Guy," I heard my dad say brightly. "How're you feeling?"

"Not so good, actually. I was wondering . . ."

All three of us knew what was coming next. I peeked around the corner, my lip curled in disgust.

". . . could you lend me a few bucks? Lennon's girlfriend, Maddie, is taking a massage therapy class at the Learning Annex. She said she'd work on my knee if I wanted, but she's still gonna charge me for it."

"That sounds like a great idea, son," Dad said. "How much do you need?"

I inched forward in time to see Cyrus shrug.

"I dunno. Sixty bucks or so."

Dad reached into his pocket and pulled out his wallet. He counted out some cash.

"Will forty-eight do it?" Dad asked. Cy looked disappointed, but reached for the money anyway.

"Yeah, I guess it'll have to."

As Cyrus headed for the back door, I watched his left hand; it was gripping the money like it was a dirty napkin

71

or some kind of garbage. There went my chemistry lab fee. There went my brother. I shook my head. Nothing seemed to leave that house quicker than family or cash.

The only reason I ever went into the basement was because the washer and dryer were at the foot of the stairs. I never made it past the utility sink; I wasn't interested in seeing what my brother had turned it into. But, for once, I felt differently. I needed a blatantly obvious reminder of exactly what my lab fee was funding.

It was hours later, just after midnight, when I stepped down onto the old shag carpet, which was almost crunchy with dry rot. Our basement had the same cool dampness of everyone else's, plus the tinge of Cyrus Smoke and some sort of decay.

The space was technically unfinished, but Dad put up enough drywall to make a bedroom. Once Cyrus hurt his knee—well, once he'd seen Dr. Frank—he asked Dad to set him up down there so he wouldn't have to deal with stairs. When I said that that made no sense and asked what the difference was between going down a flight or up a flight, Cyrus called me a bitch and my dad called me insensitive. So I shut up and tried to ignore the three weeks of hammering and sawing and Dad's horrible country music wafting from below my bedroom floor.

Cyrus had a door with a gold handle. It was weirdly shiny and new in a house filled with rusty everything. I knocked softly.

Nothing.

I tried again. I leaned my ear against the door. Cyrus could've been home, but I doubted it. It was way too early. For a second, though, I thought I could hear him, pressed up against the other side, breathing hard. Then I realized it was my pressing, my breathing.

"Cy?"

No answer.

I tried the knob. It was locked.

I walked over to Dad's tool chest and dug out a putty knife from the bottom drawer, then lodged it between the lock and the jamb like a credit card.

The door slid open without a sound. No click. No alarm. No scream of indignation. Nothing but my involuntary gagging when the smell hit me full on.

Ever seen an episode of *Hoarders*?

Welcome to Cyrus's room.

I avoided breathing in through my nose. Cyrus wasn't there, but everything else was. And most of it was trash.

I picked my way over the floor, or what would've been the floor if it hadn't been covered with clothes and junk. There was a desk in one corner blanketed in magazines and fast-food wrappers. An old PC monitor sat on the floor next to it. The flat screen Dad got Cy for his birthday was leaning against one wall, plugged into a power strip. A can of soda was tipped on its side, a pool of syrupy liquid inching dangerously close to an extension cord.

It looked like a meth lab waiting to happen. All you

needed were some decongestants and a hot plate. I couldn't believe my dad let him get away with that shit. A wave of fury crashed up against my rib cage. I got reamed out if I didn't do the dishes, while my fuckup brother could house a miniature landfill beneath our feet and Dad didn't say a single word.

I took a few tentative steps, then spotted the unmistakable translucent orange of a prescription bottle on the floor. I leaned over and moved aside a ratty pillow. There were dozens of bottles. Maybe a hundred—all empty. He'd stripped the labels off, the ones that had his name and address, but some of them still boasted warning stickers:

> **Take with Food.**
> **Do Not Operate Heavy Machinery While Taking This Medication.**
> **Do Not Chew or Crush. Swallow Whole.**

Then, right next to that, was his kit. One of them, anyway.

The glass from a picture frame. A razor blade. Straws—some from fountain sodas, some made out of what looked like pages ripped from magazines. A roll of foil. A rainbow of lighters. And an almost-full bottle of pills.

They were little and round. They looked harmless, like breath mints. Like baby aspirin. I pressed down hard on the cap. Carefully, I shook four tablets into my hand. I peered at them, transfixed. How could something so small cause so much damage?

Two thoughts entered my mind concurrently.

Take them with you. You can flush them.

Take them with you. You can sell them.

It's true that the things in my life that were the most essential seemed to be the most expensive. I still owed money to Dr. Schafer. I always needed to pay for gas. Sometimes I was stuck buying groceries. Or picking up Cy's prescription.

This could be like a refund. Like a reimbursement.

Jason's face was suddenly in my mind—his leering gaze, oily words asking about my brother—as I grabbed one of the empty bottles and let four pills slide inside. When I made it back to the door, I considered covering my tracks. But looking back over my shoulder, I was sure Cyrus wouldn't know the difference. The trash was the only thing that knew I'd been there and, as it crunched underfoot, it whispered, *Don't worry. It'll be our little secret.*

It wasn't in a ditch or a Dumpster where I found Jason the next morning. It was behind the tennis courts at school. And he wasn't alone.

When I got closer, he and his buddies gave me a slow once-over. One of them murmured "nice rack" under his breath. I crossed my arms over my chest and jutted out my chin.

"What's going on, Goth Girl?" Jason asked.

"I want to make a deal with you."

I felt awkward. I didn't know the lingo. I didn't even know what to charge. For the millionth time, I found myself faltering, thinking once again that this was a really bad idea.

75

"What kind of deal?"

I was about five feet away from the chain-link fence that bordered the court and, suddenly, I felt desperate to cling to it. Jason was wearing a shirt that said *Charles Manson had it right*. The guy next to him was covered in skulls—his jacket, his ring, the plugs filling the stretched holes in his earlobes. A couple of other guys were moving a little closer, having heard the interest in Jason's voice. I swallowed hard.

"I got what you asked me about."

"The Oxys?" He sounded surprised.

I nodded. "Yeah."

"Nice." He elbowed Skulls and grinned at the others. "I knew Cyrus would come through."

"Actually," I began, feeling indignant. Then I stopped. Better for them to think Cyrus was behind it. That I was just a middleman, not a source.

"So how many you got?" Jason was asking.

"Four."

"Cool. How much does Cyrus want?"

Crap. I had no idea about market values or any of that stuff. I should have done my homework. I was usually so good with research projects—just last week, I'd nabbed another A for my Organic Chem lab report.

"Um . . . the standard, I guess," I finally say. "What you usually pay."

Jason opened his wallet and counted out a few bills. He looked up at me, squinting.

"Two hundred, right?"

"Sure." I said. I fingered the bottle in my jacket pocket. The edge of the cap felt unexpectedly sharp.

"Great."

Jason wasn't slick. I saw him give a self-satisfied look at his buddies. I narrowed my eyes and did the math in my head.

"No, sorry—it's two hundred and forty for four. One dollar a milligram." I have no idea why I said this. I must have heard that somewhere before. It sounded right, anyway.

"What?" Jason sputtered a little, then flipped back through his wallet. "Fuck, man, all I've got is two hundred and ten."

"That's fine." I smiled, snatching the bills from his hand. "I'll tell Cy I cut you a break this time."

Reluctantly, Jason nodded. "Okay, good deal."

I reached into my pocket again and pulled out the bottle. Jason stared at it.

"What the hell is that?"

"What do you think it is?"

"I don't want that!"

He dumped the pills in his palm and threw the bottle back at me, glaring.

"What the fuck? You trying to get me arrested or something?"

I watched the bottle roll into the grass. The cap was nowhere in sight. A flush of humiliation rose up my neck.

"Whatever, come on." Jason grunted to his friends and they started to move back toward the gym doors. I checked my watch. I'd have to come up with a good excuse for being so late for English.

"Wait." Jason stepped back toward me and handed me a slip of paper. "That's my number. You tell Cyrus—whenever he's holding, I'm buying."

It wasn't until I turned to leave that I noticed Lucas. Like the other day in the library, he sort of hung back, like he was appraising the situation. He smiled at me as he followed the guys. In the breeze, his blond hair swirled above his head like soft-serve ice cream. For a second, I wanted to lick it.

I felt a sudden jolt of embarrassment, like I'd been caught with my pants down. Something about Lucas made me feel naked. It wasn't an entirely unpleasant feeling. Trying to hide my flushed cheeks, I pulled up my hood and hurried back toward the building. I tried not to think of the realities of what I'd just done—the fact that I was officially a drug dealer and that the money in my pocket was for pills that didn't belong to me. Instead, I tried to establish some sense of moral high ground. There are fewer pills for my brother to take. There was enough cash to pay off my science lab debt to Dr. Schafer.

A Wednesday feels like a Wednesday no matter what. But a Wednesday when you have cash in your pocket is a little better than normal. I found Dr. S at the end of the day. She was clapping erasers outside her window. She might be the only teacher who still used a chalkboard—even our school, tech-impaired as it was, gave all the teachers Smart Boards.

"Dr. Schafer?"

She turned around. The cuffs of her jacket were coated in pale yellow dust.

"Cecelia, hi." She frowned up at the clock. "I've only got a minute—there's a faculty meeting today." She gave me an apologetic smile.

"That's okay. I just wanted to give you this." I handed her sixty dollars. "For my lab fee."

Dr. S looked at the cash and nodded slowly.

"Right. Well, okay. You actually don't pay *me*, you pay Mrs. Fleishman, the school secretary."

"Oh."

All afternoon I was so excited to give her the money, to show her I was good for it. Instead, I looked like an idiot.

"Here." I reached for the bills. "I can take it to her."

"No, it's fine." She shook her head. "I think they just want to try to avoid money changing hands between students and teachers."

"Yeah. I guess that makes sense."

I heaved the strap of my bag back up onto my shoulder. The buckle pinched my skin, bringing unintentional tears to my eyes.

"CeCe . . ." Dr. Schafer said, peering at me. "Is everything okay?"

I made a show of unzipping my bag and finding my car keys. "Yeah, sure. Everything's fine."

"Okay . . ." She didn't sound convinced, and I felt even worse.

I forced myself to give her a tight smile before walking

back out the door. Suddenly, I knew how Dad did it, how he put on the happy face for me. All a smile required was defying gravity. It wasn't nearly as hard as admitting how you're really feeling.

8

STEALING THE PILLS WAS A HORRIBLE IDEA.

I paced in my bedroom after school, creating an ugly track in the nap of my carpet. I hoped it, and my nervous nausea, weren't permanent. When Dad's truck pulled into the driveway a few minutes later, I watched Cyrus get out, his face half concealed by the brim of his hat. Was it my imagination, or did I sense a searing combination of rage and betrayal?

It was my imagination. He never even came upstairs.

By dinner, Dad was out in the seed shed and Cyrus was either asleep, high, or out. Jane was gabbing away on the phone to her sister in Denver, so I sat down at the kitchen table alone and, between chews and swallows of stringy chicken cacciatore, considered the following:

   1. I did the right thing. That's four pills that can't kill Cyrus.

2. Let Jason shove them up his nose or in his veins or whatever. Who cares what that guy does?
3. I'm really doing my family a favor.
4. I really need the money for school.

I know I said denial is a refuge, but it's also a time-share. I could vacation there anytime I wanted when guilt threatened to steal what little righteousness I had left.

I started sifting through a stack of mail piled at one end of the table. My eyes skimmed the bills until one long, creamy envelope stopped me short.

Edenton University Alumni Foundation.

I hadn't expected an answer so soon—I'd been accepted at the end of last year, but I only recently applied for their academic scholarship. I ripped it open like it was an Emmy nomination.

And the award for "Most Desperate for Scholarship Money" goes to . . .

Dear Ms. Price,

Thank you for your recent application. We received many highly qualified entries; however, we regret to inform you that you were not selected to receive an Edenton University Alumni Academic Scholarship . . .

I didn't bother reading the rest. Instead, I crumpled up the letter and tossed it in the garbage. It landed on a Styrofoam meat tray slicked with blood. I wished it were mine.

Suddenly the kitchen felt crowded. It was impossible to see the bright side. That, or there wasn't a bright side. I got up quickly and gripped the back of my chair, a little dizzy. I didn't wait for my head to clear before I clambered out the screen door.

Normally, spring evening air would be refreshing. Instead, I felt like a wet blanket suffocating in a plastic grocery bag. It was almost too humid to breathe. Maybe that's why my tears came quick, like a late summer rainstorm. I wished they were hail, that they were hard enough to throw at something. As usual, my tears couldn't hurt anyone but me.

After-school activities, honor roll—all of it was for nothing. I could have been working, earning money, saving for my future—instead I had a "well-rounded" academic profile. What a fucking waste.

I sat alone in the dark until my eyes were dry enough that I could pretend I was just tired. My nose was still a little stuffy and I reached into my jeans' pocket, hoping I had a tissue. I didn't.

But I did have $150. And then, I had an idea. It bloomed in my head like one of Dad's perennials—all at once and kind of like magic.

I'll swipe three or four pills a week—Cyrus is clearly too blitzed out to even notice.

That's at least $750 a month—better than I could do at a part-time job.

By September, I'll have enough money to enroll in a few classes. Enough to pay for my books.

I won't have to worry anymore about paying for groceries or gas or prescriptions.

I won't have to worry anymore about waiting for money to come to me.

The back porch light suddenly flickered on and I stepped back into the darker space behind me. Cyrus came through the basement sliding-glass door, pausing to light a cigarette, then inhaling deeply. I wondered when the last time was that he took a deep breath like that of just air. Just then, a car pulled up and, after a few seconds, the driver flashed the headlights. Cy tossed the cigarette into the grass and walked toward the passenger's side.

If you had asked me two years ago if I could steal from my brother, I would have balked. We were close. We were honest with each other. On a night like tonight, I might have made spaghetti with sliced hot dogs like Mom used to when we were little, then Cy and I would have eaten it straight from the pot with forks while we watched TV. Two years ago, my encounters with my brother would have been as innocent as pasta and *SportsCenter*.

And, two years ago, Cyrus didn't have anything I needed.

I waited until the taillights faded away, the red glow splashing against the bank of trees at the end of our drive-way. Then I walked toward the basement door. When I got there, his cigarette butt was still smoking, a tiny ember flashing against the lawn.

I moved to smother the glow with my foot, but the damp air beat me to it. The butt was dead, the house was quiet, and I walked into the basement, feeling nothing but possibility.

It took less than three minutes for Jason to respond to my text message, and less than two for me to make it to my car. As I pulled into his neighborhood, I could see the silhouettes of McMansions lining the street. I forgot that Jason's dad was some kind of real estate tycoon. The image of greasy-ass Jason and expensive Egyptian cotton sheets felt like a paradox of epic proportions.

"Jason's in the basement, sweetie," his mom said with a warm, fresh-baked smile. I swallowed hard. In what world was it fair that a douche like Jason got a mom like that?

The house was enormous and the open floor plan somehow divided it into levels that were more than separate—like there was a floor that was absent between them. As I descended the stairs, I smelled the same sort of waste, the same reek of human landfill, that Cyrus had polluted our house with. I wondered what Jason's mom thought he was burning down here.

Jason was sitting in front of a massive TV, but it wasn't brand-new. It was one of those big ones that took up more space than a couch. *Call of Duty* and its video game massacres moved across the screen like snapshots.

"Jason."

He looked up at me, and his stoned eyes widened like hungry mouths.

"You made it here quick, girl. You got something for me?" he asked.

I nodded. I imagined that the Ziploc of pills in my pocket was thumping in time with my heartbeat.

"And?"

For a split second, the Jason in front of me transformed. He was in fifth grade again, trying to remember the capital of Wisconsin in the State Capital Bee. When I whispered "Madison," he never said thank you. Later, when I forgot the capital of Washington, he was busy biting a hangnail.

"You got something for me?" he repeated slowly, like I was still too stupid to conduct business. I handed over the bag.

"Sixty a pill, right?" he murmured.

"Yeah. There's five pills in that bag."

"No shit, I can count."

He got up and headed into another room. From where I was standing, I could see the side of a dehumidifier and a half-full basket of dirty laundry. I started to tally the seconds in my head, but each one felt thick and musty like the air. The higher the numbers, the heavier I felt.

Jason's hand, gripping a wad of cash, reentered the room; the rest of him followed. I just stared at the money. He looked at my expression and smirked.

"I threw in an extra ten." He handed me the money and I flipped through it clumsily.

What I thought: *You really can count.*

What I said: "Let me know when you're ready for more."

THE THING THAT'S WEIRD ABOUT A TREADMILL IS THE USELESS-ness of it, the fact that you're going nowhere fast. (Insert jail metaphor here.) According to Dr. Barnes, exercise is a healthy way of venting frustrations or anger. The way I see it, unless I'm throwing dumbbells at a plate-glass window, working out isn't going to relieve anything festering inside me.

Still, I decide to use the Behavioral Therapy gym equipment this morning. I like the idea of feeling exhausted by something other than my therapy sessions.

Today we have a guest speaker. I've heard it's a pretty regular thing, doctors or teachers or victims coming in to make us feel like crap. I can handle most of this therapy stuff. I can sit through group, I can work with Trina, I can keep my nose clean and stay out of people's way. I just don't think I can listen to someone else drone on and on about what they think will fix me or enlighten me or fill me with remorse. So I'm trying to see how long I can stall before Nathan, beefy guard du jour, busts into the BT gym and escorts me to the meeting room.

When the door finally opens, though, it's Tucker. He takes one look at me and crosses his arms.

"Since when do you work out?"

"How would you know if I work out or not?"

"Um, maybe because I'm in here every morning and this is the first time you've ever made an appearance." He grabs a towel from the shelf and hands it to me. "Come on, we're going to be late."

I glare at him. "Seriously? Are you here just to harass me?"

He shrugs. "You call it harassment. I call it holding you accountable."

"Fuck that. I'm not even going."

Tucker rolls his eyes. "Sure you are."

I keep running. My footfalls feel hollow like promises, but I fill them with all the stubborn attitude I can muster. Tucker, on the other hand, tries for chastisement.

"Come on, CeCe. Don't be an ass."

I glare at him. "You know, the last thing I need to do is listen to someone who'll make me feel worse about myself."

Tucker reaches over and pushes the red stop button on my machine. The belt stutters to a stop and I cling to the railing.

"Dude, what the hell?"

He shrugs. "You weren't getting off."

"That's because I'm NOT GOING."

Nathan's concerned face appears in the window. Tucker glances back at him, then lowers his voice.

"Look," he says, stepping closer, "these people that come in—all they do is talk to us."

"All we *do* around here is talk."

"No"—Tucker shakes his head—"all *everyone else* does around here is talk. All you do is avoid talking."

"I think they call that listening."

"In order for it to be listening, you have to actually *hear* what people are saying. And, you know, *care* about what they're talking about."

"Whatever." I snatch the towel from Tucker's hands and wipe my forehead. "What difference does it make if I'm there or not?"

"It doesn't."

"So then why are you making it your life's mission to get me there? Who gives a shit if I let some asshole lecture me this morning or if I just sweat out a few more minutes?"

Tucker doesn't answer. I narrow my eyes until his form lengthens and fades.

"Why do you always do that?" he asks. I blink hard, widening my gaze.

"Do what?"

"That squinting thing you do. Do you need glasses or something?

I shake my head, feeling stupid. "No, my vision's fine."

I busy myself wiping down the treadmill's control panel, but I still feel Tucker's eyes on me. I give up. Listening to a stranger is far less intimate than fielding his questions and dodging his gaze while something palpitates inside my chest.

"Listen," I finally say, "if I go to this speaker thing, will you get off my back? Stop bugging me so much about working through my feelings or whatever?"

Tucker looks genuinely hurt. "I'm not trying to annoy you, CeCe. I'm trying to be your friend."

"I don't need a friend," I mumble.

He shakes his head. "Everyone needs a friend."

Tucker's earnestness, while annoying on the surface, is more than that—it's disarming. So I drop my weapons—towel in the laundry basket, snarky responses left unsaid—and try to follow his lead without hating it.

Everything about Mary Jensen is big. Big head, big hair, big arms, big man hands. I'm sitting in the last row, and she still has a booming voice, like she's holding a megaphone. She's pretty young—maybe early twenties or something. Her ankles look swollen to an uncomfortable degree. I swallow hard. She looks like the Abominable Guilt Trip.

"I'd like to thank everybody for coming today," Mary says, as though this were some sort of voluntary seminar.

"I'm going to give you a little bit of background so that you know why I'm here and why you should give a shit."

It's fun when a stranger cusses. In this case, it's like a

substitute teacher tossing out the lesson plan and taking the class to Dairy Queen. I glance over at Dr. Barnes, who's sitting off to one side. He doesn't seem rattled, which is sort of disappointing.

Mary launches into what she considers an "abbreviated" life story: a full ten minutes of droning on about how she has a brother, how her parents have been married for forty years, blah, blah, blah. When she starts talking about her freshman year in college, I have to work hard to control my rising bile. There's nothing more utterly depressing than hearing about a normal person living a normal life. Everyone sitting here is far from normal, and most of us have never wanted to be anything but that.

"I was away at school when my brother discovered prescription drugs," Mary is saying. "I'd noticed a difference in him since I'd moved out, but I figured it was just the fact that he was growing up. When I was a freshman in college, he was twelve. Sixteen was a whole new ball game."

She's got a hardened look on her face, like a disguise that she wears to tell her story. Like she's separated herself from it out of necessity.

Been there, done that.

"When I graduated college, I moved back home. While I looked for a day job, I ended up working as a night manager at the fast-food restaurant where my brother worked. We were cleaning up one night and I told him to clock out. When I was cashing out the register, I looked out the window and saw him sitting in a friend's car. He was taking a hit, right there in the parking lot—lighter sparked, foil hovering, smoke disappearing into a straw clamped between his teeth. I didn't even know you could smoke pills until that night. And when I finished counting out the register, we were about two hundred dollars short."

Mary stops to take a sip of her water before continuing. I bite down hard on the side of my cheek and let the saliva pool under my tongue.

"My parents were in complete denial when I told them. Even after my brother had been arrested for possession, they still refused to believe that he was a junkie. They did, however, believe every story he fed them—that he was just holding the drugs for friends, that his urine test was positive because he'd been in the same car while others were using—the list of lies was endless. They bailed him out of jail twice, let him live at home, gave him money—at least until they realized he'd been stealing from them the entire time."

I've watched enough Lifetime to know what comes next—there will be a confrontation, a rock bottom, tearful hugs, and a trip to treatment. People think a story like that is a shocker, that it'll rock the rest of us to our very core. Try again; an intervention, rehab—that's the best-case scenario. There's a fist in my chest now and I realize I was wrong. Stories of a normal life, no matter how foreign, would be far better than hearing someone tell a story you already know by heart.

"The thing is," Mary says, her voice now a little wobbly,

"nothing stopped him. That's what people don't understand about drug addiction. It isn't the *death* of a loved one that makes you suffer. It's their *life* that's the real torture—watching them use and use and use with no sign of stopping."

Mary stands up and starts to pace in front of us, and I think, *Lawyer.* And then I think, *Televangelist.*

"What I want to talk to you about today is second chances. When you're stuck in here, the last thing you're thinking about is how it's a blessing. But this place is offering you an opportunity. You have nothing but time. You need to take advantage of that time to become the person you want to be. Like my brother, you had to hit rock bottom to get here. Now that you're here, with nothing but time, how are you going to use it?"

This is the part that's supposed to inspire us to change, to motivate us to live a life of service to society or whatever. Mary pounds one fist into her palm like a visual exclamation point and I let my eyelids drop over the world like a curtain. I sit as still as possible and try to make the room disappear.

But even with my eyes closed, I can hear Mary's fist as it strikes over and over. I can't help thinking of the phrase "it hits home" when I hear the smack of knuckles against skin. There's nothing like hearing your own life story, complete with sound effects, to make you feel like you're living it all over again.

But I'm here. And at least I got Tucker to agree to quit his CeCe Rehabilitation Initiative. I turn to remind him of it, but his chair is empty. Turns out he's the one who bolted early. I guess I should have known better. This place is full of more than just criminals and addicts—it's full of liars, too.

I close my eyes, trying to recall a time when I could trust someone—when lying didn't feel as familiar as family. I remember back in eighth grade, when a couple of girls from school convinced me to steal from Mr. Mulligan, a math teacher who had a propensity for leaving his briefcase open and keeping cigarettes in plain sight. The Marlboro Lights probably weighed less than an ounce, but, for the rest of the day, the pack was a weight in my pocket, like a gun or the Hope Diamond.

But I never considered how much cigarette smoke would actually smell like cigarettes. Or how it would linger on my clothes or in my hair like the perfume I wore too much of. My dad smelled it first; at dinner, I'd taken a helping of zucchini and he sniffed hard, then glared at me.

"Have you been smoking?"

It was a voice I'd never heard him use before, the kind of voice you don't lie to, and I wasn't going to. But my brother did.

"It was me, Dad."

I just stared at Cyrus, dumbfounded. Five minutes earlier, he'd threatened to tell my dad about the crop tops and short skirts I'd been wearing to school. The dance we did in those days was a passive-aggressive tattletale tango. Yet, every now and then, Cyrus positioned himself to take the fall. It was like I was some kind of damsel in distress. It was like he was some kind of knight in shining armor.

Back then, lying was something you did to save someone else, not just to save yourself.

"I just don't understand," Jennifer says, shaking her head.

I shrug. "Dr. Frank skipped town months ago."

"Were you going to tell me that before I went traipsing all over creation to find him?"

"I did tell you. You didn't believe me."

The week of perpetual rain has finally let up, so outside privileges have been reinstated. Jennifer and I are sitting at a picnic table in the patchy grass just beyond the cement yard. There are a handful of general population juvies hanging out on their side of the chain-link fence. I wonder if I'll be joining them after my hearing.

Jennifer reaches into her pocket and pulls out one of those "note to self" handheld recorders.

"I think this will work better than taking notes," she says, pressing a button. She sets the recorder on the table between us. "Okay, so let's pick up where we left off last week."

"Where was that?"

She consults her notes. "Um . . . you'd started selling your brother's prescription."

"Well, yeah. That was pretty much it."

"Had you dealt drugs before?"

"No."

"Had you taken drugs before?"

"No."

She raises her eyebrows. Jennifer has only a handful of expressions. This is the "I don't believe you" look.

"Look"—she places both hands, palms up, on the table—"I'm just saying that, usually, people who deal drugs *do* drugs. It's pretty unusual for that not to be the case."

"Well, it's not."

"Okay, well, that's great." She slides one hand across the table and pats my arm. It's a strange gesture; I blink for a second, then pull back a little. Jennifer gives me a sad smile.

"I upset you. I wasn't trying to. Let's move on."

It takes a lot to freak me out. Jennifer showing emotion definitely does it. She's supposed to be the concrete wall between me and the world. She needs to be impartial and practical and by the book. And that book isn't *Chicken Soup for the Inmate's Soul.*

"Anyway, let's talk about the pills. You started selling them—how did that begin?"

I squint. In the distance, I can see an old farmhouse. Piedmont is surrounded by cornfields; out here, some people still make their living by farming. Strike that. Out here, some people still *try* to make their living by farming. Some of them, like Dad, fail miserably.

"CeCe?"

I wonder what it's like, being the person who lives right next to a jail. Is it a life of extremes? You're either terrified you'll get stabbed in your sleep or you're confident the guards are doing their job? Not to mention the fences and cameras.

"Cecelia?"

I sigh. Jennifer isn't letting me off the hook anymore. We're two weeks away from court and now she wants me to bare my soul.

"Some people at school asked about Cy," I begin. "They knew what he had. They said they'd be interested in buying." Jason's face flares, then fizzles before my eyes.

"So this was a deal between you and Cyrus?"

I shake my head. "No. I just took them."

Jennifer looks surprised. "And he didn't notice?" She frowns. "Addicts keep track of their stash. How could he not notice?"

I shrug, then look back over at the fence. The inmates are gone now and the fence is just a barely there border. A chain-link wrinkle in time.

"He was high. Like, all the time—too high to see straight, let alone count. I didn't take that many at a time, and he was constantly upping his dosage anyway. I guess it never occurred to him that the disappearing pills weren't his own fault."

"So, do you think he was taking other drugs?" she asks. "To supplement?"

"Maybe."

"Any idea what kind?"

I think about that for a second. "No. I only ever saw Oxys."

"That's okay." Jennifer clicks the recorder off, then makes a note on her legal pad. "I can pick up the autopsy report from the medical examiner. It'll tell me what I need to know."

Here's what I see when she says *autopsy*: Cyrus's remains, as though a century has passed.

The borders around my hardened heart sort of fizzle inward and I can feel it—the thick, syrupy grief I've ignored since the moment I knew Cy was gone. Despite all the pain, the things I still see when I lie down to sleep are the moments when we were closest—when we were the kind of brother and sister who wanted to be in each other's space.

It was hard to transition to something less than that. But once I had, it was like I'd lost that need to link myself to another person.

And now, it's his body I think of—mummified, calcified, whatever would make it crumbly and impossible to recognize. His bones are brown and his flesh is gone. There's nothing left to love and that's good, since I'm not sure I want to anymore.

"Speaking of reports . . ."

Jennifer's holding a case folder—manila, unmarked, non-descript—in her lap. She flips through it and pulls out a yellow paper. It's thin, like tissue, and it sort of glows when the light filters through it.

"Family medical history can often be a big clue to behavior. If it doesn't answer our questions, it usually helps us ask the right ones . . ." She trails off, squinting at the form.

"So, we've also been going through *your* medical records, CeCe."

Jennifer hands me the paper; I try to soften the edges of my breathing before it accidentally tears it in half. She points to the address at the top left section.

"Do you remember this place, CeCe?"

Yes.

"No."

"We got these from your house. Your father said your mom had a great filing system."

My mom had a great everything.

"Okay."

"So, you don't remember when you went to see this therapist? After your mom passed away?"

Of course I remember. Dr. Marks was young, too young to be taken seriously. He had a nervous habit of clearing his throat, and I must have made him nervous because he did it a lot. I think he was worried I'd slice myself open and bleed on his beautifully upholstered wingback chairs.

"It was a long time ago."

"Four years."

"A long time."

Jennifer takes back the paper and scans the page. She starts to read.

"Patient exhibits extreme depression related to deceased mother. She is lethargic and unemotional, possibly self-imposing isolation to cope with loss. Major concerns—possible suicide potential."

She looks up at me. I set my jaw.

"What did he mean by 'possible suicide potential'?"

"If you're asking if I tried to kill myself, the answer is no."

"Did you ever *think* about killing yourself?"

I shrug. "Sometimes."

I glance at Jennifer's watch, then nod at the door.

"Trina's waiting for me—I should go."

Jennifer shifts in her seat. "Just tell me something."

"Sure, shoot."

"Is that something you still think about?"

"What?"

"Killing yourself."

I look at the fence again, the metal netting separating here from there. There's nothing on the other side but asphalt and emptiness; the only difference over here is that there's grass.

Somehow, there's still life on this side of the world. And, somehow, that still includes me, despite all my desires to the contrary.

"No," I finally sigh, standing up and stretching. "That window of opportunity seems to have passed."

I point up at the cameras aimed in my direction. Jennifer grimaces.

"Death isn't the answer, Cecelia," she says, eyes narrowed.

I huff out a little laugh. "Please. Tell me something I don't already know."

Death is *never* an answer. It's an end result. It's a finale. But it certainly doesn't lay questions to rest. In fact, the only thing it lays to rest is people—and, even then, I'd replace the word *lay* with *disintegrate*.

And I'd replace the word *rest* with *dust*.

June 21

For a brief moment in time, Cyrus and I wanted nothing more than to harmonize. There were whole afternoons we spent scream-singing along with the music video for Queen's "Bohemian Rhapsody." Cy would drape himself in Mom's scarves and use her round hairbrush as a microphone. The perpetual second fiddle, I settled for a black Magic Marker.

His wild, spastic dancing made me giddy. I wanted to be just like my big brother—I wanted to move and sing and breathe like him. If he jumped up onto the couch, I followed. If he knelt down, I joined him. Cy never accused me of being a copycat. It was the only time he wanted me to be his shadow.

During the slow moments, we'd shift to a rocking

sway. As the music rose to a crescendo, we traded our moves for louder and louder voices. Standing in the middle of the room, we'd face each other and yell the lyrics.

Inevitably the music would wane to a close. Our tradition always ended the same way—a plop on the couch. A deep breath. A final, slow lyric we could barely sing.

C.P.

10

AN AFTERNOON OUTSIDE WITH JENNIFER FELT ALMOST FOREIGN IN
its unfamiliarity, considering I hardly ever get fresh air anymore. But when the therapy session Barnes has been touting
all week turns out to be a field trip, I find myself almost
excited. The idea of going anywhere in a vehicle feels suspi-
ciously like possibility, and it's a little intoxicating.

Of course, a junkyard is the last thing I expect to see when
the Piedmont van rolls to a stop in front of Bertie's Scrap
Metal. Nothing good can come out of me being surrounded
by so much death, even if it's just the riddled carcasses of old
cars.

Barnes, sitting in the passenger's seat, directs the driver
through the front gate before turning around and smiling
at us.

"This is where we're going?" Aaron asks. He sounds as
skeptical as I am. Barnes nods.

"I told you we were going on a therapeutic journey."

"Yeah, but I thought that meant we were going to a Zen garden or yoga studio or some shit, not Trailer Trash Central."

Barnes shushes us as a very round woman lumbers out of the shed-like office. He hands her some cash and we pull forward between two rusty Oldsmobiles.

Minutes later, I'm standing between Aarti and a dilapidated Camaro IROC, shifting from foot to foot like I have to pee. All around are stacks of bricks, a half-dozen bowling balls, a metal bat, and a bunch of concrete pavers.

"Welcome to Destruction Therapy," Barnes says, something like triumph or pride icing his words. He is clearly pleased with himself.

"Bertie has donated this lovely piece of machinery," he continues, patting the IROC's hood, "for us to use for today's exercise. Here are the rules for Destruction Therapy:

"Everyone gets a turn.

"Use your words to communicate.

"Don't hit each other."

"If they sound familiar," Tucker says, "it's because I think they're the same ones that are posted on the wall at Chuck E. Cheese's."

"This is ridiculous," Aaron mutters.

"Eh, look at it this way—we're out of Piedmont. And we get to throw things and scream," I tell him.

He smirks. "I can do that whenever I want to."

But, in reality, no one wants to be first to attack the car.

We all spend a few awkward minutes shuffling our feet and kicking at the dirt before Aarti picks up the baseball bat. Her thick hair shifts over her face and she approaches the car cautiously, like it could wake up and snarl at any moment. The whole junkyard is eerily quiet. It's like everyone's waiting for Aarti to snap.

And then she does.

She goes for the headlights first, jabbing at them with the butt of the bat. The glass cracks on the first blow and shatters on the second.

"That's for my husband," Aarti says, "who thought I was his property."

She flips the bat around and swings hard at the hood. The clang is like a thunderbolt that echoes off the metal around us.

"Who thought he could touch me anywhere he wanted," Aarti is saying. "Who said I needed a real man to show me how to do it right."

Soon the bat is forgotten in favor of a paver, which she struggles to throw at the back window. It misses, landing with a crunch on the trunk. The paint scrapes off, leaving a skid of gray-blue primer behind. Aarti's panting and she bends over to catch her breath. Then she looks up and gives us a rueful smile.

More people go, choosing the pavers and bricks as weapons against their ex-boyfriends, their teachers, their parents, themselves. Tucker attacks his drug dealer and Leslie wails on her stepdad. Aaron goes after a friend who introduced him to meth. By the time Barnes hands me the bat, it seems sort of pointless. There's hardly an untouched surface on the car; it's been destroyed beyond recognition.

"Give it a shot," he urges. "It can't hurt, right?"

It's a weird question to ask someone wielding a bat.

I walk up to the driver's-side door and yank on the handle. When the door creaks open, I reach down and pop the hood. As I walk back to the front of the car, the air around me turns thick with buzzing, like some sort of feedback. I try to ignore it, the way you ignore the too-close rush of highway traffic beyond a strategic but too-thin line of trees.

Under the hood, the IROC is almost pristine. Someone took care of this car before it kicked the bucket. I hold the bat from the top, at the place where a home run begins. I look back up and see Tucker give me an encouraging nod. Something like irritation sears through me; this guy's still trying to be my therapist, and there's no room for another one of those in my life. So it's Tucker's face I see when I take my first swing.

"Who are you angry with?" Barnes calls out over the blows. I grit my teeth and try to concentrate.

"My dad," I finally say, dropping the bat and heading for the yet-untouched bowling balls.

"Why?"

Before I shut down and retreat, I see a handful of balls sitting side by side in the dirt, each one a marbled purple or blue or green. I pick the one closest to me and head back toward the car. I stare at the spiderwebbed cracks in the windshield glass. They've spread to both sides like a disease. I see Cyrus's face in the middle, and all the jagged lines coming from it.

"This is for being an enabler," I say. "This is for letting it all go down."

And I launch the ball toward the glass. The shatter has barely subsided as I'm picking up the next one.

"This is for my mom, for dying. For leaving me alone to fend for myself.

"This is for my college fund that doesn't exist.

"This is for my pile-of-shit future.

"This is for my past."

My arms are wobbly with exhaustion as I heave the last ball up with both hands. I come around to the back of the car and find a partially intact taillight to aim for. I watch the way the sun flashes over the fragmented surface. The red plastic rectangles wink like they're flirting, and I know there's only one thing left to say.

"This is for Cyrus."

I want to throw it hard, but my arms are too tired. Instead, I launch it underhand, but it's like a weak substitution for what I should be doing. When the ball hits the dirt instead of the car, I feel like a failure. Tears prick at my eyes. I take a step back, away from the group. Then another. Then another.

And then I turn around and start to run.

Surrounded by the forest of abandoned vehicles, I try not to compare the piles around me to Cyrus's basement bedroom. I stop next to an unrecognizable, rusted-out car carcass and sit down on the ground, my back against a tire. I let the tears fall. They are slick on my face—nothing like water and everything like blood. I want to drink them and take them in. I want to reject them and spit them out.

"CeCe?"

I ignore Tucker, even though his voice is like lace—soft and practically transparent. I try to forget the ever-changing texture of his eyes and how I can't stop comparing them to things I've touched. I don't look up when he sits down next to me, pulling his knees up against his chest.

"Are you okay?" he asks.

"I'm fine," I lie.

When I finally look up, his eyes mirror the rust around us. They've somehow aged and are completely overwhelming. He puts a hand on my shoulder and I can feel the joint melt under his touch. My bones turn to something liquid and, for a second, it feels like a memory.

"Who's Cyrus?"

Here it is—an opportunity to be honest. Still, I don't answer. I'm waiting for someone to interrupt us, for Barnes to come around the corner and scold me for "stifling my process." But another minute goes by without a sound, save for the metal-on-metal racket echoing in my mind as I stare at the wrecked cars around us and imagine their accidents. Head-on collisions, T-boned passenger doors—the physical brutality, like bruises, are easy to see. It's the internal damage that is still disguised.

Maybe it's better to tell the truth, to confess. Maybe when

you expose your injuries, you give them a chance to heal.

"My brother," I finally say.

My mouth is dry and cottony with a coating of gummy saliva. I want my tongue to lasso the words back in. Tucker moves his hand from my shoulder to my knee and my whole body shudders. He feels me quake and pulls back a bit.

"You don't have to talk to me, CeCe," he says, pulling himself up straighter, "but I hope one day you will."

Then he grabs my hand and I forget how to ask questions. Around us, the cars and trucks are so corroded, they're almost crumbling. I'm reminded of avalanches I've seen on TV, how the ice and snow become something broken-down and terrifying. Here, though, the potential threat is just a field of windshields and roofs. When I squint, we're in a movie theater parking lot or at the post office or stuck near the bus station. When I squint, I don't see anything but what's normal and I'm soothed for the first time in weeks.

But when Tucker's thumb, with its dry, scratchy hangnail and callused tip, brushes my palm methodically, I remember that normal isn't a state of mind. It's a place I don't live anymore. I start to pull my hand away, but he tightens his grip.

"Don't."

I look at him warily, then narrow my eyes, remembering his swift departure from the guest speaker's presentation.

"You're such a hypocrite," I say, shaking my head.

Tucker sort of rears back. "Excuse me?"

"You act like you want to help me or something, but

when you dragged me to that guest speaker yesterday, it took you all of twenty minutes to disappear. What the fuck is up with that?"

He drops my hand like I've burned him.

"I guess . . ." Tucker begins. Then his eyes start to close. Not close via eyelid but close via access to thoughts. He's cutting me off.

"It was all stuff I've heard a million times before," he finishes, sighing. Then he stands up. "Come on. Let's go back."

"Was it something I said?"

He smiles, and it's the first time I've noticed his teeth. They're white, but not fluorescent, Hollywood white. Natural white. Like he just inherently has good teeth. Somehow, this makes me want to trust him more than ever.

"Don't want to miss the bus," he's saying, wiping his hands on his jeans. "Not to mention I promised Barnes I'd bring you back in one piece."

"Right. Well, thanks for not hacking me up or whatever."

Tucker looks at me sideways. "You're a little morbid, you know that?"

I snort a laugh just as, out of nowhere, he swoops in and presses his lips against mine. It's a chaste, easy kiss. It feels dry and reminds me of tissue paper. When he pulls back, I blink rapidly, then open my mouth. No words come out. Tucker's smile turns from toothy to sexy in a matter of seconds.

"I've been wanting to do that," he admits, saying the words slowly, "but I didn't want to get in trouble."

One of the floor rules in BT is no romantic fraternization.

Considering how fucked up most of us are, there are days when everyone just wants someone to cuddle or grope or make out with. Sometimes a lack of human touch feels like an ache in your belly. Sometimes all you want is for the pressure squeezing your body to be coming from the outside and from someone's arms rather than from the cliché, self-imposed torture.

I force myself to inhale and the air stutters along my tongue. Tucker is watching me carefully, as though he's afraid I might combust or burst into tears. Instead, I give him something I haven't given anyone in a long time—I smile. It's a slow process, an upturn that almost hurts since it feels so foreign now. As my lips curve up, I find myself missing the sensation of grinning—the kind that makes your cheeks ache. I wonder if I'll ever be allowed to be that happy again.

I can't remember what it's called, but something makes you feel sort of high when you're happy. Endorphins, maybe? Dopamine? Regardless, there's something frenetic and unbridled coursing through me as we walk back to the bus. I'm a little frightened of the frenzy, of the out-of-control-ness. Tucker's body is so close to mine that his hand brushes my arm more than once. I try to remember what it feels like to kiss someone back. It's a giving over, if I remember correctly. I imagine Tucker kissing me again.

It's the most alive I've felt in months.

MORNING SUN ALWAYS FEELS TOO BRIGHT, ESPECIALLY WHEN you've been sitting near the back of a school bus for an hour. I squinted up at Sexton Hall, the white-columned building at the entrance of the Edenton campus. It reminded me of my second-grade field trip to Washington, DC. Those monuments felt more important than any building I'd ever seen; Sexton Hall was like the Capitol Building and the Lincoln Memorial's love child.

Natalie tugged on my sleeve. "Look at this"—she pointed to the map—"there's a Starbucks right on campus! How cool is that? Do you think they let freshmen choose their own roommates? Maybe we should fill in dorm applications today."

"Okay. Sure." I forced a smile.

When Jeremy bailed on the trip, I was sure Natalie'd blow me off, giving me an exit strategy. There was no point in visiting Edenton now; it was a club I'd never be allowed to join. And I hadn't told Natalie about the rejection letter from the Scholarship Foundation—she didn't have to worry about stuff like that. Her college was already paid for.

But she'd called last night to read me Edenton's raving reviews at collegepartygods.com. Apparently Jungle Juice and nitrous oxide were seeing resurgence at local off-campus social gatherings. Maybe that accounted for the number of people on this tour; the bus was full and a handful of seniors had come separately with parents in tow. I don't think their parents came for the laughing gas, but you never know.

Eddie, one of the student tour guides, shifted from foot to foot as he checked out cheer captain Julie Hardwick. Julie had decided it was an excellent idea to wear last night's party clothes to this morning's academic outing, along with a sexy smear of eye makeup on each lid. I always knew she was classy.

A handful of guys were quizzing Eddie's counterpart, Vince, about intramural sports, while Mr. Morton, our chaperone, was chatting with a couple of parents. I used my well-bitten thumbnail to peel the insignia from the front of my "Welcome to our expensive-ass college where the only thing you get free is this folder" folder.

"So, is this still your number-one school?" Natalie asked me. She flipped through the course catalog. "If it doesn't have a fashion program, I'm not interested."

I shrugged, picking sticker adhesive from under my nail.

I could feel bile or panic or both rising in my chest. I don't know what I was thinking—how was I supposed to make it a whole day pretending that I was actually going here in the fall? Pill money would never pay for Edenton courses. I was destined to be an alumna of Nowhere Important Community College.

I contemplated faking a sprained ankle and started scoping out something to trip over. At least then I could hang out on the bus while everyone else planned their futures.

If nothing else, I can hide out in the Starbucks, I thought.

"Cecelia?"

The voice was husky and smoky and male and, I'm not going to lie, even before I knew who it was, every hair on my body stood up and took notice.

I turned to see Lucas Andrews standing behind Natalie, hardly five feet away. His eyes were the kind of blue you see in Disney movie princes—royal or cobalt or sapphire. I would have broken into song had I been able to breathe. Natalie just looked back and forth between Lucas and me.

"How's it going?" he asked, this time looking at Natalie.

"Good." She gave him a sleepy, glazed-doughnut smile—the kind that Natalie usually reserved for her boyfriend and baked goods. The sun made Lucas's hair even blonder; I wouldn't have thought that possible. It was almost like a halo shining above his head.

"So, Edenton, huh?" Lucas said, this time to me. He shoved his hands in the pockets of his jeans.

"Uh, yeah. You, too?"

He didn't answer—just stood there, looking at me, with a smile buried under his lips so that all his mouth showed was potential. Somehow I could tell he was used to not answering questions people wanted answers to. And that was sexy as hell.

For a second, the three of us stood there like a disjointed tripod, with Natalie just staring at me as though I'd grown a few extra pairs of breasts and they were the only explanation for Lucas's attention. In the meantime, Eddie had started to herd our group into an amorphous body that, as it shifted, absorbed more and more people. The audience of thirty or forty sort of swayed as it moved toward the nearby library. Natalie glanced at Lucas again, then grinned at me before tucking her folder into her bag and moving toward the front of the crowd. I watched her curls bounce along her shoulders, then disappear from view.

Lucas and I were walking slowly and the rest of the crowd moved past us to hear Eddie's spiel. I flipped through my folder to a photocopied map. The Edenton campus was like one rectangle, divided into angles by diagonal sidewalks and buildings. We were walking toward the Commons, where there was a student bookstore, the dining hall, and mailboxes for on-campus students.

"This campus is pretty small," Lucas said. I nodded, watching him from my peripheral vision. His chin jutted with a kind of confidence. Even his face had swagger.

"Married housing is just behind this building." Eddie pointed at a series of double-wide mobile homes. They reminded me of the portable classrooms at our high school. The teachers called them "the learning pods," while the students preferred "the trailer park."

"They're first come, first serve and they fill up fast, so if you need 'em, make sure you put that on your application," Eddie was saying. "Otherwise you'll end up in the dorms."

"I can't imagine being married in college," I muttered. Lucas raised an eyebrow.

"What, you don't want to get hitched at seventeen? You might get an MTV show if you're up for it."

I grimaced. "Not unless they pay enough to cover my tuition."

We were walking through a pergola and toward the freshmen dorms. Lucas was watching me now and his gaze felt sort of spicy, like when I burn my tongue. Less painful, though. More tingly.

"What about scholarships?" he finally asked. "You're such a good student—AP classes, honor roll, all that shit."

So, he knows stuff about me? The tingle in my cheeks started intensifying and I bit down hard on my lower lip.

"The scholarship route hasn't really panned out for me," I admitted. "If I had another year, I could apply for more financial aid, but—"

And that's when Lucas stopped walking. He moved to the left, where a nearby building cast shadows over a few benches and two sad-looking rhododendron bushes. It took a second for me to realize that, in the process, he'd grabbed my hand.

"Look, I'm not here because I want to go to Edenton."

What I think: *I'm here because there's just something about you. We've hardly spoken, but there's this bond between us . . .*

What I hear: "I came because Jason asked me to."

The world righted itself. Of course.

"He's got a message for your brother," Lucas continued, one hand raking through his hair. The same hand, coincidentally, that had been holding mine a second ago. "He wants a quantity and he's willing to pay big money."

I blinked hard. "I—I just saw Jason. Last night."

Lucas raised both eyebrows and I felt the color wash over my face.

"To bring him . . . stuff," I said, suddenly wary of who could be listening.

"Yeah, I know. But Jason gave me eighty bucks to find you today and tell you to get him more."

I swallowed. "How much is more, exactly?"

Lucas shrugged. "As much as Cyrus will pass along, I guess. At least a couple dozen."

I exhaled. I knew I couldn't do that, not all at once.

"I'll check with Cyrus," I said carefully. "It might take a little while."

"Sure, sure. I understand." Lucas glanced at his watch. "Well, sweet. Easiest eighty bucks I ever made."

I felt like garbage.

"So, I think I'm gonna head out," Lucas said. "I'm starving." He looked at me, head cocked to one side. "You wanna get some breakfast?"

"I don't know . . ." I said slowly, peeking around the side of building.

Eddie and the group were still moving farther away, but I could hear him talking about elective credits while parents were taking pictures of a historic clock tower. I couldn't see Natalie in the crowd and I felt a stab of guilt for abandoning my friend. I turned back toward Lucas.

"I should probably catch at least some of the tour."

"Aw, come on—break the rules for once." Lucas grinned, moving in closer.

Something inside my chest stuttered and I watched the half smile on his face spread to whole.

"How do you know I don't break the rules all the time?" I asked, attempting to flirt without throwing up or swallowing my tongue. Lucas laughed.

"I have a feeling that you've been a good girl pretty much all your life."

Right. The good girl who sells drugs? The good girl who gives up on her dream school? The good girl who lies to her best friend and takes off with an almost stranger to get breakfast?

And that's when Lucas winked at me.

And that's when I asked, "So, where are you parked?"

The interior of Lucas's Mazda was tricked out—he had a kick-ass sound system and a built-in GPS. On the floor were black mats with a glow-in-the-dark pot leaf outline in the center of each one.

"How long have you had this?" I asked, gesturing to the car.

"For a year or so."

"Did you bring it with you from California?"

"Huh?"

"From . . . California?" I repeated uncertainly. "I thought you lived there or something."

He laughed. "No, who told you that?"

"Um, I don't remember. Someone at school."

"I'm originally from Kansas. Right outside Topeka."

"Oh. Right."

I looked at Lucas's profile as he fiddled with some buttons on the dashboard. For the first time, I noticed a thin, raised scar running down his cheek; it was long, snaking its way back behind his ear.

He messed with the car stereo for a minute, then pushed the clock button. It was 10:10 a.m. He looked over at me.

"I think I passed a diner just outside town. It's a little early for lunch, but I'll bet they serve breakfast all day."

I shrugged, pretending not to care. Being alone with him was already making me queasy with nerves. Being with him in public couldn't be any worse than us sitting in his car, our bodies barely a foot apart. I'd liked guys before, but never a guy who voluntarily spent time with me. It was a revelation, and it made me both giddy and completely uncomfortable.

In fact, something about Lucas reminded me of my very first crush. His name was Josh, but I called him Joshua, and he played on Cy's soccer team in middle school. I also liked writing the word *Joshua* on my notebook—especially when it was followed with + *CeCe*. My crush on Josh was lengthy, even after he'd figured out how much I liked him and long after he'd started mocking me to his teammates.

Cyrus was torn. Sometimes he laughed at me, like his friends. Sometimes he spent the car ride home yelling at me for being so stupid, for liking a boy who couldn't care less about me.

It's the day Cy punched Josh that I remembered best. I don't know what was said or how it started, but, from the sidelines, I'd watched my brother's shoulders sort of ripple and extend. I thought, *Just like the Incredible Hulk*, and then fists began to fly. Cy's team lost the game. My parents grounded him for a week and Cyrus learned that even he faced consequences.

Of course, from then on, Cy wasn't so fiercely loyal to me. From then on, he was just fierce.

When Lucas and I got to University Diner, the hostess seated us in a wide booth by the front window. I could hear the crunch of gravel as cars pulled into and out of the parking lot. For a minute, we read over our menus. Well, Lucas read over his menu. I pretended to look at mine, but the laminated surface was too shiny for me to focus; all I could think was that Lucas had driven an hour to come find me. Eighty bucks might have covered a tank of gas, but not breakfast.

"You want to split some French toast sticks?" he asked. His eyes met mine over a photo of omelets and my brain felt scrambled.

"Um, okay. Sure."

"So, Edenton—yes or no?" he asked after the waitress took our order. I shook my head.

"No. It's really too expensive."

"How much is too expensive?"

"Like forty grand a year."

He gave a low whistle and shook his head, then checked his phone. Nervously, I fingered the paper ring around my napkin.

"So, how'd you meet Jason?" I asked, needing to fill the silence.

"I never really met him." When I looked confused, Lucas laughed. "He's my cousin."

"Oh." The fact that Lucas and Jason were related seemed impossible. Two people had never looked more different.

"That's why we moved here," Lucas was saying. "Mom and Aunt Wendy are twins—they do everything together. Every time they've ever lived in different places, one of them always ends up moving to be closer to the other. They finish each other's sentences, all that twin stuff. It's super annoying."

"I think that's actually sort of great," I admitted. I tried to imagine a world where I didn't want to get as far away from Cyrus as possible.

Lucas reached for his soda. It wasn't until his mouth hit the straw that I realized I'd been watching his lips like today's feature presentation. He must have noticed, because I could see a smirk start to bend the corners of his mouth. I was becoming unhinged, so I tried to regroup.

"Do you have any summer plans?"

I almost cringed at the lameness of my question. Lucas just shrugged.

"Get a job, I guess. Work on my car."

"What about the fall?"

He shrugged again. "Community college, maybe? Honestly, I don't have the grades for much else. School's just not my thing."

I nodded. That's how Cyrus was, too, but he always had to keep a 3.0 to remain eligible for soccer.

When our food arrived, I forced myself to take a French toast stick, even though I was anything but hungry. The still-hot grease burned my fingers, but Lucas was chewing his like he couldn't feel a thing.

"What's wrong?" He motioned to my stick, now drowning in syrup.

"It's too hot."

He peered at it; a wisp of steam rose from one end. Then, leaning across the table, he looked at me, pursed his lips, and blew.

The steam disappeared. Inside my chest, something cold and hollow started to melt.

"So . . ." Lucas lifted an eyebrow at me, then dipped another French toast stick into the syrup.

"So," I echoed. I could feel a warmth spreading over my cheeks and I forced myself not to bite my lip.

"Do you have a boyfriend?"

I blinked at Lucas and his smile was less curious and more

sure. Like he already knew the answer. I shook my head.

"No—I don't."

"Hmm." He chewed and swallowed, then leaned back in his chair. "Then I think I'm obligated to tell you that that information pleases me."

I smiled shyly. "Oh—um, well . . . I guess I'm glad it pleases you."

"Good."

Lucas kept eating and I tried not to stare at his mouth. Boys had always made me nervous, and I forced my hands under the table and sat on them so I didn't start fiddling with my silverware.

I began thinking up mantras.

I will not write his last name behind my first.

I will not follow him around.

I will not ruin this before it's even started.

"You've got beautiful eyes, Cecelia."

From that moment on, the way Lucas Andrews looked at me felt like a miracle. I licked my lips and reached for a French toast stick, no longer caring if I got burned—by anything—in the process.

12

THE FIRST TIME LUCAS KISSED ME, IT FELT LIKE A FOREIGN LAN- guage in my mouth. I didn't know how to reciprocate—not well, anyway. Everything I did seemed slightly off, as though my self-consciousness zoomed straight from my brain to my lips, practically paralyzing them against Lucas's soft, coaxing mouth.

As we pulled apart, he leaned back in the driver's seat and adjusted the radio, trying to get rid of some of the static. I wanted to tell him it was useless, that we didn't get reception in my driveway, but I was too busy noticing the way my mouth felt, even without his still on it. It was sort of numb, like I'd been shot up with Novocain.

"So, when you suggested coming to your house, did you mean inside or just in the general vicinity?"

He gave me a lopsided smile and I felt a surge of panic. I didn't know what scared me more—being alone in here with Lucas or risking him running into Cyrus the Oxy-idiot. When he'd offered to drive me home from Edenton, it only seemed polite to invite him inside.

"I don't know . . ."

Lucas looked up at the interior light. The bulb was blue, making his skin a little zombie-ish.

"We could hang out with Cyrus or something, right?" he suggested, still looking at the ceiling. "Do you think he's home?"

Fuck.

"I'm pretty sure he's out . . . he had an appointment today. Or something."

"Oh, okay. Some other time, then."

Lucas leaned in and brushed his lips against my cheek. They were dry and, for some reason, I felt the threat of tears rising in my throat.

"So, I guess I'll see you around?" he asked. His lips traveled closer and closer to my mouth. I felt his breath and I wanted to close the gap between us. I wished he'd say he'd call me tonight. I wanted him to *want* to see me again.

But I said, "Sure. I'll see you around."

Lucas laughed. "How about we make 'around' be 'ASAP'?"

I'd never felt so much promise in so few words. "Yeah, sure."

Then I was out of the car and waving and he was on the road and out of sight, and I was standing in the driveway feeling dazed and throbbing, unable to stop my brain from running in circles that had more words in them than actual thoughts. I touched my fingers to my mouth. I wanted to lick my lips, but I was afraid I'd lose their current sensation. It was almost like an aftertaste, an echo I couldn't quite hear. It was the first time I'd been intoxicated.

I tried to be quiet when I opened and closed the front door. As I made it to the top of the stairs, I heard the yawn of the furnace coming on a floor below me. Jane was still at work and Dad was making the two-hour trek to the closest farm supply store for more weed-and-feed. So, when I heard the scuffling, I knew who it was. It sounded like raccoons were digging in the garbage, but it was a different kind of bottom-feeder.

Dad hadn't had a lot of luck selling his seeds wholesale. He'd gotten some mail-order business, but he made most of his money from farmers' markets. Because he was naive or trusting or both, he kept his cash box in the kitchen. He really should have hidden it. Then again, he really shouldn't have had to.

Cyrus had the metal box up on the counter, the top tray pulled out and tossed aside. He knew the bigger bills were at the bottom. I watched him stuff the money in his pants' pockets.

"Cyrus."

His name tasted like poison. It used to slide over my lips like a smile. Cy jumped a little at the sound of my voice and whirled around.

"What the fuck are you doing home?"

His eyes were completely black. The warm golden brown

irises we used to share had been overthrown by the strength of something dark and needy. In the past, drugs had made Cyrus lazy and tired, absent and unable to function. They'd never made him like this—driven by something ugly.

"Cyrus," I repeated, trying not to let my voice shake. "Don't do this. Please. Dad needs that money. *We* need it."

"Just shut the fuck up."

He turned back around and grabbed the rest of the cash before shoving the box back against the Mr. Coffee. I stepped forward and touched his shoulder, and it was like I had electrocuted him. Almost instantly, he had me pinned up against the pantry door and his hand was at my throat.

"Jesus, Cy," I managed to croak, "relax. I'm just—"

"You think you're so perfect." His breath was hot and rank. I struggled to breathe.

"You never make mistakes, do you, CeCe? You always do everything right. And you think that makes you so much better than me."

"Cy?" Tears filled my eyes. I squeezed them shut.

"Oh, please," he scoffed. "Bitches don't cry. They don't have feelings."

That word—*bitch*. That word snapped me into action and I pushed him away.

"Go to hell!" I yelled into his face. "Don't you realize how much you're costing us—costing *all* of us? We've already lost Mom and now you're just trying to make the swiftest fucking exit possible? Don't you care what that would do to Dad? To me?"

I shook my head then, the venom racing through my veins.

"But you know what? You wanna fuck up your life? You want to spend your days and nights in an Oxy-stupor that's going to ultimately kill you? Then do it—but you better do it right. Because it would be a hell of a lot easier—and a hell of a lot *cheaper*—for all of us if you just overdosed and ended it."

I didn't get a chance to say anything else before Cyrus shoved my face backward and my head slammed into the pantry door with a crack. The last thing I saw before I hit the floor was the cash box, gutless and gaping like a victim.

"Fuck you, Cecelia. Fuck your perfect, bullshit life."

The pain swiftly migrated from my head to my ribs as his boot connected with my body. I tried to open my mouth, to speak, but there was something about words that felt too impossible to even attempt.

"You think I like this? You think I *want* to be this way? I had everything, CeCe. I had the kind of life people dream of. I didn't ask for my knee to get fucked up. I didn't ask for my soccer career to go down the fucking tubes. I have nothing left—don't you get it?"

With all the strength I had left, I turned my head to see his face. His eyes were crazed and glassy and I wondered if he could even see me.

"I have nothing left," he repeated under his breath.

I curled up in a ball, prepared to ward off another kick.

"You stay the fuck away from me—you stay out of my

business and out of my life." He leaned down and grabbed my chin. "And if you breathe a word of this to Dad—I'll fucking kill you."

When his hand slammed my head back into the floor, I felt everything all at once.

And then I felt nothing. Or, more specifically, I felt *like* nothing. Like the world was nothing and I was nothing and my body was inexplicably cracking in half, starting at my heart and working outward.

When I opened my eyes, I was lying on the kitchen linoleum. I don't know how long had passed. I put a hand to my rib cage and winced. There was a tender place right over my heart; something was broken in there. I felt fractured. Torn apart.

Cyrus was gone. Maybe his pills saved him from a sense of guilt or responsibility. Then again, it was what we'd become—I was perpetually broken and Cyrus, *my* Cyrus, had disappeared for good.

I couldn't remember a time before that day that physical violence entered the doors of our house. In fact, the only time Dad ever spanked either of us was the time Cy played with matches. It was evening and cold out in our playhouse. Cy collected branches and tore up some newspaper—it wasn't thirty seconds before the flames reached the four-foot-high ceiling. Dad put out the fire with a bright red extinguisher, and I was little enough to think it was exciting, as though he were a real live fireman, the kind I'd read about in books.

When the smoke began to clear, Dad grabbed Cy by the

arm and turned him over his knee, right there in the yard. Cy didn't cry. He just took it, absorbing the hits like a sponge soaks up something sopping and liquid and easily disguised. Dad said that he wanted Cy to learn a lesson, but he never said what it was. Seems that the lesson my brother learned that day was how, when someone does something wrong, you can hurt them with your hands. That and, as long as you're stronger, you're right.

I crawled like a dog down the hall to my room, where I managed to hoist myself into my bed. The sun was still high and bright when I fell asleep; when I woke up again, my room was dim in the fading dusk and I felt like I'd been hit by a car. I teetered to standing and moved in front of the full-length mirror to assess the damage. I looked like an art project—evidence of Cyrus's freak-out was splayed across my chest and shoulder. The what-would-be-bruises were still red, the blood beneath having leached to the surface. There was a shadowy mark along my cheek, which must have been caused by my run-in with the kitchen floor. When I moved my jaw, it clicked.

I heard someone moving around in the living room. When the TV came on and football blasted down the hall, I was sure it was Dad—and that meant I needed to make a decision. I'd been here before—standing in my room, debating whether to tell my dad another truth about Cyrus that he would find a way to forget or ignore. I grabbed some concealer and started smearing it on my cheek. Maybe this way, I'd be the one to forget or ignore.

Dad was getting ready to go back out to the seed shed when I made it out to the living room twenty minutes later.

"Hey, sweetheart." He glanced at me briefly, but he didn't really see me. I may not have needed the makeup after all.

"Hey."

"Any plans tonight?"

I shook my head, then immediately regretted it. The pain was immediate and so sharp, I could almost hear it.

"All right, well, I'm gonna be in the shed if you need me, okay?"

The sliding-glass door screeched open and the pounding in my temples spawned a wave of nausea. I gripped the edge of the table and tried to swallow the bile in my throat. After a few deep breaths, I managed to microwave a mug of water, then found a peppermint tea bag in the back of the cabinet. Through the window, I could see Dad raking the recently tilled beds as clumps of dirt and rock scattered at his feet.

I held the mug in both hands and slowly sipped the barely steeped tea. Directly across from me on the refrigerator was the last picture we took as a family before Mom died. It was the Fourth of July. Mom had on a sparkly headband with glitter antennae over her wig. My dad was smiling in a way I hadn't seen in years, and Cyrus and I were both holding sparklers. It was a time when stuff like hanging out as a family and playing with fire didn't feel so dangerous.

I finished my tea and tried to lie back down, but every time I closed my eyes, I saw Cyrus. His face was screwed up with rage—red and somehow jagged. He looked at me like I was a traitor. An enemy.

Outside, a patchy fog was settling over the farthest fields. On evenings like that, I could usually see all the way to the tree line. At that moment, I couldn't see past my house, my brother, and the disaster that had bloomed around me.

When the front door opened, then closed, I panicked. I wanted to hide, and I went so far as to look around the room at what I could possibly crawl under or into. When I heard Jane's high heels click along the wood floors, though, I exhaled. Cracking the door an inch, I saw her hanging her coat in the hall closet.

If Dad can't see me—can't see what's happening here—maybe it's time I talk to Jane . . .

But, of course, talking to Jane involved *talking to Jane—* something I'd never been particularly good at, despite the fact that she'd been in my life for years.

Mom had been dead for nine months, three weeks, and two days when Dad told us about Jane McPherson. He'd met her at the grocery store. They had both reached for the last pint of Ben & Jerry's Cherry Garcia. Apparently a similar taste in ice cream was enough to base a relationship on.

I wanted Dad to be happy and I could see how he lit up when Jane was around. At first, she seemed to understand where there was room to slide into. She made dinner for us, but never wore Mom's apron. She watched movies with us, but never sat in Mom's recliner. It wasn't until later that she became integral instead of extraneous.

My first high school dance was the spring of my freshman year. Jane volunteered to take me dress shopping, something everyone seemed to recognize as a rite of passage and a Mom-Job that had been left vacant.

But once we were at the mall, Jane tried on more dresses than I did. She looked beautiful in black and green and even orange. "It's my coloring," she told me when I said something about it. I couldn't disagree. She bought two dresses for herself and one for me that I didn't even try on.

Jane had a new wardrobe. Dad had a new girlfriend. I had a dress I never wore to a dance I didn't even go to. Sometimes the picture you paint is more important than the life you're living, I guess.

Now I cleared my throat and Jane turned toward me.

"CeCe?" She blinked at me and I noticed she was wearing more eyeliner than normal. "I was just getting off work—is your father in the shed?"

"Yeah."

My voice was little more than a croak. Jane frowned.

"Are you sick?"

I thought about that for a second. "Sort of—I, um . . . I had a run-in with Cyrus."

Jane rolled her eyes. "I've been telling your father that we need to get that boy out of the basement and into a job. What did he do this time? Hit you up for money?"

I'd have laughed at the irony of her statement if there was

anything funny about it. Instead, I opened my mouth to tell her the truth—but Jane had already turned to walk back to the kitchen.

"Don't worry about it, CeCe—he's been a drain on all of us. Try not to give him any more money and maybe he'll actually get out there and apply for work. Not to mention— if you see him again tonight, tell him to clean up that hovel downstairs."

She disappeared around the corner and I leaned up against the door jamb. Apparently, only the house could support me in a way my father and Jane couldn't. At least it was there for me to lean on. It may not have seen me, but it certainly stuck around longer than anyone else had.

I considered calling Natalie, seeing if I could come over and spend the night. She knew Cy was injured and living at home—knew we fought a lot and that he wasn't in college like the rest of his friends. She probably knew he was doped up, too, but we never talked about it. I never *wanted* to talk about it.

No, I needed to do something else—something for myself, something to get closer to being away from this family and closer to being out on my own.

It took a supreme effort to get down the stairs. When I finally made it to the bottom, I leaned on the washing machine and listened hard. Nothing. Not that that meant anything. Cyrus was usually dead to the world when he was blitzed. I reached over and started the washer, dumping in some nearby towels. Still nothing. No creaks, no shuffling, no crumpled paper underfoot. I grasped his doorknob. It was unlocked.

When I was little, maybe four or five, I used to sneak into Cyrus's room at the old house. His walls were dark—navy blue or hunter green, I can't remember which—and whenever I went in there, it felt cooler than the rest of the house. Cooler like cold, but cooler like awesome, too. Already, he'd had trophies lining his dresser. I used to take them down, running my little fingers along the engraved plates at the bottom of each one. I'd press hard where it said *Cyrus*, and his name would be stamped in my skin for a few seconds before fading away. Sometimes I did it until it hurt, hoping to make the letters permanent like a tattoo.

There were some trophies down in the basement, too, but they weren't exactly a focal point. In a room like that, the disaster morphed and widened and somehow the sprawl looked different than the last time I was down there. I stepped over a pile of garbage and found what I'd been looking for—Cy's stash. First came the bile, then came the fury. I swallowed them both and reached for the box.

The foil was gone, but there were still some straws, some tipped with what had to be gray smoke smears. A little bit of powdery residue gathered in one corner of the container. The bottle of pills, now half full, was tucked under a folded envelope.

And then I saw the syringes.

There were five of them bundled with a rubber band, capped with orange plastic stoppers. A few used ones lay in the bottom of the box, along with a spoon, whose handle was bent over in resignation.

I wanted to be shocked, but I'd run out of that emotion. Instead, I thought about how Cyrus used to be afraid of needles, how he'd scream in terror when it was time for booster shots or blood draws. I closed my eyes. Cyrus and his fury were waiting for me there. They backed me into a corner. The choking wasn't any worse in my mind. The only difference was that I was ready for it this time.

I pocketed the remaining Oxys. Each pill I sold would be a sucker punch aimed right at my brother's gut, and each pill I sold would get me one step closer to college, one step closer to Lucas, and a hundred steps away from this life I've been living.

"Did you count them?" Jason asked me. I nodded, trying to focus on the handful of little white pills in his cupped palm, and not on Lucas's gaze as it traveled over me.

"There's forty pills," I said, shuffling my feet. "That's twenty-four hundred dollars."

Jason didn't even bat an eyelash as he whipped out his wallet. I glanced around his well-appointed basement again—at the leather couches and a pool table and covered hot tub in one corner. I suppose it figured that a guy with that much money would want to flush it away on drugs. I couldn't decide if I felt guilty for fueling his downfall or giddy for finding available cash.

Jason tucked a wad of bills into my hand, and I tried to

decide if it was tacky to throw it up in the air and let it rain around me like confetti.

"Yo, Jay," Lucas said, sauntering over to Jason and laying a hand on his shoulder, "you mind if CeCe and I play a game of pool?"

Jason nodded. "Sure—I'm taking this shit upstairs anyway. My parents aren't home." He glanced from me to Lucas. "You all want to come up and hit this first?"

I wondered if Jason smoked or snorted his pills—or if he'd moved on to syringes like my brother. For a second, I just blinked at him, then shook my head.

"No, I—uh—I don't do that shit."

Lucas gave a little shake of his head and Jason shrugged. He didn't look back as he headed up the stairs. I heard a door shut softly behind him.

When I looked back at Lucas, he was smiling. His lips were sexy in the way that guys' lips can be sexy—thick and full without any semblance of color or gloss or liner. The contradiction of sharp masculinity and something rounded. I could feel my own mouth begin to curve up.

"Do you play pool?" he asked.

I shook my head. "Not really."

He shoved his hands in his jeans pockets, giving me the opportunity to watch the way his arms wore muscles.

"We don't have to play," he said, nodding at the pool table. "I just wanted Jason to give us some time alone."

His eyes traveled over the room and landed on the hot tub. He looked back at me, the same eyebrow raised.

"I don't have a suit," I said, feeling a little flush travel over my cheeks and down my neck.

Lucas grinned. "Yeah, I guess that's a problem."

I was positive that he'd tell me we could get in naked, or in our underwear, and no matter how much I wanted to feel Lucas touch me, I knew I wasn't ready to take off my clothes in any capacity. When he didn't push, didn't do anything but move over to one of the couches and flop down on it, I felt a loosening somewhere in my chest. Something was breaking free. Something like my guard was slowly coming down.

"We could just talk," he suggested then.

And what was left of my guard crumbled apart.

It was hours later—almost midnight—when I pulled back into the driveway. I shifted the Honda into park and squinted up the hill at the seed shed. The lights were on. Through the blinds, I could see my dad moving from one side of the room to the other. I thought about the money he'd lost, the empty cash box he probably didn't even know about yet. It made the money in my pocket feel even more vital.

For the first few minutes of the drive, I was drunk on Lucas—on his eyes crinkled at the corners and his husky laugh and, most of all, the way his lips brushed along my jaw and down my neck as we sat, legs intertwined on Jason's basement couch. But once I'd made it halfway home, I'd been terrified of getting caught with that much cash and an empty bottle of OxyContin; I'd spent more time looking in my rearview mirror for flashing lights than I did looking at the road in front of me. Somehow, an internal GPS-like voice, robotic and stern, had echoed in my ears. It ordered me down the street, out of the neighborhood, along the road, up the driveway, out of the car, and into my house. Do not pass Go. You already collected your two hundred dollars. And then some.

Once I was back inside my house, though, the adrenaline-fueled momentum had disappeared and I felt like I was wading through honey. There was a thickness to my stride and it weighed me down like guilt. That lasted only until I saw that the door to my bedroom was wide open, the same door that I'd shut tightly when I left. The honey around my legs became loose and liquidy. As I pushed the door open, my legs became loose and liquidy, too.

Inside, a tornado had hit and nothing had been spared. My desk chair was overturned and papers were strewn all over the floor. Clothes were pulled from my dresser and closet, only to be thrown on the floor. My mattress was askew from the bed frame.

Usually when something happened that was Cyrus-induced, like money gone from my wallet or mildewed piles of his clothes by the basement stairs, I found a way to ignore it. It wasn't worth getting Dad involved, especially when it put me on the defensive against two people desperate to deny the elephant stomping around the room. But this disaster was somehow bigger and louder than the elephant.

Of course, this time, I wasn't faultless. Still, when my dad started down the hallway toward me, sweaty and tired, I didn't tell him to turn back around. Instead, I stared at the implosion and considered what my lifeless body might look like lying in the middle of the mess. What if I'd been here? Would the destruction have included me? I clenched my jaw against the thought, then winced at the immediate pain. It was a sharp reminder of what Cy had already destroyed today.

"What's going on?" my dad asked, for once attuned to my facial expression. I gestured to my bedroom's implosion and watched that ever-present optimism on my father's face slide off into the surrounding air and swirl, eddy-like, to the littered floor.

"Jesus, CeCe. What the hell happened?"

I looked at him, then back at the room. "What do you think happened, Dad?"

"Cyrus did this?"

I nodded.

"I can't believe it. What—why? Why would he do this to your room? Was he looking for something?"

"I—I don't know." Lying felt beyond natural, like blinking.

Dad looked up at the ceiling, then back to the ravages of my room. I knew what he was doing in his head—trying to come up with excuses for Cy, reasons why he'd do this. This time, though, Dad's face looked broken. It reminded me of how I felt lying in bed earlier—fragmented. Shattered. Unable to hold it together.

"I don't think I really understood . . ." Dad trailed off, then shook his head. He stepped over a pile of clothes to look out the window. "I should have put a stop to this sooner. I should have seen exactly how bad things had gotten. It's just—well, after your mother—after we lost her, I just didn't want to do anything to make you kids feel unloved. Unwanted."

I blinked at his back, letting the lines of his flannel shirt crisscross through my watery gaze.

"I know you love me, Dad. I just don't think you see me."

He looked at me then, his eyes filled with the same unshed tears as mine.

"I see you, CeCe. I see all of the good—*only* the good. It's why I can ignore trashed basements and doctor bills. When I look at my children and see nothing but love, my heart hurts less than it did the day before."

I narrowed my eyes. "What about needles? Did you see those when you were ignoring everything else?"

He blinked at me. "What are you talking about?"

I shook my head, exhaling hard. The last shreds of respect I'd had for my father seemed to exit my body with my breath.

"He's shooting up, Dad. I'm not even sure for how long, but I know it's true. And I know that Cyrus is way, way beyond a pill-popping addict. He's a junkie."

Dad's eyes narrowed as though he wanted to deny it, to deny it along with everything else he'd been denying for so long. Then he just swallowed hard.

"I—I didn't think it would ever get that bad."

And I wanted to throttle him, to grab him by the hair and force him downstairs into the pit of Cyrus's waste and personal destruction. Instead, I wrapped my arms around my middle and squeezed just enough to remind me of the bruises on my ribs and the ache in my heart.

"He needs help, Dad. We need to help him."

Unable to meet my gaze, my father stared over at my window. The blinds were slightly raised and bent inward from something Cy had launched at them in his rage.

"You're right." Dad said it sadly, then he sighed. "We need to get him help. Immediately. And I can't believe I've let it go for this long. I'm so sorry, honey."

It was the only apology I'd ever gotten—through the doctor's appointments and heated fights and missed dinners and lack of money and everything Cyrus said and did, Dad had never admitted that there was something wrong. Or, at least, that there was something to be sorry about.

I almost said, "It's okay." But that lie wouldn't have been quite as easy as the other one.

Instead, I let him pull me in for a hug, which felt like so many things at once. Mostly it was a consolation prize. I hugged him back and, somehow, bits of me were soldered back together. My dad was hugging me and I was crying and Cyrus had left or passed out or died and neither of us wanted to know which.

JUNE

PRESENT DAY

13

THE WORDS *VISITING DAY* ARE ONLY A POSITIVE THING WHEN IT comes to zoos or grandparents and you're about five years old. When someone you love is planning to visit you in a treatment program, in a jail, it's not exactly an exciting prospect. So it's probably a good thing that no one's coming to visit me today. Usually, our only access to the unincarcerated is through a bulletproof window. But Barnes maintains that "family and friends are an integral part of the healing process."

I watch Tucker as he walks across the room and leans up next to a motivational poster. His hair is curling a bit and is still slightly damp from his morning shower. I feel a shudder of something like desire race over my skin like goose bumps. Since the junkyard, Tucker has kissed me exactly twice— once when we'd somehow ended up alone in the hall and last night, when he'd pulled me into the shadowy side of the common room, next to the soda machine.

"You know that kissing is pretty much a carnal sin around here," he'd murmured against my lips in the dark. I'd shrugged and looped my arms around his neck.

"It certainly won't be the first sin I've committed."

I let my fingers drift up over his cheekbone and down to his lips. He grabbed my wrist and pressed a brief kiss against it before leaving me next to the humming soda machine, its warm side pressed into my back like a body intent upon sheltering me.

But today? Today we have to face our families. Or, at least, Tucker has to face his. I don't really have *one* to face anymore, and I certainly don't think my dad will be coming here today. I think part of me aches with this knowledge and the rest of me sighs with relief. I'm not sure what we'd say to each other now anyway.

Before long, the common room is overflowing with emotion and I'm a cannonball sinking into a pile of feathers— something heavy and immovable and everyone else can walk on air. People are hugging and I want to move away from it. The closer the bodies get to each other, the farther I fold into myself.

Next to the door, Tucker is still leaning against the wall. He glances down at his feet, then up at the ceiling. Then he looks over at me, grins, and looks away. When a woman, tall and lithe like a ballet dancer, hesitates in the doorway, he stands up a little straighter before reaching out to her.

"Hi, Mom."

"Oh, Tucker. Hello, dear."

Tucker's mother's face is blank as she moves farther into the room. He follows her like a puppy. I think about how I used to follow my mom that way, too. The gesture is so childlike and familiar, it's almost painful.

I try to switch my focus to the families that are starting to assemble in clusters around the room. A few head outside to walk along the concrete slab of patio.

"How's your recovery going?" Tucker's mother is asking him as they walk toward the sliding-glass door. Her eyes are a clear blue, the kind that are usually filled with light. But her face looks waxy and a light sheen of sweat glazes her forehead.

Tucker doesn't answer his mother's question. Instead, he steers her in my direction and I feel myself start to panic. The hyperventilation starts in my stomach and works its way through all the veins in my body.

"Mom, this is Cecelia, one of my friends from the program. CeCe, this is my mom, Debbie."

I give her a weak smile, not trusting myself to speak. She returns it, kind of. Both of us sort of stare around each other, but not at each other, as though trying to respect some sort of first-meeting-at-a-psych-ward-prison-combination boundary.

"Well," Debbie finally says, gulping back her discomfort, "I'm glad that Tucker's making friends."

I don't know what to say to that. Tucker sort of shuffles his feet and I realize he's nervous. Then I remember the stolen college fund and the car driven through the living room. I guess I'd be nervous, too.

"So—Dad's not coming today?" he asks. His mother gives him a noncommittal shrug.

"He—he just isn't ready yet."

I look down at my shoes, trying to think of something to say to make me feel less awkward.

"Hey, Tucker."

The three of us turn to see Mary Jensen, guest speaker extraordinaire, standing about ten feet away. The armchair in front of her cuts her off at the waist, making her look legless, like a life-size Russian doll.

I look at Tucker. His face is even paler than before; Debbie has moved from his side and starts to walk toward Mary. Before she reaches her, Mary rushes forward and gathers Tucker in her arms.

"I missed you," she says, her voice muffled against his shoulder.

The fragments of this situation feel like kites on strings, but too close and tangled, impossible to separate. Then memories curl up and over me like a smoke I can't help but inhale. When I'd confronted Tucker about skipping the guest speaker, he'd said, *It was all stuff I've heard a million times before.* Now I can see the resemblance between brother and sister. I can't believe I didn't notice it when Mary had been onstage.

All at once, there's something with wings flapping around inside me, something clawing at my rib cage and trying to escape. I don't wait for a formal introduction or handshake with anyone else Tucker loves. Instead, I leave him and his family reunion, feeling inexplicably tattered from the inside out.

Or maybe not tattered. Maybe just broken into pieces, with half those pieces missing. My dad. My mom. My brother. All my broken, jagged parts are completely unrecognizable compared to the person I used to be and the family I used to be a member of. I've never wanted to belong to something as much as I do right now—and I've never felt as alone as I do as I walk out the door, leaving everyone's family behind me except my own.

Trina is wearing a different pair of glasses today. Pink frames. They're weirding me out. I don't see her as pink—more gray or taupe. A good neutral color. Like a mass-produced household appliance.

She takes a deep breath. "You know, this is our last session before the hearing—"

"Yeah, I know," I cut her off. My nerves are still rubbed raw from witnessing Tucker's impromptu family reunion. The last thing I want to talk about is court.

"Well, I thought you might want to dictate what we do today. Within reason, of course."

I snort. "There goes my plan for hopping the red-eye to Vegas."

Like Jennifer, Trina's eyes never look happy. They're either sad or sorry, at least whenever she's looking at me. I wonder if she's that way with all her patients. Like a volunteer at an animal shelter, she has nothing but empathy for even the most useless, the too-far-gone.

"Anything on your mind?" Trina asks, settling down into the desk chair. We're in Dr. Barnes's office this time; most of the conference rooms and therapy suites are occupied with family sessions today.

"Not really," I say, shaking my head. She eyes me skeptically.

"Somehow I don't believe you."

"You *never* really believe me, so what's the difference?"

Trina shrugs, her shoulders sharpening into a place I can't lean on, even if I wanted to.

"I guess," I begin, searching my hands for some sort of cheat sheet. I feel like I've left all the answers in my other body. "I guess I'm just done with people."

"What do you mean, 'done with people'?"

"Done like done—I'm tired of trying to have friendships. I'm tired of talking."

"Why?"

"Because people suck."

Trina crosses one leg over the other. "Want to be more specific?"

I shrug. "They just—I mean, I used to believe the best in people before—before everything went down."

"And now?"

"And now I'm either just focusing on my disappointment or I don't give a shit anymore."

"So what I hear you saying," Trina says slowly, "is that people are always falling below expectations. That they don't live up to the hype."

"Exactly," I say, pointing a finger at her. "That's it right there—they don't live up to the hype."

Trina watches me for a minute, then pushes her glasses back on her head, sunglasses-style. "Okay, I lied."

"About what?"

"I told you I wasn't going to make you do any more visualization, but we're going to try it one more time."

"You've got to be kidding," I groan. At this point, anything I "visualize" won't make a damn bit of difference. I'm still going to court next week. I'm still stuck in here. My brother's still dead.

"Go ahead and get comfortable," Trina directs me, and I ease myself back against the chair. We do some breathing exercises, which always piss me off. Breathing is one thing that I can do by myself, thank you very much.

"All right, CeCe," Trina says quietly. "Go ahead and close your eyes."

I tilt my head up toward the light above me; eyes closed, I try to imagine it's the sun, that I am ten years younger, and that I've never heard the words *Piedmont* or *OxyContin* or *visualization techniques*.

"I want you to picture yourself in a safe place," she begins, her voice sort of lilting and rhythmic. "Imagine you are in a location you always found comforting when you were growing up or a place you thought of as home."

I clench my jaw. It's hard to remember a time I was safe or comforted. When a memory actually surfaces, I'm floating in the middle of Lake Erie.

"Now," Trina's saying, "try to picture a moment that makes you feel warm inside. A moment that is both present and past."

Mom's family is from upstate New York. Every two years, we'd drive up for the family reunion, staying outside Buffalo in a waterfront cabin. I remember how the lake was so big, it reminded me more of oceans than any lakes I'd seen at home. On the second day, my aunt or cousin or someone had brought a canoe and Cy was determined to try it out. I was far less interested.

"C'mon, CeCe," he'd said, his voice cracking from the onset of puberty. "It'll be fun."

"Why can't you just go by yourself, then?" I'd asked.

"Because, stupid—it's a CANOE. Canoe means TWO."

"Don't call me stupid!" I'd screeched, chasing him down the dock.

"Can you tell me what you see?" I hear Trina ask. But I'm not ready to leave just yet. It's the first time I've seen Cyrus this kind of alive in years. It's the first time I've really wanted to remember him.

Once we'd made it into the canoe without tipping it over, Cy tried to show me how to paddle. I was pretty bad at it; my arms were short and my oars barely reached the water.

"CeCe, I might as well be out here on my own," he'd complained. I remember his oars tugging us through the water, his arms doing all the work my arms couldn't.

I remember thinking about how he was starting to look like Dad, like a man instead of a boy.

"Nah," I'd said, giving up on paddling and lounging back in the sun instead. "You'll never be out here on your own. Canoes mean two, remember?"

"Yeah, well—not if you're not helping."

"I'm helping you not tip over," I'd said. "We're keeping each other afloat."

And then the canoe and the lake and my brother vanish, snapping back into my head like a rubber band on fire. My eyes fly open and my face is still tilted toward the fluorescent lights above me.

I don't look at Trina. I don't look anywhere but up.

When I close my eyes again, I can still feel the sun on my face and the rocking of the water below. For a minute, it's like my brother is there across from me.

And then, just like that, he's gone.

"Open your eyes."

Trina is peering at me and I blink at her, then let my eyes flicker over the room. They drag along the creases, where the walls meet the ceiling and the floor. They feel like folds. I feel boxed in.

"Can you share with me what you just experienced, CeCe?"

I swallow hard. I don't want to share this memory— it feels like a gift. It feels like a secret.

"It was about my mom," I lie. "I was thinking about my mom."

Trina nods slowly. "And what about your mom?"

I sort of shrug. "About . . . about her smell. What she smelled like—it's something I try really hard not to forget."

For a lie, I sure am managing to make it true.

"Smells are often an impactful memory," Trina is saying. "They pull us backward rather than propelling us ahead."

That makes a lot of sense, considering what I think about when I remember my last moments with my mother.

"I'm going to ask you to do something for me, CeCe."

I sniff. "Okay."

Trina pauses, then clears her throat. "I want you to tell me about your mom when she died."

I let my gaze grow fuzzy and I bite my lip. I want to say no. I want to run. I want to catch fire or drown or freeze or fizzle up. I want to be anywhere but here.

"Very soon, you are going to have to answer questions about your family," Trina says, her voice softer around the edges than my vision. "Maybe it would help to tell me something right now that's true."

I swallow hard.

I could say no. But I've said no so often lately—no to Tucker and no to Barnes and no to Cam and no to Jennifer.

But something about Trina—maybe her glasses or her slim build or her overwhelming genuineness—makes me want to say yes.

I take a deep breath.

"Can I write it?" I sort of croak.

She thinks about that.

"How about this? You tell me one memory now, then you write something in your journal later. That way, you've shared two things—and we're two steps closer to you being more comfortable exploring your feelings."

"Okay." I swallow, then look up at the ceiling. "Do you think you could give me a prompt—I mean, like something to talk about? A suggestion."

Trina taps her pencil against her bottom lip. "Hmm. How about—tell me about something your mom disliked. Like, liver or spiders. Something she really couldn't stand."

I don't even have to think about that one.

"Pain medicine."

Trina's eyebrows rise. "Pain medicine?"

I nod. "We knew she was feeling really shitty when she actually took hers. The bottles would move from the kitchen to the bathroom to her bedside table—closer and closer the worse off she got. And she hated it—said it made her loopy and lazy, two things Mom never was before she got sick."

Trina shifts in her chair. "What kind of medicine was she taking? Do you remember?"

I sniff. "A bunch of different kinds. About six months after her diagnosis, her doctor prescribed her Oxys. It seemed like a numbing haze was the greatest and only gift we could give her. After taking the Oxys, Mom couldn't, or wouldn't, get out of bed at all."

I go quiet, thinking of those little orange bottles. Mom's name printed boldly on the sticker. The white childproof caps always a little askew, making them anything but childproof.

Trina is completely quiet, completely still. When I look up at her, there's a bloom of recognition on her face.

"Cecelia?"

"Yeah?"

"When did your brother first try Oxys?" she asks slowly. The question hits me like so many things at once—most of all, like an accusation.

"My mom didn't give my brother drugs, if that's what you're asking," I practically spit at her.

She shakes her head. "No. I didn't think that. But when your mom was gone . . . were there pills left? In your house, I mean?"

I shrug for what feels like the thousandth time. "Some, I guess."

"Do you think Cyrus took them?"

"He could have," I admit. "I—uh—I never really thought about that."

Trina nods and looks up at the ceiling. "Here's the thing, CeCe. With addiction—sometimes it's programmed in our brain. Cyrus may have tried painkillers, maybe your mom's or a friend's, before he ever hurt his knee. It could have just been a matter of time—a different injury, perhaps—that the drugs would have caught up with him."

I stare at the floor. Its bumpy unevenness feels forgiving. Acceptable. Familiar.

"It's not something you could have helped."

The feeling I hate most—the lump of tears that feels like a

ball gag—enters my throat and I try my damnedest to swallow it down.

"I should have said something," I choke out.

Immediately, I wish I could take my words back. Trina's eyes fill with the pity I hate most. The pity that says, "You've lost your whole family and your freedom and your future." The pity that says, "You've lost everything."

"Said something to who?" she asks.

I focus harder on the floor—its flecks of pretend igneous rock, its shoddy caulking.

"To Dad."

"You never did?"

I rub my eyes. "I did at the beginning. Not at the end. Not when I should have."

Trina comes toward me and kneels down, forcing me to look her in the eye.

"Cyrus's addiction—and his death—wasn't your fault, CeCe. Neither was your father's choice to enable him. Your father saw what he wanted to see."

I almost laugh at that, but a tear rolls down my cheek instead.

"He never saw me."

Trina smiles at me, then grabs my hand and squeezes.

"I see you, Cecelia," she whispers.

And for a second, or maybe longer, I believe her.

June 27

Mom wanted to die at home.

This was something Dad hated, because we were all completely ill-equipped to save her life. It was only when there was no hope left, when "saving" became an empty promise that Dad finally agreed.

But sometimes there isn't dead or alive. Sometimes it's not that simple. My mother, still breathing, fell asleep during Jeopardy on a Thursday night. Dad carried her to bed. She never woke up, but she didn't die either. Dad was torn—there was no protocol for half-life. What would she have wanted him to do?

He called 911.

At first, the hospital smell was a foreign combination of latex and disinfectants. After a few days and nights, however, it became as familiar as fabric softener. It seeped into our clothes and hair like smoke or grease. Just because it was the smell of clean didn't mean it didn't make you feel dirty.

Mom's bedding was from home—it was the only way we could give her the death she'd asked for. Two hours after she stopped breathing on her own, I lay my head down next to her and inhaled everything I could. I smelled all that was fleeting and all that was home—my mother's hair, our generic detergent, and something like life. I wanted to ingest as much as my body would hold. I wanted to never exhale again. Things that ride the air, like scent and breath, always disappear first.

For weeks after, I would search our house, looking desperately for that smell—I buried myself in Mom's sweaters and my own grief. It took months for me to stop looking for that familiar scent. It took far longer for me to stop wishing I could find it.

C.P.

14

THAT EVENING, I DON'T GO LOOKING FOR TUCKER AND I DON'T think Tucker went looking for me. Instead, we just appear, we manifest, in the same place at the same time. I'd call it a magic trick, but I'm still pissed about Sister Mary Jensen. The only magic I'm interested in is disappearing.

"Cecelia."

Tucker's voice is kind of husky, but with sparks, like a match scraping the flint before being lit. I narrow my eyes but I'm not squinting. I'm glaring.

"Cecelia," he says again. I open my eyes wide enough to roll them.

"So, she's your sister," I say. It's not a question. Tucker shrugs.

"She's my sister."

"Did you know she was coming here?" I ask.

He shrugs again. "Not really. I mean, I knew she wanted

to be a guest speaker. I didn't have the right to tell her not to. It was supposed to be helpful."

"And was it helpful?"

"For me?" He shakes his head. "I ducked out of there early. I didn't stay to hear about the failure that is my legacy."

"Yeah, I noticed. I thought you were just being an ass."

"Well, yeah. That, too."

"Whatever."

I turn to leave, but Tucker reaches out and grabs my wrist. I try to yank back, but he's stronger than me. For a second, I'm furious. Then, all of a sudden, this capture feels less threatening and more intimate. The anger begins to leach from the veins in my wrist and pool in the space around me.

"I didn't lie to you," he says.

"Okay."

"I don't owe you any explanations."

"I know that."

Tucker lets go of my wrist and I rub it like it's sore, even though it isn't.

"My sister volunteers," he says, as though he didn't hear me. "She usually talks to high school kids."

"Were you pissed when you saw her here?"

Tucker's mouth lifts at one side in an expression that would be a half smile if there were any happiness behind it. Instead it's kind of a cartoon grimace.

"I don't know if I was pissed, exactly," he is saying. "The thing is—well, it's her story, too, you know? I may have been the fuckup, but she was the one who got fucked over."

I digest that for a second. Outside, there is a misty, foggy rain that is more hovering than falling. It's the kind of weather my dad loves—he could plant and water at the same time. Sometimes nature was on his side.

I look back at Tucker.

"My brother almost drowned once."

He blinks at me, confused. Then, I think he gets what I'm trying to do. I'm trying to tell him something about me—about my family. To even the score, I suppose. I've met his sister. I've seen his world. Maybe I should give him a window onto mine. Or maybe I just finally want to.

"I was little," I continue, looking down at my hands. "Like, really little. I didn't understand breathing or that you couldn't do it underwater. I didn't know that floating wasn't always good. It was really the only kind of swimming I'd ever done.

"Mom had jumped right into the pool with her clothes on. When she pulled him out and started to give him CPR, I didn't know what she was doing. I thought she was kissing my brother good night."

I smile at that—I remember her explaining the truth later when Cy was resting and after the paramedics had left. That she'd been breathing for him because he couldn't breathe for himself.

"I couldn't wrap my head around the idea that something invisible was what made us exist."

Tucker nods, his motions carefully calculated as though not to scare me. I swallow hard against the overwhelming desire to clam up, to shut up and run.

"My brother, Cyrus—he was hooked on Oxys, too," I manage to say. "Like you."

Tucker's eyebrows lift. "Yeah?"

"Yeah."

"He's doesn't take them anymore?" he asks. My hands clench at my sides and I try to stay unlocked, unblocked. I try to stay open for him.

"He's dead."

Tucker is silent for a second. Finally he says, "I'm sorry."

"Yeah, well . . ."

In the silence of the room, it's impossible to ignore the rhythm of my breathing, which is now jagged and stressed. If air could palpitate, it would be palpitating. Like the rain outside, the oxygen in the room hovers like an eavesdropper. I take an intentionally slow breath. It's like inhaling a mouthful of bleach.

"It was my fault."

Tucker's brows furrow.

"What was your fault?"

I scrub a hand over my face. "His death. My brother's dead because of me."

Tucker doesn't say anything to that. I'm exhausted from so much talking, from so much honesty, so I sit down. I choose an armchair and Tucker settles himself on its matching ottoman. It's the first time I've gotten dibs on something in a long time. In my house, the oldest or fastest always got the best choice of everything.

161

But it's here and now that I've been dreading. This moment when someone starts asking all the questions Jennifer is asking and Trina is asking and all the questions I'm asking myself and I still don't really have any answers. I'm grateful we aren't in group right now. I'm grateful Tucker's the only person here. And some small part of me is grateful that he knows a piece of my truth.

"If you could be an animal, what kind of animal would you be?"

"What?" It's the last question I expect to hear. Tucker's looking at me sideways and I stifle a laugh. I know what he's doing. I don't know if I'm glad. Changing the subject gives me an out, but I don't really deserve one.

"I'd be an elephant, I think," he says thoughtfully, his eyes squinting up at the fluorescent lights above us.

"Yeah? Why's that?" I ask him.

"Because, you know, they're strong and tough. They can be fast if they want to be. They're nice to their kids. They hold each other's tails in a row and that's sort of cool."

"So you're saying you want to use your nose to hold someone's tail, which is inextricably connected to the place they shit from?"

Tucker cocks his head, clearly reconsidering. "Maybe everything but the tail part, then."

But I feel bad for him giving up on his power animal so easily. I shake my head.

"I don't think you'd get shit on or anything. You'd just have to pay close attention. But I'm sure elephants have

162

enough manners to wait until no one's holding their tail to do their business."

"Unless it's like holding someone's hair back when they puke."

We lapse into silence and I think about dolphins, the stereotypical girl animal, or horses, another popular girl choice. I could say unicorns and just be an asshole. Instead, I try for a genuine response.

"I think I'd be a prairie dog."

"Really?" Tucker looks appalled. "Aren't they just, like, glorified hamsters?"

"No!" I'm indignant on the prairie dogs' behalf. "They are really fast. They live in a series of complex holes and tunnels."

"Like moles."

"Yeah, but they can see. And they work together and they live in families. You never see one prairie dog at a time— they're always in a group."

"Like a cult?"

I ignore him. "They're my favorite exhibit at the zoo."

"Well, that doesn't count, then."

"What? Why?"

"Because if you only know them as zoo animals, you can't possibly understand their indigenous character. You have to see them in the wild."

"Let me get this straight," I say slowly. "You've seen elephants in the wild?"

"Well, no . . . but I've seen them on TV."

"Seriously?"

"They were *filmed* in the wild."

This time, I let myself laugh. The sound is almost unrecognizable.

"You know, you look really pretty when you smile." His eyes, now crinkled, have turned a little coppery, like shiny new pennies gazing right at me. I duck and shake my head.

"You just never see me do it," I say. "It's a foreign concept."

He brings his hand up to the right side of my face. I think he's going to lift my chin, to make me face him, but instead he just lays it flat against my cheek. The warmth is soothing. I put my own hand on top of his. There we are, my skin and bones and blood sandwiching his. I've sort of captured him back. And he's still got me confined, but in a different way now.

Our lips meet two feet above the space between chair and ottoman. If we were smaller, we'd fall through. If we were smarter, we'd stand up. Instead, we use our free hands to hold the furniture together, and we kiss and kiss and kiss until the rain looks more like sun and the air feels endless and sweet.

Jennifer clears her throat. "Can you state your name for the record?"

"Cecelia Price."

"And where were you born?"

"Roanoke, Virginia."

"And please describe what your childhood was like."

I bite my lip. It tastes raw. I must have been biting it earlier, though I can't remember doing it.

"Are you really going to ask that question?" I complain. Jennifer takes off her suit jacket and throws it over a nearby chair.

"Yes. I am. We need to set the stage of your happy childhood. However, I've also told you again and again that you need to be prepared for multiple lines of questioning. The prosecution might try to paint your family as perfect and you as the black sheep. Or they might go another way."

Rehearsing is never something I've been good at. I wasn't much of a studier. I didn't do a lot of prep work before a test. I just managed to do pretty well on my own. So rehearsing for my hearing feels more than phony—it feels itchy. I'm sitting straight up in a wooden chair wearing a long-sleeved shirt and a stoic expression. There is nothing natural about anything that's happening in this room right now.

"Look." Jennifer pulls up a chair next to me and sits. We both face the picture-less wall. "Now is the time to ask me any questions. What are you worried about? What do you think it's going to be like? What outcome are you prepared for?"

I consider the courtroom in my future. Maybe I'll be quiet. Maybe I'll protest the details. So far, I don't think I've argued once. That's my lawyer's job.

"I guess I'm worried about seeing my dad," I admit.

"Yes." Jennifer nods solemnly. "That will be difficult. You haven't seen him since you've been here?

I shake my head. "I haven't really talked to him since Cyrus . . . since I got here."

"Right."

"So, yeah. Other than that, I'm not sure much could throw me off-kilter. Wait, do I have court clothes?" It occurs to me that I'm currently stocked with nothing but jeans, hoodies, and flip-flops.

"I'm going to bring something with me—you can dress before we drive to the courthouse."

The future is full of contradictions. On top of the worry or regret or anger or fear is the anticipation of getting out into the world again. I haven't been in a car since Jennifer drove me here. At night, sometimes I imagine I am driving my Honda up and down the hills near my house. Like being on a ship, I can almost feel the pitch forward and back of the car's momentum.

"What time will you be here?" I ask as Jennifer stands and pulls her jacket from the back of the chair. She's wearing a gray suit today, a shade darker than my sweatshirt. Her white blouse has the faintest purple pattern. It's the flashiest thing she's ever worn here.

"I'm going to get here by eight; we need to leave no later than nine," she answers, shrugging her jacket over her shoulders. "Can you be ready by then?"

Talk about a question that's impossible to answer. I shrug.

"I'm sure Tom or one of the other security guards will wake me up."

Today, Jennifer escorts me back to my room. I walk in to see Aarti, sitting cross-legged on the floor in front of our full-length mirror, carefully applying eyeliner. She looks like Cleopatra and I wonder if that's the point. We all have our disguises.

"See you tomorrow, CeCe," Jennifer says over her shoulder. The door shuts behind her and its vertical rectangle of glass reverberates with the solid almost-slam.

"Your lawyer?" Aarti asks, even though she knows. Aarti knows more about me than I've ever told her—it's a side effect of being my roommate.

I lie down on the under-fluffed comforter on my bed—it's really more of a blanket than a comforter, considering its lack of weight and complete failure in comforting me. Aarti continues to apply her makeup and I prop my head up on one arm to watch her.

"Where'd you get that anyway?" I ask. The attendants had confiscated my cosmetic bag when I got here, not that it had much in it.

"Victoria let me have it. We had a good session." Victoria is Dr. Barnes's second-in-command. "I only get it for today."

We lapse into silence and I watch her sweep powder across her cheeks.

"How did you learn how to do that?"

"Do what?"

"Put on makeup and stuff. Did your mom teach you?"

She shakes her head, holding a mascara wand a few inches from her eye.

"My sister showed me. In India, you wear makeup for ceremonies and such. Even when you're young."

She brushes on the mascara and it's sort of hypnotizing.

Mom never really showed me how to do the makeup thing. I mean, I figured out the basics—lipstick is for lips, eye shadow is for eyes. But I still don't know which colors to choose or how to blend them. I don't know what brushes are used for what jobs. It's like there's this entire portion of womanhood that I'm ignorant about, like I missed the femininity class for a week and lost out on knowing how to be beautiful.

"Do you want me to show you?"

I blink at her as she motions for me to join her on the floor. I pause for a second, considering the silent, lonely alternative. Then I take a few tentative steps and sink down next to her.

"My foundation will be way too dark for you, but I could show you how to do your eyes and lips."

Aarti smiles, tugging her dark hair behind one ear. When she reaches out to tilt my chin up, I force myself not to flinch.

"I've never had anyone do my makeup before," I admit as she starts sorting through her compacts and brushes. She squints up at me as she selects a palette of purple eye shadows.

"Your mom never taught you?"

I shake my head. "She was . . . she died before I really started getting interested."

I wait for the pity smile, but Aarti doesn't give it to me. Instead, she just says, "Close your eyes."

So I do.

"You have court tomorrow?" Aarti asks. I feel her brush shadow over my lid and up to my brow bone.

"Yeah."

"Nervous?"

I exhale. "Yeah—really nervous."

"Think you'll end up back here?" She moves on to the other eyelid and I give a little shrug.

"I don't know—I mean, there aren't a lot of alternatives in my case."

"Hmm."

We both fall silent then. I exhale slowly as the brushes coast along my skin and try to remember a time I felt something so lovely, so perfectly comforting and completely pleasurable. Then I remember Tucker's kisses and realize it was only an hour ago that I had the same kind of simple, sweet escape.

"Okay, look at me." Aarti is peering at me when I open my eyes. "You need some liner—and mascara will do wonders for your lashes."

She grabs a black eyeliner pencil in one hand and a tube of mascara. I close my eyes automatically as she gets to work.

"You must really miss your sister," I say as Aarti begins to draw a line along my lashes.

"Yes—she's the best thing I have left in this country. The only thing, really. I'm hoping that when I turn eighteen, I can move to be closer to her."

"How did you manage to get married so young—if you don't mind me asking?"

My lashes flutter open and I see her shrug before I shut my eyes tighter.

"My husband was on a sabbatical trip in Calcutta. I was

looking for a way out and I thought he was the proverbial—what do you call it? Knight in shining armor?"

"Yeah." I swallow.

Even across the world, the sense of needing someone to save you is pervasive. Still, it's kind of inspiring to see her trying to save herself.

"So was it worth it?" I ask her.

There's a long pause and I feel the heel of her hand rest softly against my cheekbone as she sweeps a larger brush over my forehead.

"Yes," Aarti finally says. "It was worth it—because my life in Calcutta . . . it was predetermined. Despite everything, I'm here now. I'll be able to make my own decisions eventually, even if they're being dictated to me for now."

I swallow. The bright glare of her hope for the future shines directly through my closed eyes, and I'd wince if it weren't so beautiful.

"All right—take a look," Aarti says.

Blinking, I turn toward the full-length mirror, a little afraid of what I'm going to see there—that is, until I open my eyes fully and see exactly what my roommate has done.

"Wow."

She's taken the black liner and created a frame around my eyes that competes with the shadowy circles below, that makes them less noticeable, especially with the contrasting lavender shades above.

My eyes look less sad, less broken, than they did only hours ago. I don't know if it's Tucker's kisses or Aarti's makeup or even Trina's therapy that's done the most good. I don't really think it matters.

"Thank you."

Without thinking, I reach across the space between us and hug my roommate, this almost-stranger who has heard my nightmares and watched me eat and has averted her eyes when I needed privacy. It's taken until now, until I'm almost-maybe gone for good for us to finally connect. I'd feel bad about wasting so much time if I wasn't so grateful for the last ten minutes. For the last few hours. For the last week.

If nothing else, there is this: a makeup lesson with my roommate, a counseling session that didn't make me want to pull my hair out, and a kiss from a boy who asked for nothing in return but my kisses. A boy who took Oxys and betrayed his parents. A boy like my brother, but not my brother. A boy who is still alive.

AFTER THE DETONATION OF MY BEDROOM, CYRUS DIDN'T COME home. My dad was full of conspiracy theories, but for the first few days, we just assumed he'd been staying with a friend. Dad tried calling a handful of Cyrus's former soccer teammates, sure that they were the ones Cy still turned to. I didn't say what I was thinking—that Cy's only friends were drug connections more than buddies. That he hadn't talked to his teammates in almost a year.

He'd been gone for a few days when I invited Lucas over to my house for the first time. Dad was gone—off to some farmers' market that he was scoping out—and Jane was at work. Without Cyrus, the house was more than just quiet—it was peaceful in the most foreign kind of way.

"Do you want to watch TV?" I asked Lucas. He was peering at a framed picture of me when I was in elementary school. He looked up and shrugged.

"Sure. You were adorable, by the way." He gestured to the picture, then sidled closer and wrapped one arm around my waist. "In fact, you're still pretty adorable."

"You think so?"

"Mm-hm."

I turned the TV on—some kind of morning news/talk/entertainment monstrosity filled the screen and the silence—but I don't think Lucas or I even noticed that there was anything happening in the room outside the press of our bodies against each other. He'd backed me toward the couch and had me lying down before I could even imagine saying no. Not that I'd wanted to. The pressure of his weight against my skin and bones and muscle was the very best kind of pressure—the kind you aren't afraid of and the kind your body lives for.

"Lucas," I gasped out as his hand brushed over my stomach, then beneath the hem of my T-shirt.

"Do you want me to stop?" he murmured against my skin, kissing along my collarbone.

Want? No.

Need? Kind of.

"Yes—I . . . I'm sorry. I'm just not . . ."

He lifted off me and shook his head. "Don't worry about it, CeCe. That's not what I'm here for."

He cupped my cheek with one hand, then settled back against the couch cushions before grabbing the remote. I snuggled down against his shoulder and he started surfing channels. The simple mundaneness of this moment—of having a boy at my house, of watching TV with him in my living room—made me forget just about everything that wasn't simple in my life. At least for the moment.

And once another week had passed, it was hard to keep turning a blind eye to what was happening around me. I'd become as bad as Dad—my room was still lying in many pieces of its former self, since I hadn't even bothered to clean it. The morning I finally decided to straighten up, I sat on my mattress and listened to my dad on the phone with Jane. He was getting frantic about Cy's disappearance, his voice high-pitched and tinny.

"He could have been jumped or something!" Dad yelled. "Maybe they left him somewhere to die!"

I imagined my brother's funeral and I felt sick with relief. Then I imagined having to pay for it. The unfamiliar silence in the house was so welcome, so fresh, and yet at the same time it hung in the air like a stench. Like the smoke Cy took with him when he vanished.

All week, Jane came and went without a word; the only time she and Dad talked was on the phone. She said she was assisting with a big case at the firm. I heard her tell Dad something about it being "her chance to advance" and I thought, *Advance like move forward? Or like move away?* I saw her for a few minutes every morning and evening; each time, she was holding a mug of coffee and wearing a look that was far from home. There was a blush on her face that was the opposite of camouflage. I could smell her wistfulness from a mile away.

Outside our family, I didn't tell anyone that Cy was missing. Instead, I went to school, although most days I left with Lucas before the eight a.m. bell even rang. Seeing him had become my daily necessity, like personal hygiene. Swoon was evolving to smitten. I was a goner.

"Hungry?" Lucas had asked on a Thursday as he maneuvered his car through the faculty lot and back out onto the main road.

I shook my head and watched him tap two Camel Filters out of his pack. Looking at him in the morning, I could tell his rumpledness was authentic—no shower or shaving before school. All I could think was: *This is what it would be like to wake up next to him.*

This is how I decided that midterms were irrelevant and that I didn't need a diploma.

"Third day in a row of blowing off classes." Lucas grinned, handing me a cigarette. He watched in amusement as I inexpertly lit it. "Guess you were serious about not going to college, huh?"

I just shrugged, attempting to take a cough-less drag of my cigarette. I rolled down the window and exhaled, watching as we pulled into McLaughlin Park. The municipal park was now our go-to spot. There was nothing to interrupt us, save the staccato punctuation of tennis balls hitting the nearby courts. That kind of white noise, that proof of life just beyond our periphery, was sort of arousing. There's nothing like being almost alone to make you take advantage of privacy.

Kissing was more natural since I'd been practicing on

Lucas every day, too. Sometimes when my eyes were closed and all I could feel was Lucas, I thought about soccer—about how Cyrus used to get up at all hours, how it took every bit of his strength and interest and hand-eye coordination. That when he was done, it was still morning and he was already spent. That's how Lucas made me feel. I gave him all I had and there was nothing left for anyone else. It was particularly convenient at a time when I should have been feeling so many other things, like guilt or fear or regret.

"So, tell me something," Lucas said, his lips pressed against my neck. We were parked at the far end of the park's upper lot. Fewer people came up here this early and, at that moment, it felt like we were the only two people on earth.

"Mmm?"

"At school. In school, I mean. Is it, like, easy for you?"

I shifted to look at him and winced; the parking brake was lodged between us like an extra limb.

"What do you mean, 'easy'?"

Lucas shrugged. "I mean, you got good grades and shit. I know we were joking about it before, but we both know you're going to college."

I snorted. "Not the good kind." Then I bit my lip, knowing how that sounded. "I mean, not like a university."

"I know what you meant."

There was silence for a second and I thought I'd offended him. Then he reached out to stroke the soft, fleshy side of my pinky. I gave him a half smile, then let my fingers intertwine with his.

"You could get good grades, too," I said softly. It was Lucas's turn to snort.

"Please. Ever heard of a lost cause?"

Yeah. I live with one. Lived with one.

"There's no such thing as a lost cause," I lied.

He ran a hand over his hair, then let it rest over his eyes. "I'm not cut out for school."

Moments like this confounded me. I'd read enough books and watched enough movies to know I was supposed to be trying to make Lucas a better man, the best possible version of himself. That I was supposed to get him to turn his life around or something. Instead, I linked a free finger into a belt loop of his jeans.

"Maybe tomorrow you can stay for first period."

He barked a laugh, as though I'd suggested something impossible and I glanced at the clock on the dashboard. I was missing Dr. Schafer's lecture on acidity and alkalinity. I felt bad about skipping her class—really, I did. I just couldn't help it—I felt a gravitational pull toward Lucas. It was inexplicable, but I had a few hypotheses, and mornings like this were my opportunity to collect data.

Lucas was showing me different sides of himself. Like this morning, when I'd seen how he'd tucked an Oxy under his tongue as I climbed into the passenger's seat of his car. He'd never asked me for them, so I could only assume he was getting them from Jason. Something about that concept made me feel dirty. And there were other things. Sometimes he chain-smoked. Sometimes he laughed too loud.

Sometimes he reminded me of Cyrus in ways that made me sick and scared.

Still, Lucas was soft around the edges and his hands already felt like home. It sounds weird, but they almost felt like my mom's hands when he smoothed back my hair or touched my cheek. Soon enough, though, they learned to slide down the front of my jeans. And then I didn't think about my mom anymore.

I didn't think about anything but how his touch was the center of my universe, my gravity, my reason for being. In all ways, Lucas had become my drug. In all ways, I'd become an addict—just like my brother. And I would have hated myself for it if it hadn't felt so damn good.

That Friday, I told Lucas that I had to go to school, that I needed to at least attempt to pass my classes. That, and I wanted to talk to Natalie, who had pretty much disappeared off the face of the earth in the last week or two. It was like when Cyrus split, Natalie went with him.

"I've called you a couple times, Nat," I said quietly. We were standing by her locker in the morning before Chem class. She shrugged.

"Look, you do you, CeCe—you wanna slum it with Lucas Andrews and his buddies, that's up to you."

I narrowed my eyes. "What happened to the girl who thought he was hot? Who left me alone with him on a college tour?"

Natalie sighed. "Look, Jeremy told me that Lucas and

his cousin are into a bunch of shady shit."

"What kind of 'shady shit'?"

"The dealing drugs kind. Jeremy said that Jason kid offered him OxyContin in the locker room. That's pretty hard-core, CeCe. It's not, like, pot or whatever. I don't think that's something you want to get yourself wrapped up in."

I sniffed, forcing my voice to stay even. "Look—maybe Jeremy just misunderstood."

"Misunderstood being offered drugs?"

"I don't know—maybe." I sort of tossed up my hands. "I've never given you a hard time about the guys you date. Can't you just be happy for me?"

Natalie looked like she'd eaten something sour; her expression was decidedly pinched.

"Honestly—no. I don't think I can. Not this time."

Then her eyes widened a bit. She pulled a book from her locker and slammed it shut.

"I gotta go," she mumbled, hurrying off. I frowned at her retreating back.

"Good morning, beautiful."

I spun around and grinned at Lucas, who was standing with his hands shoved in his pockets and wearing a hundred-watt smile.

"You're here! Are you actually going to first period?"

But he put a finger against my lips as though he needed me to hold in a secret.

"Listen, I need a favor."

I frowned. "Of course. What's up?"

He sighed and scrubbed a hand over his face. "Jason's dope sick like shit. He's out of pills and falling apart—he's gonna have a seizure or something. We need to get him something to keep him from ending up in the hospital."

"He needs more?" I couldn't help the incredulity in my voice—I'd sold him a shitload of pills hardly two weeks before.

"You know I wouldn't ask if it weren't an emergency," Lucas said, lowering his voice a little. "You think Cyrus can spare a few more?"

He reached forward then and toyed with a lock of my hair. For a second, I imagined he was weaving it into something splendid. Something we could cloak ourselves with, something we could fly away on. Then he dropped his hand to his side.

"I'll see what I can come up with," I said finally. Past Lucas, I could see Dr. Schafer at the end of the hallway, talking to another teacher. I'd skipped her class three times this week. When our eyes met, she just looked at me like I was a new student, like she didn't know me at all.

"I need to go to Chem today," I said, turning back to Lucas. He nodded, but looked distracted. A few feet away, some of Jason's friends—Lucas's friends, too, I guess—were standing in a semicircle.

"I'll text you." His lips brushed against my cheek and I fought the urge to grab his face, to pull him closer and not let go.

During class, I thought about competitions—how there seemed to be some sort of game involved in being with someone, but I was a novice and I didn't know the rules. If this had been a year ago, I'd have talked to Natalie about it. I might have even gone to Cy for advice—he always had a good outlook when it came to love. For me, it was just an elusive commodity, something to be coveted. Cy wasn't as unhinged by the opposite sex as I was.

Maybe I should've been honest.

"Lucas, I can't get the pills."

"Cyrus took off. We haven't seen him all week."

"Maybe Jason should go to the hospital. I mean, someone who takes that many pills has got to have a problem . . ."

The thing about honesty, though, is that it's a deluge, not a drip. Once you stop, the release turns to relief so quickly, you hardly remember what you've said. As soon as I started confessing things, I wouldn't be able to stop. Who could guess what would come out?

"I've been stealing Cy's pills. That's why he left."

"I haven't wanted anyone to touch me since my mom died."

"I'm just a shattered person and you almost make me whole again."

I probably shouldn't have been surprised when Dr. Schafer asked me to stay after class. I guess I wasn't surprised, per se. Uncomfortable, yes. Definitely uncomfortable.

"You want to tell me what's going on with you, CeCe?"

She asked it so matter-of-factly, so straightforwardly, that I was almost unable to respond. I looked down at my shoes, then back up at my teacher.

"I'm sorry—I know I've been absent a lot . . ."

"Please." Dr. Schafer rolled her eyes. "Absent is when you are sick or when you have an appointment. What you've been doing is cutting class."

"I—" I didn't know what to say, considering she was right. "I'm sorry."

She shook her head and sank down into her desk chair.

"You're so bright—so talented, CeCe. You have your whole life ahead of you. Now, so close to graduation, is *not* the time for you to throw all that potential away."

I nodded. "I know that."

"You know that you can talk to me if you need to." Dr. Schafer gentled her tone and I clenched my jaw.

"It's okay, Dr. S," I said finally, giving her a weak smile. "I'll be fine."

"So, then, I will anticipate seeing you in every class from now on, right?"

I swallowed hard. "Right."

I told myself it wasn't a lie when I wasn't positive of the outcome. And I guess it was good enough for her, because she let me leave without another word.

I pulled into the driveway after school and had to pause for a duck couple to cross over the gravel. As I parked, a hand-ful of Jane's French hens were scratching around in the dirt next to the seed shed. When you live on a farm, you're never alone. It's something I'd learned to get used to. It took me a little longer, though, to see the person sitting on the porch, the rocking chair next to the door leaning backward ever so slightly. When I got closer, my stomach lurched.

Cyrus looked strangely small in the chair, but gangly, too, like his body was growing too fast and his limbs had nowhere to go but out. He was dirty and his eyes were closed. I watched him, waiting for the telltale rise and fall of breath. His rib cage didn't expand. I pressed a hand against his chest.

Then, like him, I stopped breathing.

I couldn't remember much after that, at least not until we got to the hospital and I realized where we were— a place far more familiar to me than I liked admitting. London County General's waiting room still had the same pressed-wood chairs upholstered in vinyl. It was like a table-cloth, but depressing—the opposite of a cheerful, checkered pattern in a bright color. I think this one was called "puce." Some earwax-looking foam was busting through the seams like the aftermath of an explosion.

Jane was sitting in a chair across from me instead of the love seat/couch thing that was right next to me. We could have been swapping magazines. Instead, we didn't even speak. I watched her foot shake and at first I thought that she was nervous. Then I realized those nerves weren't from worry—they were from impatience. They were sign language for *I've been through this enough. Cyrus will never get his shit together.*

Dad was back in Recovery with Cyrus and the team of

doctors and nurses who revived him. It was the first time Cy had been a part of a team in a long time. He was a pretty integral part, too. Everyone had rallied around him.

At the house, I'd had enough wherewithal to call an ambulance. Now, at the hospital, I could barely flip the pages of my *People* magazine. My hands were shaking like Jane's foot, but they had less to say. My shaking wasn't nerves, either, but it was evidence that I cared. There was worry wrapped up with hunger. The last time I ate had been that morning and my stomach was growling loud enough to embarrass me.

When Dad came out through the automatic double doors, the kind that sweep in two different directions, Jane and I performed the obligatory "rise for the news" and stood in front of our respective chairs. Dad headed for Jane first, wrapping his arms around her middle like a small boy. I didn't know if I should have been jealous. Part of me wished he'd have come to me first. The other part of me knew that him clinging to me like that would be the landlocked equivalent of drowning.

"Janey, oh, Janey," Dad was half sobbing into her shoulder. Her face was sort of impassive and I winced on my father's behalf. Watching the beginning of their end was becoming excruciating.

Finally, Dad let go of Jane and came over to me. He let a hand smooth over my hair. His eyes were red-rimmed and watery, as though he had a terrible case of hay fever.

"We're so lucky, CeCe. You were there just in time. Had it been much longer, well . . ." He choked on another tortured cry and I pressed my lips together until they hurt under my teeth.

"You helped save his life, baby."

I hadn't been a baby in a long time and I really hadn't saved anything. I couldn't help but wonder if I'd done a good deed or created a monster.

"Can we see him?" Jane asked in an uncharacteristic show of concern. Dad nodded.

"As soon as they move him to a room. They want to monitor his vitals overnight, but we're hoping he can go home tomorrow."

Jane exhaled hard and I remembered she was in a hurry. She wanted to see him to get it over with. She gripped her purse in one hand like she'd bolt at any minute.

Cyrus was moved to a double room, but was alone in it when we got there. The bed closest to the door was stripped down to its plastic cover. I could see a metal bedpan on a side table and tried not to gag. Just beyond the curtain divider, I saw Cyrus's feet and ankles, pale and flaccid like dead birds. There was a time, not that long ago, when all his strength resided there.

"How you feeling, son?" Dad asked. I pulled the curtain back to make room for Jane and me to stand next to the bed. Cyrus was hooked up to an IV that was pumping him full of clear liquid. He had electrodes attached to his chest that were wired to a beeping monitor. It beeped out of habit, as opposed to beeping as a warning. It was like trying to sleep through a firm alarm when the battery wants you to replace it.

Cyrus tried to clear his throat, but it was a dry, scratchy attempt. He closed his eyes and shook his head.

"I'm sorry, Dad," he managed to croak.

Maybe it was an apology that was supposed to make things better. Instead, I wondered why he couldn't have just left his apology without assignment, as a blanket statement. Unless, of course, he was sorry only for what he'd done to our father.

"Shh," Dad said, putting a hand on Cy's forehead as though checking for a fever. "We're just glad you're okay."

I sat in one of the folding chairs, but Jane's time had run out.

"I need to head back to the office . . ." she said, trailing off a bit as she glanced at the clock. She leaned over to give Cyrus a halfhearted hug before she left and Dad followed her out. I could hear heated whispers outside the door. I looked at Cy. He looked at me. I looked at my hands.

"Thanks for calling 911," he said quietly. His voice was a little stronger.

"Sure."

"I'm gonna get clean, CeCe."

And, at first, I thought—*How? I mean, with the IV and electrodes, he can't possibly shower.*

Then I realized what he really meant. I watched him carefully. Suddenly, he was the one looking at his hands. His knuckles were swollen to the size of globe grapes and were almost as purple. Along the backs of his hands, the bruises followed the path of his veins and I knew they weren't from the hospital.

"You were shooting up, Cy."

He followed my line of vision where it rested at the crooks of his arms. Then he coughed.

"I know. It was stupid. I—you probably won't believe me when I say this, but I was actually trying to save money."

I stared at him then, trying not to shake my head or spit in his face.

"You're right," I finally said. "I don't believe you."

Cy shrugged. "It's a stronger high—it takes less to get you where you need to go. So I wouldn't need as much. Wouldn't have to use as much or go to the doctor as much."

"Oh. So you were an efficient junkie?"

I could've killed him right then. Right that second, lying there in that hospital bed with all those doctors and nurses and saviors to help him. I could've literally strangled him until he turned blue.

But then I saw him smile.

"Yeah." He grinned. "An efficient junkie. Never took me as one to pinch pennies, huh?"

I swallowed. That smile struck my heart like a bullet—like a fist somehow infinitely harder than the ones Cy had sent flying in my direction. Harder than the linoleum floor. Harder than anything I'd imagined hitting me since the moment my mother left this earth.

I hadn't seen my brother's smile for almost as long. And I wanted to see it. I wanted to see it again and again and again.

"I know you don't believe me," Cyrus said. "I wouldn't believe me either. But, really, I can't—I can't keep doing this shit. I'm miserable. I'm gonna kill myself. I've got nowhere to go but down."

He was already living in the basement and hanging with the dregs of society, so I didn't actually think there was much further to go. But I didn't say that. Instead, I said: "Well, I hope you're serious."

And Cyrus said, "As a heart attack," which was both completely appropriate in an ironic way and totally inappropriate in a cheating-death way.

"And I guess I should thank you for taking my pills," he said. "I mean, I got super sick and shit, but it forced me to get here. To get clean."

"How do you know it was me?" I asked him.

"Wasn't it?"

I shrugged. Better not to admit anything that could bite me in the ass later.

"The last time we were here was for Mom," Cyrus said. "To pick up her personals."

I blinked several times, then nodded. "Right."

In the silence that followed, I remembered what my mother was surrounded by when she passed away—her favorite sweater, an afghan from her grandmother, framed pictures of our family, and total silence. There was no one in the room when she breathed for the last time. In the wake of second chances, I tried not to be angry and wish for a swap of family members.

I was willing to make a fresh start. I was. For the sake of the family we had left.

"I'm going to prove myself to you again, CeCe," Cyrus promised.

I stared at him. I nodded. I leaned in for a hug and felt his warm breath, still circulating through his system, still keeping him alive.

And then I did something stupid.

I decided to believe him.

16

IT'S AMAZING HOW MUCH POISON A BODY CAN HANDLE. ACCORDING to Cy's doctor, he was taking enough Oxys a day to sedate a handful of barnyard animals. It was no wonder that, when he came home, he was still shaking like a leaf. Even after a week of hospital-monitored detox, he was still in withdrawal.

I never really got Cyrus's fear of getting "dope sick," but once I'd seen it in person, I understood what he'd been trying to avoid. There were moments when he was folding in and over on himself like something was trying to hide inside his body. At other times, he was practically clawing off his own skin, as though something was trying to force its way out.

That's how the drugs escaped Cy's life.

My life, on the other hand, still relied on them. Or at least the money they were bringing me. And the people they bound me to.

I'd made excuses to Lucas about Cy running out of pills early. I didn't say anything about him getting clean. Really, since I wasn't sure I believed it, I'd convinced myself that there wasn't a point in sharing the news.

Cyrus was camping out on the living room couch until he felt better—that way, Dad and I could get to him quicker. I didn't really mind helping out. This soberish version of Cyrus was nicer than the drugged one and even said "please" and "thank you." But it was hard to strategize when I was busy frying up grilled cheese sandwiches that weren't for me or digging blankets out of the linen closet that I didn't need.

I was starting to think that Cyrus's sobriety was my way to duck out of the game. At that moment, I had a little less than two grand in a shoe box at the bottom of my closet. It was enough to enroll in a few classes if I went to a community college. Sure, it wasn't Edenton, but the first two years of college are mostly just required courses anyway. With a few semesters under my belt, I could transfer wherever I wanted.

"CeCe?"

Cyrus's voice had gotten stronger since he'd stopped puking every few hours. Now he could call for me instead of stomping his foot against the wood floor. When I left my room, I closed the door behind me. Suspicion still won out over potential change.

Somehow I'd thought that Cy's slovenliness had been an Oxy-effect, but I was wrong. In the three days he'd been home, our living room was no longer livable for anyone but him.

"What do you need?" I asked him, picking my way around the clothes, magazines, and trash that littered the floor.

"Dad said we're out of orange juice." His voice still had a croak to it, like a career smoker or an amphibian. "Would you mind running to the store?"

It wasn't really a question of minding. If I didn't do it, Dad would have to go out, and he'd been doing just about everything for Cyrus.

"Yeah, that's fine. Anything else you need?"

"Maybe some more magazines?"

I looked at the ones littering the floor and raised an eyebrow. "Done with these ones, I take it?"

At least he had the decency to look sheepish.

"Sorry. I'm a slob."

I bent to pick up some of the trash. "Don't worry about it."

I pushed away a persistent thought—that cleaning up after Cyrus had become the rule, not the exception.

I texted Lucas to see if he wanted to take me to the grocery store—not exactly my finest date option. Still, it was time to tell him the truth and I wanted to get it over with. I'd run out of reasons not to have pills. I'd run out of energy to figure out what story to make up next.

Car's out of commission, he texted back. **Can u pick me up?**

The Honda was low on gas, but I caved. I convinced myself a twenty out of the shoe box wouldn't even make a dent.

Lucas lived in the only apartment complex in town; it was adjacent to the only town house community. When I pulled up, he was standing outside his building, hands shoved in his pockets. I watched the way his fists unfolded, one reaching for the passenger door handle. I was beginning to love his hands best of all. I was beginning to love him, period, but I swallowed those three words when my heart vomited them into my mouth.

"Hey," I said instead.

"Hey yourself."

He leaned in and gave me a kiss, his mouth pressing hard against mine. Something hard bit my lip and at first I thought, *Teeth*. But when he pulled back, I saw the small silver stud at the bottom of his lip.

"New piercing?"

He nodded. "I got bored."

The boys in my life equate boredom with needles. I tried to forget about the piercing.

"So, what are we getting at the grocery store?" Lucas asked, scrolling through my iPod. He'd downloaded a selection of heavy metal in an attempt to "broaden my musical horizons." The music had an angry edge that made me uncomfortable. I could do angry all by myself. I didn't need guitar angst or drum fury.

"Orange juice," I answered, wincing when he settled on Sonic Youth.

"That's it? You could hit up 7-Eleven for that."

"I might get a few more things. Cyrus is . . . sick."

The parking lot of Kroger was about half full; I picked a space next to the "Expectant Mother" spot. I looked at the little stork on the sign and thought about the conversation between Jane and my dad, the one where Dad talked about having another baby. I pictured taking care of two brothers— one adult, one baby. I couldn't decide who would be more needy.

Despite my nonexistent shopping list, Lucas insisted on getting a cart. It was squeaky and a little wobbly, but he didn't seem to notice. Suddenly, I was involuntarily catapulted back a few months to the day he and Jason came to see me in the library, and that squeaky wheel on the book cart. Lucas and I hadn't even spoken yet. I hadn't felt anything but his gaze, but even that had made me hot underneath my clothes.

There was chemistry between us; I wasn't imagining that. And as we moved through the produce section, stopping at the bananas to grab the ripest ones, there was something purely domestic about the whole scenario. He was here. He was shopping with me. There weren't Oxys involved. He wasn't getting any action, save for when he grabbed my ass by the avocados. Maybe there was a chance of him staying with me, despite my losing the only asset I'd acquired.

"So, listen," I said as we rolled down the dairy aisle and toward the refrigerated juices, "I need to tell you something."

Lucas stopped to look at the yogurt and made a face.

"That Greek stuff tastes like shit. How come so many people are buying it?"

"I have no idea. Did you hear me?"

"Yeah, sorry." He leaned in and pressed a chaste kiss against my mouth. I felt a surge of something hot and heavy fly into my face—I think it was a combination of lust and blood and fear.

He made a gesture with his hand, as though giving me the floor. This was not an acceptance speech, but I took a deep breath anyway.

"You know how I said Cyrus is sick? He was—he just got out of the hospital a couple of days ago."

Lucas raised his eyebrows. "Overdose?"

"Um, no. Withdrawal, actually. I found him passed out on our front porch. He wasn't breathing, but the paramedics revived him. They kept him at the hospital for a week to detox.

"Anyway," I said quickly, wanting to rush through the rest of it, "he's clean now. Or getting there. He's still detoxing, but it isn't as bad as it was."

Lucas nodded. I couldn't read his expression.

"So, no more Oxys from Cyrus."

"Yeah. He—he said to say he was sorry for leaving you guys dry on such short notice."

Lucas shrugged. "It is what it is. Oxys are fun, but they're expensive as shit. That's what I keep telling Jason. If he wants a supply, he needs to go right to the source."

"The source?" *Wasn't I the source?*

"Go right to a doctor and get a prescription."

"Oh. But you need to have something wrong with you, like an injury or whatever. That's how Cyrus got them in the first place."

"Nah." Lucas shook his head as we pushed our cart toward

the front of the store. "It's easy enough to fake it. Change the name on an X-ray, cry in the office, that kind of thing."

I didn't ask him how he knew all that. At the self-service registers, I started scanning items as he handed them to me. This is how I used to help my mom grocery shop, handing her items from the cart to place on the conveyer belt. This felt eerily similar, with the role reversal throwing me off-kilter.

"So, Cyrus gave you a cut, right?" Lucas asked.

I frowned, looking back at him as he handed me the bananas. "Cut?"

"Of the money."

"Oh, right." I nodded. "Yeah, he did."

A 100 percent cut, in fact.

"I was just thinking that you might miss that money, you know?"

I was quiet as I scanned the orange juice and winced at the price. I should have gotten Sunny D.

"I guess," I said finally. Lucas bagged the last of the groceries and I paid with Dad's debit card. I held my breath, waiting for the transaction to go through. You never knew with Dad. The receipt shot out of its slot and I exhaled.

When we were back in the car, Lucas switched off the radio and turned to face me. His hand reached up to cup my chin, and I felt small—not insignificant, but special. Precious.

"So, what if *you* went straight to the source?"

I looked at him. Lucas was staring up at the ceiling, as though calculating an equation. Then he looked back at me.

"Cyrus saw that Bethany guy, right? The one in Williamsport?" he asked.

Apparently Dr. Frank was as notorious as I'd been told. I nodded, still unsure of where this conversation was headed.

"What if you went to see him yourself?"

I blinked. "Why?"

He looked at me as though I'd missed the answer to an easy question. "To get Oxys."

Which is when my brain started gushing something like water in and around all my thoughts. I couldn't process the suggestion because even my own ideas were drowning.

"No—no, I could just get a part-time job for the money," I managed to say.

"Babe." Lucas tipped his chin down and regarded me. "We both know a part-time job isn't going to make nearly as much money as this would."

I swallowed something like bile or blood or both, then stared out the windshield, knowing Lucas was watching me. The cars around me felt like enemies and I wanted to run and hide. Maybe the enemy was in my car with me.

But I couldn't let myself believe that.

So instead I said, "Let me think about it."

In the end, it wasn't Lucas who convinced me to go see Dr. Frank. It was my father. Or, more specifically, the farm.

I came home from the grocery store with orange juice and a pounding headache. Cyrus was asleep on the couch, but my dad was in the kitchen. I set the bags just inside the door.

I didn't need conversation. I didn't know what I needed, aside from two Advil and a time machine.

In an effort to clear my head, I walked back out onto the porch and breathed deep. The air was damp and felt thick in my lungs. I wished for winter. I wished for snow. Something to clear up the scenery, to give my life a blank canvas. Something crisp and nothing like the world around me.

"Honey? You all right?"

Dad poked his head out the door, a spatula still in one hand. I willed a smile to my lips.

"Yeah, Dad. I'm fine. I've just got a headache."

"Maybe you should eat something."

"Maybe."

I followed him in, the creak of the stairs like a knife to my temple. Headaches like this would drive me to Dr. Frank on their own.

"You want some double H?"

I leaned against the kitchen door jamb and watched Dad stir his version of Hamburger Helper—a combination of macaroni, chopped-up burger patties, and tons of chili powder. Lately his cooking had taken a cue from Jane's spicy tendencies. I think he was trying to make up for the meals she hadn't made recently.

"Sure, I'll have some," I said. "Want me to set the table?"

"That'd be great."

We fell into an old pattern like it wasn't old at all—the way he used to cook when Mom was too sick to stand in front of the stove. The way I'd set the table when she was still well enough to come sit for meals. I felt a familiar tug somewhere in my chest. It was like being a part of a family. I could barely recognize it anymore.

"So, CeCe, listen," Dad said, dishing out our dinner onto paper plates, "I wanted to talk to you about a couple of things. I know it's been kind of crazy around here lately, what with your brother and the hospital and all. But you've done a great job helping out. I really appreciate it."

"Sure." I shrugged, as though it weren't a big deal. In reality, I wasn't doing much more for Cyrus than normal. This just involved less driving.

Dad ran a hand over his face. He looked more tired than usual and the smile he was so good at faking was missing. In fact, I hadn't seen it at all today. Which is why I shouldn't have been shocked by the next thing he said.

"Jane left."

His eyes held a kind of sorrow that was far too much like what he felt when Mom died, and I wanted to bristle with indignation on her behalf. But I managed to stave off my bristling. Instead, I asked the obligatory questions:

"Why?"

"What happened?"

"Are you getting a divorce?"

According to Dad, Jane couldn't handle the responsibilities of a full-time farm, a full-time job, and a full-time marriage to a man with grown kids. I figured that probably was close to the truth, except that I would have banked anything on the fact that she was banging either a) her boss or b) someone very much like her boss. Or both.

"There's something else."

Now he'd tell me she's banging her boss.

"The bank's foreclosing on the farm."

A few things happened at once. First, blood rushed to various parts of my body—my heart, which started pounding; my ears, where the sound of it was like gushing water; and my temples, which throbbed with the superfluous supply. Then there were my eyes, which both twitched and widened like I was having a seizure. Dad was watching me closely. I think he might have been afraid I was actually going to start swallowing my tongue.

"What does that mean?" I finally managed to get out. Jane leaving was inevitable. I wasn't expecting today to be the day, but I'd known it was coming. Foreclosure was probably inevitable, too. Somehow I'd been able to ignore that fact.

"Well," Dad was saying, his head resting on one hand, "that means that we'll have about a month or so until we need to find somewhere else to live."

One month. One month would be graduation. I'd put on my cap and gown, get my diploma, and head home to my cardboard box on the side of the road.

I swallowed nothing. I hadn't taken a bite of dinner yet and I knew I wasn't going to.

"So—so what are we going to do?"

In an irritating turn of events, Dad's eyes actually looked less worried or heartbroken about being homeless with his kids than about losing a probably cheating wife. I wanted to slap him hard across the face when he shrugged and pulled on a string at the cuff of his shirt.

"I don't know. I wish I did. I've been trying to come up with some options. I've talked to the bank a handful of times—there's just no way to pay the money they're looking for."

I blinked for a while, trying to decide if the tears that threatened to fall were out of sadness, anger, or frustration.

"So I'm going to shut down the seed business and get a job," Dad said.

I was surprised by that—up until now, it seemed like he wasn't planning on taking any action during the downfall of our family.

"Where are you going to get a job?"

"Anywhere that pays enough to try to get an apartment, I guess."

I tugged at the macaroni and meat on my plate with the prongs of my fork. I thought about the money I'd saved. I thought about how I could get more. I thought about the rights and wrongs in life and how the line was far too thin between them.

"I've got some money saved up, Dad. Do you think . . . ? I mean, if you can make a mortgage payment, will the bank maybe do something for us? Help us out or something?"

But he'd shaken his head.

"Sweetheart, that's so wonderful of you and I really appreciate you saying that. But we're almost six months behind on the payments. The bank's long past second chances. It's over."

And then, finally, the tears came. His, not mine. Mine still pooled, but never fell. His were an overflowing ocean of regrets. My regrets, like everything else about me, stayed tucked inside where only I could hear them.

When we buried Mom, we buried so much money that I couldn't help but think about it. As the one who wrote the checks while my father was immobile in his grief, I was burdened with the details of each expense. Death isn't just about loss. It's about math—and, more specifically, about subtraction.

But life is all about math, too.

Subtracting this house from my family.

Multiplying the expenses I'd thought I had.

And dividing my father and brother and mother from me.

I didn't even excuse myself from the table when I left to call Lucas. And I didn't even greet him when he answered.

"I'll do it," I said quietly when he picked up the phone. "I'll go see Dr. Frank."

ON TUESDAYS, INDIVIDUAL SESSIONS ARE IN THE MORNING INSTEAD of group. The only people who are awake right now are the ones who have to be. Except for Tucker. He's sitting next to me, his pinky tentatively brushing up against the side of my hand. He got up early to see me off. He says it's just because he's hoping Jennifer is bringing a short skirt for me to wear to court. I know his flirting is an attempt to distract me from myself because it doesn't come naturally to him. His teasing reminds me of middle-school slow dancing.

"I wish I could go with you," he says after a long silence. I swallow, unsure of what to say. Do I wish that? Am I grateful that he can't?

"Thank you," I say, because it's polite and the only thing I can think of. Tucker moves his arm around my waist. Our kissing has given him a new confidence about touching me, which would annoy me if it weren't so desirable. I think about grabbing his hand and pulling him back toward my room. In hushed whispers, we would slip under the covers of my bed. Our snuffles and giggles would be muffled by our mouths and their real intentions. Aarti might wake up, but she wouldn't tell. I'd find a way to make love in this place where there isn't any love left at all.

Instead, I move in closer to him and rest my head against his too-bony, almost-sharp shoulder. It's like leaning against a bookshelf, but I pretend it's soothing.

When Jennifer comes in, she's carrying a plastic garment bag over one arm, the kind you get at the dry cleaners. She blinks when she sees Tucker, then nods at him. I stand up and take the bag.

"I—I guess I'll go change," I say. Tucker stands, too.

"I better get back . . ." he says, trailing off. There's nothing for him to get back to, but I understand. We've reached the end of whatever kind of solace he can offer me. We walk back toward my room and Tom the guard tails us from a few yards away.

"Listen," Tucker says in a hushed voice when we reach my door. He takes my hand. "I don't have anything to say that will make you feel any better. I can't give you anything but me. But, for what it's worth, you have all of me that's left."

It's such an intimate thing to say, so adult and almost foreign. I blink, unable to respond. Then he places a Polaroid picture in my hand.

"I'll be here when you get back."

And then he's gone, back down the hall with Tom still

behind him. Technically, Tom probably shouldn't have let Tucker be out and about at all this morning, but I think he feels sorry for us. Maybe he sees something star-crossed in our faces.

I look down at the picture. It's Tucker's "bio-pic," the picture they take of you the day you arrive at BT. They paste it to the wall by your room, allegedly to give you a sense of ownership over your surroundings. I think it's in case there's a new staff member who can't put names to faces yet.

And the thought I can't get rid of is: *He gave me a picture to remember him by. As though I won't be back.*

Tucker disappeared before he could see my outfit, but it wasn't much to write home about. Jennifer had decided to go conservative, not that I'm surprised. The navy blue skirt is long enough to cover my knees and reminds me of her ever-present suits. The white shirt is crisp with sizing, not ironing. The shoes feel like weights fastened with tacky buckles. Jennifer nods when I come back out, though, so I guess I fulfill whatever vision she had of "Cecelia Price—Defendant."

Leaving BT feels surreal. The hallway seems to narrow as we move closer to the detention center's territory. We're getting more boxed in as we get near the reflective double doors. We walk through them and we're at our first check-point. The deputies review Jennifer's credentials, my court documents, our IDs. It isn't until we're out in the sunshine that I really open my eyes. It's not like I haven't seen life moving around me. We have windows and doors and picnic tables and grass. But somehow, because it's monitored and fenced in, that kind of outdoors feels more like an imitation.

Jennifer's car is exactly what I expected—a reliable Camry, a few years old but in good shape. It's clean, but not recently washed. Everything inside is stock. Her GPS is the kind you plug into the cigarette lighter.

"Any requests?" she asks, flipping on the radio. I shake my head. Honestly, I'd prefer silence, but then she might feel compelled to make me talk. I'm saving all the words I have for when I'm forced to say them.

Our second checkpoint is at the razor wire–topped gates at the edge of the detention center grounds. We go through the same procedures. This time, a sheriff has us step out and takes a look through the car for contraband. I can't imagine what he's afraid we'd smuggle out.

It's been months since I've been in a car. It doesn't take long before I start feeling queasy; the bumpy back roads into town were a bad choice. I feel my stomach lurch as the Camry swings around a curve. To attempt to stifle my vomit, I decide to ask questions.

"So, could they take me into custody today?"

Jennifer gives me a sideways glance. "Yes."

"Would I be placed back in BT?"

Jennifer shook her head. "No, if the proceedings don't go our way, they would transfer you over to the detention center."

"And if it does go our way?"

"You'll be acquitted."

"Right." I look down at my shirt and run a hand over the pearly buttons. I've never had a shirt like this before. Lately, my life is filled with far more firsts than I'm comfortable with. I close my eyes and lean my head back, hoping that I won't puke all over the nicest thing I've ever worn.

Imagine what you expect a courthouse to look like—brick, somewhat old, possibly a little grimy. The intention would be stately but the effect would be outdated. That's how the London County Courthouse looks. It's a knockoff courthouse—one that looks legit, but really doesn't have the same style or flair as a legit courthouse with pillars and statues and a garden outside.

We go in through a back entrance. Two uniformed officers meet us at the door; Jennifer nods to them and steps farther into the dingy hallway. It's the color of dust and smells like an underground subway station. I can feel the cinder blocks judging me with every step I take.

I've been to this courthouse twice before. Once with Cyrus—he got a speeding ticket right after he got his license. And with Dad, when he was picking up his marriage license. It's funny how a place like this can be a place of anger and sadness or hope and new beginnings. Kind of like the hospital. Kind of like life.

I keep my head down and stare at the floor. Unlike my room at BT, this might really be marble or granite. I can't really tell the rocks apart. Geology wasn't my best unit in science. For some reason, it makes me wonder if Dr. Schafer is here, if she's one of Jennifer's character witnesses speaking on my behalf. I doubt it. The list of people on my side is short.

Suddenly, these shoes I'm wearing feel like burdens, like I'm weighed down by my very roots. I try not to consider it a metaphor. Instead, I force one foot ahead of the next. The repetition would be soothing if it weren't leading me directly to my worst nightmare—a courtroom full of people I don't know at all and a handful of people I actually do.

"Thank you, Your Honor."

The prosecutor takes a step toward Judge Collins and gives him a toothpaste commercial smile. His name, Bruce Mason, makes him sound like a game show host—which I guess makes sense since he's putting on quite a performance.

"Cecelia Price was always jealous of her brother, Cyrus. He was talented and successful and got a lot of attention from her parents. After Leona Price, Cecelia and Cyrus's mother, died of cancer, Cyrus was even more determined to become successful to help support his family. And then, in a dramatic twist of fate, Cyrus was injured during a game. His knee was never the same again."

Jennifer warned me about how this was going to go. I thought I'd steeled myself for the onslaught of indigna- tion I'd feel when a stranger, who would've busted Cyrus without a second thought, stands up and talks about him as though he's a close friend. Painful prickles of something like fury begin to travel up the back of my neck. I stare straight ahead when Mr. Mason turns and gestures in my direction.

"Ms. Price's lawyer will weave tales of a boy who was a

junkie—a boy who stole money, who shot up drugs, who took advantage of his father and his sister. But this boy they speak of was just that—*a boy.* Cyrus was dealing with the loss of his mother and the loss of soccer—the two things he loved most of all. He wasn't perfect, but he was struggling and suffering through a painful time. Even more important is the fact that Cyrus Price had made the difficult and admirable decision to stop taking narcotic medications. Only weeks before his death, he was hospitalized through a week of medical detox.

"Cecelia Price is a selfish girl who is directly responsible for her brother's death. The witnesses speaking today and the evidence you'll see will make it abundantly clear that there is only one person to blame for the fact that Cyrus Price is dead today, and that person is his sister."

I'm stuck on the word *witnesses.* Evidence was one thing—pictures and plastic bags called Exhibit A or B couldn't hurt me. People were a whole other thing entirely. I try to be surreptitious as I turn my head to look at the benches behind the prosecution. There are a handful of people I don't recognize—experts in whatever field they are in, I'm sure. Behind them are a couple of Cy's teammates. Then there is the officer who arrested me.

"It is the state's recommendation that Cecelia Price remain detained at the Piedmont Juvenile Correctional Facility until her eighteenth birthday," Mason continues, "upon which time she will be transferred to an adult facility."

With that, the prosecutor seemed to be finished demonizing me. Really, he couldn't make me feel any shittier and, in the end, the facts wouldn't change. There were many truths in his opening statement. Combined with the truths that are etched in my brain, I can hardly keep track. Here are the ones I remember best:

1. I am/was Cyrus Price's little sister.
2. I was jealous of the attention he got from our parents.
3. First, I resented his talent. Then, I resented his injury.
4. Cyrus was clean for three weeks, two days, twenty hours, and six minutes.
5. He died from an overdose when he injected OxyContin into his left arm.
6. I might as well have done it for him.
7. The pills weren't Cy's. They were mine.

18

I NEVER COULD HAVE PICTURED JASON OLIVER ON THE WITNESS stand. Court didn't exactly seem like a place he'd want to be voluntarily. Then again, maybe it wasn't voluntary. I would imagine his testimony was quite a "get" for the prosecution.

Jason didn't bother dressing up for court, but I think he actually showered. His hair looks a little less greasy than normal. His face is pale in a way that makes me think he hasn't been eating. What had they promised to him if he testified against me? What had they threatened him with to force him up onto the stand?

Bruce Mason moves forward like a snake unfurling its body. He is practically stretched across the room from his table to the witness stand where Jason is sitting. He promises to tell the truth, the whole truth, and nothing but the truth; still, I can see a kind of doubt on his face. This is the same guy who wore spikey wrist cuffs and worshipped serial killers. Somehow, the obvious intimidation looks wrong on his face. If they were in a darkened alley, there'd be no question of who'd come out on top. Here, Bruce Mason is the heavyweight.

"Mr. Oliver. Tell us. How do you know Cecelia Price?"

Jason looks right at me, then quickly glances back at Mason.

"We went to school together."

"And what would you say you knew about Cecelia, up until the last six months?"

Jason shrugs.

"Nothing really. She was quiet, I guess. Good student."

"Uh-huh." Mason has a finger pressed to his lips as though deep in thought. "So I'm sure it came as quite a surprise the first time she offered to sell you drugs."

The empty chasm in my stomach widens to a canyon. I should have seen this coming. Add "narcotic solicitor" to my list of offenses. Jason never would have fessed up to approaching me first.

"Yeah," Jason says, nodding, "I, uh—I didn't know she was dealing, you know? But I guess she said her brother had a supply of pills that was pretty steady. She made it seem like it wasn't a big deal."

"But you never actually spoke with Cyrus Price?"

"Nah." Jason wipes a palm on his jeans and I want to shudder. "I always just dealt with CeCe."

"Thank you, Jason. Ms. Reinhart is going to ask you a

few questions now."

Mason recoils into a spool of a man; everything about him is so tightly wound that, if given the opportunity, he'd either snap or strangle you.

"Your witness," he murmurs to Jennifer, his eyes filled with something like amusement. I want to deck him. Jennifer scoots her chair back and clears her throat.

"Mr. Oliver, did you have classes with Cecelia Price?"

Jason shakes his head. "Naw. I think she was in a bunch of AP classes or something."

"So, then, since you didn't have classes with Cecelia, how did she find you?" Jennifer says, eyebrows raised.

"Find me?"

"You know—find you to sell you drugs."

"Oh, right." Jason considered this. "The library, I think."

"Hmm." Jennifer moves back to the table and takes a paper from a folder in her bag. "Your Honor, I'd like to submit this as Defense Exhibit A—this is an affidavit from Mrs. Joyce Lennon, the librarian at London High School."

She hands the judge the paper before facing Jason again.

"So, Jason, would you like to rephrase your statement?"

"Uh . . . would I like to what?"

"Rephrase your statement." She doesn't wait for his response. "Your Honor, this affidavit states that Cecelia Price spent every lunch period in the school library. It also states that in March of this year, Jason Oliver came there to see Cecelia Price. In fact, the only time Mrs. Lennon ever recalls seeing Mr. Oliver in the library at the same time as Cecelia Price was one day, in March, when Cecelia was assisting her by shelving books. According to the affidavit, Oliver approached Cecelia first."

Judge Collins has eyes that scream "bored" or "hungry." He waves a hand at Mason before taking the paper from Jennifer's hands.

"You may step down," the judge says, and Jason stands. He looks a little wobbly, like a baby deer. If I blew hard enough, I might knock him over with the sheer force of my breath.

"Your next witness, Mr. Mason."

As he passes by me, Jason's eyes flicker over and meet mine. I expected to see something like disdain or maybe anger—being dragged to court seems like quite the buzz kill for someone like him. But the only expression I can read in his gaze is something a little too close to pity. If I felt queasy before, it's nothing compared to the kind of sick I feel now. If someone like Jason feels sorry for someone like me, I've sunk into the furthest depths I can imagine.

Not that I wasn't there already.

I've been to a parade a couple of times. They're pretty popular in small towns—the cheerleading squads, the volunteer fire companies, and all the veterans who ever lived in a fifty-mile radius. In general, a parade celebrates something. If nothing else, it's a reason to clap and cheer and smile.

But the parade of witnesses Mason called was nothing to

clap or cheer or smile about. There was a medical examiner and an ER doctor. There were Cy's old soccer coaches from all the way back when he played Pee Wee ball. There were former classmates and teammates, ex-girlfriends and people who had just wanted to know Cyrus when he was in his prime. The tapestry they wove was of a doomed hero, a tragic figure of Macbeth-like proportions. They were painting what they knew five or ten years ago. Jennifer just kept asking them the same two questions over and over and over again:

"When is the last time you saw Cyrus Price?"

"When is the last time you saw Cecelia Price?"

And for most of them, the answers served her purpose. *Our* purpose. The Cyrus they knew hadn't existed for years. Some of them hadn't even seen him since Mom's funeral. Most of them didn't know me at all, or knew only what they'd heard.

But then Lucas comes through the double doors, and I feel all the bravado in my body melt down and condense. It quickly turns to nausea and, to my horror, tears. I haven't seen Lucas since the day before Cyrus died. It has been impossible to erase his touch for so long, I am almost aching now when I think of it.

I watch him walk up the aisle and into the witness box. Lucas's hair has gotten long. It's still as blond as ever. When I'd first gotten to BT, I'd sent him letters every day for two weeks. After I didn't get a response, I'd stopped trying. He'd never come to see me. Now we are magnets flipped over and around; I'm drawn to him with a force beyond reason. He's propelling his body as far away from me as possible. He doesn't even look my way.

"Mr. Andrews," Mason begins, "we've heard a lot about Cyrus Price from the people who knew him best. However, I want to ask you about Cecelia Price—I want the perspective of someone who loved her."

I swallow hard. We never said that to each other, even if I'd felt it. So, really, Mason was already coming up short. Not that it really mattered.

"How long were you dating Cecelia?" Mason asks. Lucas clears his throat.

"A month or two."

Hearing his voice is like a punch to the gut. I try to remember to breathe. Why did he still affect me this way, despite everything that happened? How can I possibly still feel his hand on my hip bone, tracing the waistband of my jeans?

"And what impression did you get about Cecelia's relationship with Cyrus?"

"Objection!" Jennifer is up like a shot. "Speculation, Your Honor."

"Sustained," the judge says, nodding. Mason almost shrugs it off.

"Mr. Andrews, how many times did you meet Cyrus Price?"

Lucas shakes his head. "I didn't meet him."

"Hmm," Mason taps his finger against his too-thin lips.

"But the pills Cecelia was selling—she told you they were Cyrus's medication, correct?"

"Yes."

"And she made it seem as though he was in fact a part of the deal. That he was willingly providing the pills to be sold."

"Right. That's how I understood it."

I blink at him. I can't even squint.

"However, Cyrus got clean. He stopped taking medication. What happened after that?"

Lucas has a face that is almost too symmetrical. When he frowns, it's a perfect arch.

"That's when CeCe went to see Dr. Frank—er, Dr. Bethany."

Mason moves away from Lucas and toward the prosecutor's table. He picks up a plastic bag with a prescription bottle inside. I already know it's mine.

"I'd like to submit this as Prosecution Exhibit A—a prescription bottle for OxyContin." He walks back to Lucas and shows him the bottle. "Mr. Andrews, can you read me the name on this bottle?"

Lucas squints. "It says Cecelia Price."

"And you remember when she picked up this particular prescription?"

"Yes, I was with her when she got it. She sold half to Jason, my cousin."

"Thank you, Mr. Andrews. The State rests."

As Jennifer scoots her chair out, I reach for her arm. She

looks at me and I shake my head.

"Don't."

Her brows furrow. "Don't what?"

"Don't cross-examine him."

Jennifer grits her teeth and leans toward me.

"CeCe—I can't *not* question him. He's a witness. He was your *boyfriend*. We need to prove his influence on you."

I look up and over at Lucas and our eyes meet. For a second, I feel like I'm falling forward. I imagine there's a rabbit hole that I can't see, some kind of vortex that can suck me away from Lucas and into the floor. Instead, I just look at him and he looks at me and something inside me starts talking.

"CeCe?"

Jennifer's eyes are quickly becoming something between alarmed and irritated. I shake my head again.

"Never mind. Go ahead."

Who am I trying to save here, anyway? We're all too far gone. The vortex begins to spin and pulse like a carnival ride and Jennifer heads right for it—the past, the present, the future, all swirling.

Here they are, my world in miniature: the judge, the ex-boyfriend, and the plastic bag holding the murder weapon.

"HOW DO YOU KNOW THIS IS EVEN GOING TO WORK?" I ASKED.

Lucas ran his thumb up the inside of my palm. Then he lifted my hand to his lips and kissed it.

"It's going to work. I promise."

We were sitting outside Dr. Bethany's office. The Mazda was dark inside—between the tinted windows and the gloomy day, it was hard to see anything clearly. I looked down at the envelope in my hands. Jason ended up stealing an upper-body MRI from a friend of his mom. How much trouble could you get in for falsifying medical records?

I took a deep breath and ran through the sequence of events in my head. I'd pay the $250 office fee. I'd wait until it was my turn, then I'd tell Dr. Bethany about my imaginary neck and shoulder pain. Right now, it wasn't far from the truth.

"Listen," Lucas was saying, "whatever he offers you, just take it. Oxys, benzos, whatever you can get."

I nodded, my throat tight. I tried to remember my mantra: *I'm doing this for Dad. I'm doing this for the money. I'm doing this for college. I'm doing this for . . .*

"Do it for me," Lucas said.

I looked over at him, this boy who'd found a way inside me. Who'd found *all* the ways inside me. I'd given him just about everything I could. Feeling something like love was by far the most visceral and motivating force in my life. It was my drug. If I would do something this illegal for Lucas, what wouldn't I do?

Out of principle, I'd always stayed in the car to wait for Cyrus during his appointments. Today, I felt the pavement under my feet for the first time in the Bethany Pain Management parking lot. I looked around at the dozens of cars parked up and down the lot. There was even a makeshift auxiliary lot on one side of the strip mall. Like some kind of college house party, trucks and cars older than me parked in invisible spaces, their big bodies askew from what was the norm. I felt askew from the norm, too.

Dr. Frank's waiting room was like any other doctor's office, except there were no magazines and hardly any room between the dozens of patients. I didn't really mind either of those anomalies. I could hide among the others—the comers and goers, the waiters impatiently shaking one foot as they held MRI envelopes just like mine.

I moved toward the sliding-glass window where a heavy woman in scrubs sat at a counter with a stack of blue pocket folders at least a foot high. I approached with something like trepidation. She felt like a gatekeeper. She *was* a gatekeeper.

"Good morning," I managed, trying to smile. My lips, dry and cracked already, felt like they were splitting open. The woman glanced up at me, then back down to the clipboard in front of her.

"Name?"

"CeCe—I mean, Cecelia. Price."

She scanned the paper, then reached for a folder. She handed me some forms to fill out.

"There's a HIPAA privacy notice in there," she explained. "That's yours to keep. And I need to collect your fee. Office visit is two hundred and fifty dollars."

"Do you accept cash?" I asked, fingering the stack of twenties in my pocket. She shrugged.

"Don't make a difference to me. You need a receipt?"

I shook my head. That last thing I needed was a record that I'd been here.

In one hour, you can get a manicure, watch a soap opera, or get a prescription for a month's worth of OxyContin. I was used to the view from the parking lot as I waited for Cyrus during his appointments. Now I could see the patients up close as they filtered in and out of the waiting room like they were getting no more than handshakes and Happy Meals. This place was less of a doctor's office and more of a drive-through. Or walk-through, as it were. In the front door with your desperation, out the front door with a square of paper and the promise of something bordering on relief. Or release. Or whatever the fuck you wanted it to be.

Dr. Bethany practically demanded I call him "Dr. Frank." So much of him was "almost" something. His hair was almost completely gray, with a hint of black. His body was almost fit, with a bit of a belly. He was almost a good doctor, too. The way he sat down next to me in his office, instead of behind the desk, made me think he wanted me to feel comfortable. That there should be a sense of camaraderie. But when he put his hand on my knee and squeezed, I realized that camaraderie was not exactly the feeling he was going for.

"Do you, uh, want my MRI?" I asked, scooting my legs out of reach so I could get the envelope. Dr. Frank stood and moved to his desk, glancing down at the blue folder with my name printed on the front.

"Cecelia. You're here for . . ." He glanced at a paper in the folder. "Neck pain?"

I could only nod, then I wanted to hit myself. If I had neck pain, nodding would hurt. *I am an idiot.*

But Dr. Frank either didn't notice or didn't care. He took the MRI envelope from my hand and pulled out the printed report. He didn't even touch the films. After all the time we'd spent making the MRI look like it was mine, it probably didn't even matter whose name was on the damn things.

He moved closer to me. His scent was anything but doctor-like. The aftershave he wore was cloying and sweet.

"Can you tell me if this hurts?"

He reached over and tested a few spots on my neck, then pressed on my shoulders. I winced now and then, hoping my pain looked believable. My heart was pounding and I felt like I might throw up or burst into tears.

Dr. Frank stepped back and wrote something in my folder.

"Your neck is stiff—really stiff. I'm thinking some heat therapy will do you wonders. Do you have a heating pad at home?"

"I-I think so," I stuttered.

He opened a drawer and pulled out a white prescription pad and a pen. "And I would imagine a month of painkillers would be helpful as well?"

"Um, yes. That would be great."

Dr. Frank gave me a knowing smile, which made me think *Cheshire Cat* and also *The Joker.*

"Are you allergic to any medications?"

I swallowed and shook my head, unable to speak. Could it be this easy?

It was.

When I turned to leave, prescriptions in hand, Dr. Frank leaned in and touched my shoulder.

"I'll see you in a month, Cecelia."

I gave him a painful, chapped smile because I felt like I had to. I imagined blood gushing over my lips and down my chin. For a second, Dr. Frank looked like a vampire. And then I realized he was—a vampire that sucks the life from your body and replaces it with something else. Something dark and dangerous and inhuman. Something that makes you come back, again and again, for more.

Getting the prescription, filling it, bringing the bottle home—it had all been uneventful in the best possible way. Lucas was disappointed that I hadn't asked for the benzos, but he got over it once we left the pharmacy. When he dropped me off at my house, he leaned in for a long, slow kiss that promised so much more than kissing. I felt the breath in my chest turn to helium and I wanted to rise up off my seat and float to my bedroom with him behind me.

"I'm gonna go pick up Jason and come back, okay?"

I nodded, smiling. "Sure. Text me when you're on your way."

As his car backed down the driveway, I gripped the paper bag in one hand. No more relying on the unreliable. I had my own resources now and I could make my own way. Going to college for the first time must feel like this—independence personified.

It must have been a while since someone had checked the mail—the stack inside the mailbox was almost too thick to hold in one hand, and I had to put it down on the porch chair to unlock the front door. I didn't really think about going through it until I was already up the stairs and in the kitchen, looking for something to eat. I started flipping through the bills after I stuck an Easy Mac in the microwave. I couldn't help but wonder what other bills Dad wasn't paying—if he couldn't afford the mortgage, would we be losing water or electricity soon, too?

Chase Visa.

Potomac Edison.

Verizon.

Capital One.

The envelopes were like a roll call of Fortune 500 companies. Until I saw the one from Edenton University.

It was a bigger envelope. The kind that colleges send— thick paper, logo in the corner—and I immediately felt my heart rewind itself. It was late November and snowing the day I'd gotten my acceptance. It was March and about to rain when I'd found out they weren't offering me a scholarship. What else could Edenton have to tell me?

Dear Ms. Price,

The Science Department of Edenton University is proud to offer you a Freshman Fellowship for the upcoming school year. This fellowship provides a stipend of $10,000 per academic semester. All Freshmen Fellows were nominated by their high school science teachers and applications were assessed through a judging panel at the university. Details will be forthcoming about your duties as a Freshman Fellow . . .

I blinked at the words, almost expecting them to disappear.

I couldn't believe it. I didn't believe it. And I knew better. Really I did—when something seems this good, something else has to go wrong. It's just the way things work—it's like a rhythm written by nature. A scientific fact.

I tucked the envelope into my bag just as my cell phone vibrated from the inside pocket. I glanced at the screen.

On my way.
- L -

I'd promised that Jason would have first dibs on the Oxys and I knew he had the cash. I hated the idea of Jason in my house, but it really made the most sense to have him come here. Cyrus was finally well enough to go out, so Dad had taken him to get some new clothes. Everything he had was ruined by the hovel he'd lived in—mildew ran rampant and the trash was practically procreating. None of us had breached the basement boundaries yet; the cleanup would be a job of epic proportions. Half of me was scared I'd get jabbed with a needle when I started the process of purging the house of Cy's old life.

When I opened the front door a few minutes later, Jason looked as greasy as ever, but his eyes were almost gleeful.

"How many you got, Price?"

He was practically licking his lips and I felt a shot of revulsion roll through me. I looked at Lucas, who shrugged and gave me an easy smile.

"I've got ninety," I said. "But you don't get all of them—so, how about half?"

Jason crossed his arms over his chest, looking pissed. "If I've got the money, why the fuck won't you sell me the whole bottle? You know I'm good for it. Shit, you gave me double that much last month."

"Yeah, but I'm not going back to Dr. Frank until next month. You want more—you can buy more later."

For whatever reason, my conscience was screaming at me to be the voice bordering on reason. Jason had gone through dozens of pills in a few weeks. If he was going to OD, it wouldn't be on my watch.

He rolled his eyes at Lucas, who punched him in the arm.

"Be grateful, dude. Did I get you the hookup or what?"

"Yeah, yeah."

Jason's voice was grudging and I felt a little put out. I'm the hookup, now? Shouldn't I get a little more credit than that? Lucas only drove the getaway car.

I shook half the pills into a Ziploc bag and counted them out by fives.

"Forty-five pills—that's . . ." I swallowed, looking back at Jason. "That's twenty-seven hundred if I cut you a deal—twenty a pill."

Jason whipped out his wallet and counted out the money by hundred-dollar bills.

"I thought it would be more than that," he said, stuffing the leftover money back into his wallet.

Lucas smiled at me again, then nodded at the doorway. "We really need to get going. Family dinner tonight. You know how it goes."

He really couldn't have picked something I was less

familiar with than a family dinner, at least now, but I just nodded. He shuffled toward me a little bit and dipped down to kiss my neck. I smiled up at him shyly and grabbed my bag off the table.

"Hey—I, uh, I got this today."

I handed him the letter from Edenton. He scanned it, then smiled at me.

"Nice—that's what you wanted, right?"

"Sort of." I shrugged. "I didn't know the fellowship existed until today. I guess Dr. Schafer nominated me. Makes me feel kind of shitty for skipping her class so much."

"Eh, I wouldn't worry about that." Lucas tucked a lock of hair behind my ear. "I think we learned quite of bit of chemistry in my car at the park."

I felt the blush curl up my neck and I glanced at Jason. He was obviously getting impatient.

"So, do you want to come back over tonight and pick me up?" I asked Lucas in a low voice. "After your dinner thing?"

Lucas shrugged. "We'll see. I'll hit you up later, okay?"

I nodded and he gave me a quick kiss before turning back to his cousin. They were out the door and down the stairs before I even had a chance to exhale.

20

IT HAD BEEN A WHILE SINCE I'D GIVEN THE HOUSE A GOOD CLEANING.
The kitchen table was covered with incoming junk—the
various items that entered the house and never made it
where they were supposed to go. I grabbed two of Dad's
jackets from the back of a chair and took them out to the hall
closet. If nothing else, I could at least start getting this place
in order. It wouldn't be long before we were packing things
in boxes and getting ready to move.

"CeCe?"

I spun around to see Cyrus at the top of the stairs. He was
leaning against the railing wearing a look that could only
be called enigmatic. Usually I could read Cy's face; at that
moment, he looked like a stranger.

"Uh, hey," I said, slowly. My heart was in my throat and
I turned back around to hang the coats. My fingers shook
as I zipped them up. "I thought you went out with Dad."

Shit, what did he hear?

He shook his head. "I wasn't feeling great, so I stayed here."

"Oh."

I faced him and waited for what I already knew was coming. Cyrus ran a hand through his hair and I noticed how much color his skin had—it was all coming back, all the blood and health and life. I hadn't known that was possible.

"So, I've got a question for you," he asked.

I tried to school my expression as "impassive" or "apathetic" despite the fact that I felt anything but either of those emotions.

"Sure," I finally said, swallowing. "Shoot."

Cy scratched his nose. "Do you remember Mom's macaroni and cheese?"

Not exactly what I was expecting him to say . . .

I nodded. "Of course I remember."

He turned and flopped down on the couch. A dust mote rose and flickered in the sunlight filtering through the bay window.

"It was the best. When I think about things I wish I'd asked Mom, I really wish I'd asked her for that recipe."

I smiled and shook my head. "I have it somewhere around here—if you want, I can teach you how to make it."

His eyes brightened. Cy's sober eyes were so much more vital, more focused than I'd become used to seeing.

"That would be awesome. Eating it was my favorite postgame meal."

I glanced across the room where Cy's soccer portraits scaled the wall, then gestured to them.

"Think you'll try to start playing again?"

Cyrus inhaled deeply before shrugging. "I want to. I don't know how many of the guys are still around. But summer break is coming up—I might be able to join an intramural league or something while people are home from college."

I smiled at my brother.

"That sounds amazing, Cy."

His cheeks reddened a bit and he shrugged again.

"We'll see how it goes."

I bumped his shoulder with mine, then slapped the thighs of my jeans. "You know what? I'm going to see if I can find that recipe now. Maybe I can make it for dinner."

I was standing, then walking, then almost out the door when Cyrus's voice broke through my hazy, foreign happiness.

"So, who were those guys?"

I stopped in my tracks, then turned around. "What guys?"

Cyrus gave me a look that said, *Seriously?*

"Those two guys who left a little while ago."

"Oh, them." I fiddled with the beads on my bracelet. "Lucas and Jason—I go to school with them."

"Uh-huh." Cy crossed his arms and watched me. I could feel something within me begin to puddle around my feet. It was either resolve or bravado.

"So, did you tell Dr. Frank I said hello?" he finally asked.

I just stared at him and his strange expression began to

morph into a sort of sad smile. I shook my head. "I don't—I mean, I didn't—"

Cyrus held up a hand.

"Come on, CeCe. Even if you hadn't just sold half a bottle of Oxys in our kitchen, I would have known. I took the appointment reminder call yesterday. I knew you were going. I just had no idea you'd become such an entrepreneur."

I swallowed hard but I didn't say anything.

"Did Dad tell you about the foreclosure?" I asked.

Cy nodded. "Yeah. So, is that why? You're trying to save the world?"

"Not *the* world. *Our* world."

I felt bitter all over again. Cyrus, on the other hand, was getting some kind of sweet satisfaction from this role reversal.

"Does that mean you're the new head of the household?" he asked, snorting in disbelief. "Should I ask permission before I go out?"

"Just forget it." I started to walk back down the hall, but Cyrus grabbed my arm.

"Give me the rest."

I pulled back, hard enough that I heard my shoulder crack.
"What? Are you serious?"

Cy nodded, his expression almost grave. "You aren't the only one who needs cash, CeCe."

"Maybe not—but why would I give them to you after you got clean?"

"So that I don't tell Dad," he said. "And because you took pills from me."

I bit down hard on my lip, feeling cornered. It's not like I *liked* selling drugs. I liked the money it brought me. I liked the potential it gave my future.

But if Cyrus could get rid of them for me?

Then I could like the money and the potential without having to face a moral dilemma on the regular.

"You aren't going to take them?" I asked. "I mean, like, *take them*, take them . . ."

Cyrus shook his head. "No—of course not. It took me this long to get clean—you think I'd jeopardize that? Look—here's the truth: I know more people in the game than you do. Your boyfriend and his buddy are small-time. I can get more money than you can and I don't have any allegiances."

He moved closer and looked me in the eye.

"You can trust me this time, CeCe. I can start making things right."

There was nothing "right" about any of this, and I knew it. I'd known it all along—but something made me press forward. Something made me want the cash more than to be able to look at myself in the mirror.

"Think about it," Cy said, "I won't have to ask Dad for money. It'll take some of the pressure off. Don't you think he deserves that?"

Which was ultimately what broke me. Not quite in half, but into two unequal parts. One fragment held my heart, which wanted to wrap itself around my brother and squeeze.

The rest of me—my brain, my hands, my wide-open eyes—
saw the promise of some kind of redemption. I didn't consider
failure an option. That was my biggest mistake.

Lucas never called that night.

When I got to school the next day, he wasn't there, either.
I tried not to let it bother me. Instead, I went to Chemistry
and paid attention as though it were the day I'd learn everything I'd need to know for the rest of my life.

I don't know if Dr. Schafer knew the reason, but she
seemed happy to have me back. I thought about what life
would be like in the fall—working on research projects as a
Freshman Fellow, being able to help out Dad with rent, and,
hopefully, still going strong with Lucas. He wasn't interested
in going away for school and he'd seemed happy that I was
still planning on living with my family. I was honestly starting to think that it was possible to love someone and not lose
them.

I stayed after class to talk to Dr. Schafer about the fellowship. I suppose she knew why I was hanging back, because
she greeted me with a grin as I approached her desk.

"I take it you got the letter?" she asked.

I nodded. "I did—I can't believe it. It's so exciting."

Dr. Schafer beamed. "You earned it, CeCe. When it came
down to it, you were the only candidate in my mind. You
were the only person I recommended."

I felt a pleased blush spread across my cheeks. "Thank
you so much. Really—I don't know if I would be going

to college at all, and definitely not Edenton, without your help."

It was true—even with the money I'd saved, Dr. Schafer's lessons and now her recommendation letter to the Freshmen Fellowship panel were far more influential than anything else in my life.

A shadow passed over her face then. "Of course, I wrote that letter before you started skipping my class—so I still expect you to attend every day, just like we talked about."

"Of course."

She smiled at that, then splayed her hands wide on the desk in front of her.

"Congratulations, Cecelia. I know you're going places— and I truly hope I'm around to see where life takes you."

I bit my lip on the smile that felt a little too wonderful to be real.

"I hope so, too," I said shyly.

And I meant it.

I felt almost idyllic on my drive home as I thought about next year. When I got home from school, however, the house was quiet in an uncomfortable way. That morning, Cyrus told me he was meeting up with a few buddies to kick the soccer ball around. He'd seemed so happy about it that I couldn't help but grin back at him. It had been a while since Cy had attempted to kick anything but me or his bad habits. He hadn't said so, but I was pretty sure his plan was to sell the rest of the Oxys today. When I'd mentioned that his soccer friends had always seemed to have disposable income, he'd just smiled.

"Cy?"

I knocked on his basement bedroom door, but he didn't answer.

"Cyrus?"

It was slightly ajar, so I pushed against the buildup of trash behind it and slipped through. I couldn't believe he was sleeping down there again. We'd clean it up next weekend. Between the three of us, we could make the basement livable again.

But livable wasn't something the basement would need to be.

As soon as I saw him, I knew. He was sitting, sort of, at an unnatural angle on the couch. His head was slumped over as though it weighed more than what you'd expect.

"Cy . . ."

I kept saying his name, over and over and over again. At least until I got closer and saw the syringe still balanced in the crook of his arm.

"Cyrus!"

I practically threw myself forward, terrified to touch him and desperate to check to see if he was breathing. When I tentatively pressed two fingers against his wrist, and then again to his neck, all I could think about was thunder—it echoed in my ears and shook my body as though the world were ending and I'd never be safe.

There was no pulse.

There was no breath.

There was nothing but my brother's body and I felt the panic rising up and over me like a tidal wave of guilt.

When Cy and I were little, we used to play this game called Rabbit Hole. During a thunderstorm, we'd pull the big blue blanket off our parents' bed and drape it over the dining room table. Underneath, we'd stash all the things that were important to us—his Redskins hat, my ballerina music box, his soccer ball, my Harry Potter books. Then we'd take some canned vegetables from the pantry and some rice or pasta—just in case—and we'd wait for the storm to end. Sometimes we'd fall asleep there, curled up inside the blue cave we were so sure would protect us from danger.

I hated Cy's room more than any place I'd ever been—even the hospital, even the funeral home. But, still, I sat there for a while, holding his hand and staring at his body. I just couldn't leave him.

I wondered if I stayed long enough whether he'd start changing color. When does the blue begin on a corpse? Is that a morgue thing—blue by refrigeration? Or does blood just say "fuck it" and leach out of pores like sweat?

I thought about my dad. I knew he missed Jane in a way he'd never let himself miss Mom. The difference between Dad and me was that he needed a replacement. I didn't want someone there that wasn't my mother—someone who would never be enough.

Would I be enough to fill another new void in Dad's heart? Or would he break down into a million pieces, unable to find his way back to whole?

A pile of magazines chose that moment to lose its battle with gravity; as though in slow motion, they toppled from the desk and came crashing to the floor. They made the kind of noise that would wake someone if they were sleeping. I forced myself not to hope for a miracle. I needed to be rational. I needed to think.

We were losing the house. The seed business had gone under. Dad was looking for a job. The only money I had was contingent on selling drugs. My Edenton fellowship wouldn't be enough to pay for school by itself. There were no open windows to make up for closed doors, and funerals were expensive. Shiny wooden caskets, engraved granite headstones. It all cost money that we didn't have. I might as well bury Cyrus in the backyard like a dog. At that moment, my brother and I had approximately the same number of options.

As though in slow motion, I reached over and gently pulled the syringe from Cyrus's arm and tossed it in the nearby trash can. There was a drop of dried blood where he'd injected himself. I wanted to throw up.

No. I was *going* to throw up.

I leaned over the side of the couch and gagged. Not much came up. Still, when I straightened, I felt even emptier than before. I wouldn't have thought that possible.

I looked at the table next to the couch. The bent spoon, the cotton ball, a lighter—the cliché leftovers of a drug overdose. I picked up the spoon and examined the charred underside. Next to it, my Oxy bottle was tipped over beside the lighter. Then I looked back at Cyrus.

His face had lost all sense of life—not just the moving and breathing part, but the sheen of sweat and the tinge of color in his cheeks, what little there had been. I dropped my head into my hands. As the tears coursed down my face, I tried to remember beautiful things—my mother's smile, my dad singing in his seed shed, Cyrus on the soccer field. But I could see only things I wanted to forget—Dad writing checks to Dr. Frank, Cyrus lying on the floor in his own vomit, being thirteen and sitting in the waiting room of the hospital. Being seventeen and doing the same thing.

I couldn't believe I gave him that bottle of pills.

What in the fuck was I thinking?

Now, in every way, my brother was gone. I'd lost him for years to soccer, then to his addiction. Now I'd lost him to my carelessness and my stupidity and my greed and my plans for the future.

I was no better than Jane or my father.

I was no better than Dr. Frank.

What am I going to do?

It was a far bigger question than I was ready to answer. Instead, I made it smaller.

What am I going to do right now?

Like so many things, the stairs felt impossible to overcome. I stopped in the foyer and looked out at the yard. The way the sun filtered through the trees was like a miracle. I wanted to believe it was a soul leaving earth. But I didn't believe in anything anymore. So I reached for the phone instead.

Operator: 911, what's your emergency?

Caller: My—my brother's dead.

Operator: I'm sorry, you said your brother is dead?

Caller: Yes. He's—he's in the basement. He isn't breathing.

Operator: Did you attempt CPR?

Caller: No. I told you. He's dead.

Operator: Ma'am, how did this happen? Was he injured?

Caller: He—I—it's my fault. I did it. I did it.

Operator: Can you repeat that?

Caller: I said it's my fault. [sobbing] He's dead and it's my fault.

Operator: [pause] Ma'am, can you tell me your name?

Caller: [unintelligible crying]

Operator: Ma'am? You're going to need to calm down. Can you hear me?

Caller: Y-yes.

Operator: Ma'am, can you tell me your name please?

Caller: [pause] It's Cecelia.

Operator: Okay, Cecelia. I'm sending assistance immediately, but I need you to stay on the phone with me until they arrive.

And that's when I hung up.

WHEN WE'D PRACTICED, JENNIFER HAD ALWAYS CALLED ME AS HER first witness. Today, she passes me over in favor of Trina.

"Doctor, could you please state your name and job title for the record?"

"Dr. Trina Galinitus. I'm a psychologist with Parson's Cognitive Therapy."

Jennifer sends a pointed look at Mason, as though rubbing Trina's doctorate in his face. Mason yawns. The tit-for-tat in this room is becoming palpable.

"Dr. Galinitus, you have been working with Cecelia Price during her time at Piedmont Behavioral Therapy, correct?"

"Yes. I see CeCe once or twice a week."

"Could you describe the nature of those visits?"

Trina pushes her glasses back up the bridge of her nose and I want to wince at her helpless nerdiness.

"Cecelia has experienced a lot of trauma in her life. The

death of her mother, her brother's drug addiction—"

"Objection." Mason narrows his eyes at Jennifer. "Cyrus Price is not on trial here."

"Your Honor, the witness is merely recalling subjects mentioned in the context of her therapeutic sessions."

"Overruled. Please continue, Counselor."

It was the beginning of a consistent four-way banter between two lawyers, a doctor, and a judge. Trina would make a remark about the problems Cyrus caused in my family, Mason would object, Jennifer would contextualize or defend Trina, and Judge Collins would either allow Jennifer to continue or make Mason happy. It was tennis doubles in a wood-paneled courtroom.

I have to give Trina credit. She made me look good—well, I mean, as good as she could make me look. She described the visualization and journaling as though I'd made dramatic headway in therapy. She defended my reticence. She shot sympathetic glances my way now and then. Her loyalty was almost jarring. I am a defendant. Jennifer is my public defender. But Trina? Trina was really *defending* me up there.

"So, Dr. Galinitus, would you say you've seen an improvement in Cecelia Price?"

"Absolutely." Trina nods vigorously. "Cecelia hasn't had it easy. She knows she's made mistakes and she takes responsibility for that. However, Cecelia needs healing, not jail time. She does not belong in prison, where she might lose that momentum to work toward something better. Right now, in Behavioral Therapy, Cecelia is getting well. That's what needs to be encouraged. An environment where Cecelia can get better and make amends and move on."

"Thank you, Dr. Galinitus."

Jennifer looks like she might be gloating, which she shouldn't. Mason would slam Trina now if we were starting to feel confident. But instead he surprises me.

"No questions, Your Honor."

And, like that, Trina is excused. She gives me a smile as she steps down. I try to smile back, but it feels a little more like a grimace.

"The defense calls Cecelia Price."

For some reason, I'd hoped Jennifer had decided to pass me by. That she wouldn't need to question me at all. But, of course, you don't really ever have the right to remain silent.

Standing up felt sort of foreign and walking felt like I might as well be on the moon—slow-motion treading across a territory I can't even imagine navigating. I had to make the conscious choice to lift my feet and propel forward.

I've made my promises to Trina and Jennifer—I'll tell the truth and everything that comes along with it. The court reporter, who I've been ignoring for the last few hours, suddenly feels like a buoy in a sea of something impossible. Is she an asset, this woman taking down every word I say? Or is she the enemy I never anticipated—the one who is writing down every word I say to use it against me later?

"Cecelia?"

Jennifer's in front of me now and I try to focus.

"Cecelia, I know this is going to be difficult. But I need you to take us back to the day your brother died."

I clear my throat. I don't think I can take a deep enough breath to fuel everything I have to say.

"It was a Wednesday. I came home from school around three."

That afternoon was the last time I did so many things—the last time I drove the Honda, the last time I sat in Chem class, the last time I unlocked the front door of our house. I take a breath.

"Cyrus was planning on meeting up with friends that day, but he was supposed to be back before I got home. I didn't see him, so I went downstairs and knocked on the door. When he didn't answer, I went in. And found him."

Sympathy emanates from Jennifer like fumes. She clasps both hands in front of her waist like she wants to pray for my very soul.

"In what condition was Cyrus when you found his body?" she says quietly. The court reporter stops typing and for a moment, the entire room is waiting for the same thing—my description of my dead brother.

"He was—it was . . . he was sitting on the couch. There was a syringe still—it was still stuck in his arm. There wasn't any blood or anything. So, I knew—you know? That he'd overdosed."

"Did you call 911?"

"Not right away."

Jennifer takes a breath before lowering her voice a few octaves.

"And why did you wait to call?"

I blink, then shake my head. "I don't know. I didn't think it mattered if they couldn't save him."

"Would you say you were in shock?"

"I guess so."

Jennifer nods. "Now, before you called 911, Cecelia, can you tell me what upsetting items you found near your brother's body?"

"A spoon. Pills—leftover pills and a bottle. A lighter."

"And what were those pills, Cecelia?"

"They were OxyContins."

"And whose pills were they?"

The weight in my chest spreads over my body like something contagious. I want to be honest. People know the truth, anyway. But, still, somehow, being honest was so damn hard.

"Mine. They were my pills."

"Right. They were pills *prescribed* to you." Jennifer pushes herself off the table and starts walking away from me and toward Mason. Suddenly, she spins back around.

"Cecelia, did you inject your brother with drugs?"

I blink. "No."

"Did you put them in his mouth?"

"No."

"Did you crush them up and force him to inhale them?"

I'm beginning to understand what she's trying to do. "No," I say again.

"But when you called for assistance, you said that your brother was dead and it was your fault?"

"I —" I can feel my eyes beginning to pool with tears, something I was desperate to prevent. I look down at my hands.

"Cecelia?"

"Yes?"

"Did you say that to the operator? That it was your fault?"

I feel a shudder of shame ripple over the front of my body and settle into my skin like sunscreen, minus the protection.

"Yes. I said that."

"What did you mean by that?"

I look up at Jennifer, brows furrowed. "I don't understand."

She moves close, closer than she's been since when we were seated side by side.

"I mean, Cecelia, that if you didn't put the drugs into your brother's body, how could it be your fault?"

I know that this is the question Jennifer has wanted me to answer since the day she met me. When she agreed to be my defense attorney, she wanted me to help her out—to give her something to defend. She felt pretty strongly about my innocence—that giving Cyrus pills wasn't like pulling a trigger. We could never agree on that. She didn't see Cyrus as helpless. She didn't see me as diabolical.

"Cecelia?"

I open my mouth, then close it. Jennifer's smile turns almost smug.

"I have no further questions, Your Honor."

246

Mason hardly waits for her to move to her seat before he pounces. I force myself to look him in the eye.

"Ms. Price, I only have one more question," he says, his voice sort of slick. "Did you give your brother the Oxy-Contin that killed him? Did you give him the pills that stole his life? Did you pass him a murder weapon with the full knowledge of what he could do with it?"

Jennifer is up and out of her chair like a shot. I hear her objection, but I'm focusing on Mason's eyes. They're an unnatural shade of green. You could find them in a Crayola box.

"Sustained. You don't need to answer that, Miss Price," the judge says calmly. Mason shoots Jennifer a smug look.

"I have no further questions," he says in an almost whisper.

And he retreats, smiling at me in a way that makes me terrified and nauseous. I look around the room and I force myself not to squint. I know when they're wide, my eyes look sad, but that's just something we'll all have to live with.

"I gave him the pills," I say, my voice calm and almost vacant. "It's my fault he's dead."

Mason turns around to look at me as Jennifer's eyes will me to be quiet. She should have known better than to trust me. She should have listened when I said not to put me on the stand. Or maybe she should have entered a guilty plea. I hate making her look foolish.

"Giving him those pills was like pulling a trigger," I say, using the exact words I know she'll hate to hear.

Jennifer is up and moving toward me within seconds.

"Your Honor, I think the witness needs a break. Would it be possible for a short recess while I confer with my client?"

"No."

It's my voice, not the judge's, that rings out. I shake my head hard so I don't have to see the faces staring at me.

"I deserve to be punished. My—my brother is dead and I made it happen. I can't be innocent when I'm so guilty."

The silence is the only thing that isn't shocked by my outburst. Even Mason looks like he's been slapped. Suddenly, I understand why I'm here. Jason, Lucas, me—we were doomed before we walked into the room. We're all addicts and dealers and bad seeds. Unlike Cyrus, though, we're not dead. We have to accept our fates as they're handed down to us. In the end, it's people like Jennifer I'm trying to protect here. Jennifer, who's worked so hard to be someone who could save me.

Despite my best intentions, I begin to cry and the world around me starts to melt. I hear Jennifer's voice and feel her grab my arms as she pulls me up to stand and starts to lead me out of the room. All I can think of is how her hands are icy cold. That and how, somehow, the grip of her fingers feels like handcuffs.

Jennifer's been a lot of things. Frustrated when I won't talk. Sympathetic when I do. Tired pretty much always. But this is the first time she's been legitimately angry. It's actually kind of terrifying.

"How could you do that? You basically begged for a

guilty verdict," she practically spits, pacing back and forth in front of me. I'm sitting on a bench outside the courtroom, smoothing my hands over my skirt.

"Do you have anything to say?" Jennifer asks, stopping in front of me.

"What do you want me to say?"

"How about 'Sorry I totally screwed up my not-guilty plea'?"

I shrug. "I didn't think it mattered?"

"Are you kidding? You could have pled the Fifth, CeCe! Instead, you incriminated yourself!" She just stares at me like I'm a crazy person. "I don't get it, CeCe. It's like you *want* to go to jail."

I don't say anything. Jennifer mutters something I can't hear and clenches a piece of paper in one hand.

"I'm going to make a phone call, then we're going back in there and performing some magic. I'm not letting you fuck yourself over."

Wow. I've never heard her use the F-word.

She spins on her heel, saying something to the officer guarding me before heading down the hallway.

"Can I go to the water fountain?" I ask the officer. He shakes his head.

"No, miss. Sorry."

It's the first time anyone has apologized to me in a really long time. I'm disproportionally grateful.

I stare out the window at the moving traffic, the gray office buildings, the signs of city life I haven't seen in forever.

It feels weird to be out in the land of the living again, like I've been sleeping or dead for a lifetime and now I have to get reacquainted with what living really means. I don't know if I'm ready for it. All the more reason to stay exactly where I've been.

The clock on the wall has hands that are sort of gothic and lacy. It reminds me of the kind of clocks you see in antique stores, the ones that haven't worked for years and maybe never will. This one does, though. It's almost one. It's almost time to go back in.

I smooth a hand over my skirt again, wishing it were pants. I hate that my legs are showing, even if I'm wearing pantyhose. Everything I am is covered in something synthetic right now—something fake. 100 percent polyester, rayon, and lies.

22

THE WALK BACK TO THE COURTROOM FEELS LONG AND HOLLOW, like some kind of death-row rehearsal. I realize the death penalty isn't on the table here, but that doesn't mean I can't imagine what it would feel like. I sit in my chair, stiff and unyielding, as Jennifer calls her final witness.

"Medical examiner" is just a nice way of saying "corpse cutter." As Dr. Jefferies walks up to the stand, I picture him taking a scalpel to my skin and slicing until all my secrets spill out. He's wearing a pale gray suit. I imagine that his lab coat is in the backseat of his inevitably nice car. When he sits down facing me, I look away. Jennifer does the opposite.

"Dr. Jefferies, could you state your job title for the record?"

"Lead medical examiner, Bryson County."

"Thank you. Now, Mr. Jefferies, you were brought in from a neighboring county as an expert in your field. Could you please tell the court about your findings regarding the body of Cyrus Price?"

"Based on the autopsy, Cyrus was a longtime intravenous drug user," Dr. Jefferies begins.

"Objection, Your Honor!" Mason shouts, springing up from his seat. "We're well aware of Cyrus's past mistakes."

"Sustained."

"Dr. Jefferies," Jennifer continues, as though she hadn't been interrupted, "what drugs did you find in Cyrus Price's system?"

And again—"Objection, Your Honor. We've already spoken to a medical examiner. Cyrus Price died of an overdose—no one can dispute that."

But this time—

"Overruled."

Jennifer's smile taunts her opponent before she turns back to the witness.

"Dr. Jefferies?" she prompts.

"Cyrus Price tested positive for one narcotic substance—OxyContin. However, he also had promethazine and Xanax in his system."

"Can you tell us anything about these medications?"

Jefferies nods and I think about veins—the one in his neck is bulging above his collar. I wonder if it has to work harder to keep up with his big brain.

"Promethazine is an antinausea medication. It's often prescribed to recovering addicts to help with withdrawal symptoms."

"And Xanax?"

"Well, that's typically used for anxiety."

Jennifer reaches over the defense table and pulls out two bags—one of pill bottles and the other paper.

"I'm submitting these as Defense Exhibits B and C. These are the prescriptions, both the physical bottles and the physician's orders, that Cyrus Price received at the hospital in March, less than a month before his death.

"So, Doctor," Jennifer continues, turning back around to face the witness stand, "are narcotics usually prescribed alongside equally strong doses of Xanax?"

"Xanax is a benzodiazepine—combined with narcotic medication, it can depress the respiratory system in dangerous ways. It's not unheard of that they be prescribed together, but it would be carefully monitored by a physician."

"And what if someone took a large dose of narcotics with their benzodiazepine? Could one dose be potentially lethal?"

"It could, yes."

If Jennifer were a snake like Mason, she'd be coiling now. I can feel the venom, the need to strike. This doctor isn't the enemy, but he is at her mercy.

"Dr. Jefferies, in your expert opinion, what killed Cyrus Price?"

"A drug overdose."

"And that overdose included all three of the aforementioned medications?"

"Yes."

"So, would you say that one of those drugs alone would

have been lethal? Or did it take all three drugs to cause that reaction?"

"Objection," cries a beet-red Bruce Mason. His face is stained with a little fear and a lot of anger. "This is speculation. How could Dr. Jefferies possibly predict a variable other than medical fact?"

Jennifer spins to face her opponent and I picture her in a wrestling match, breaking a folding chair over the back of his expensive suit jacket.

"Because Dr. Jefferies has a medical degree, Mr. Mason. And he's been a medical examiner for over ten years."

Mason rolls his eyes and turns back to the judge. "Your Honor, we already had a well-respected medical examiner present his findings to the court. I move to have Dr. Jefferies's testimony be stricken from the record on the grounds that it's superfluous."

The judge looks frustrated, like a parent refereeing an argument between brother and sister. He opens his mouth, then closes it, as though he's considering all options.

"I'll allow Ms. Reinhart to continue, provided that she has an ultimate destination for this line of questioning," he finally says.

"I do, Your Honor."

"Then please get to it. Quickly."

Jennifer faces the doctor again and I swallow hard. My ears pop like I'm at an elevation much higher than this, and I wonder where my body thinks I am.

"Dr. Jefferies, in your opinion, did OxyContin kill Cyrus Price?"

In District Court, the entire room is made of wood. Wood-paneled walls, wooden tables and benches, and my wooden heart, hollow and somehow still thumping.

"I believe Cyrus Price overdosed through a combination of OxyContin, an opiate, and the benzodiazepine Xanax."

"And do you believe that the quantity of OxyContin—*just* OxyContin—that was found in Cyrus Price's body would have caused an overdose?"

Dr. Jefferies's Adam's apple dives downward toward his collar. I think about the bungee cord it's connected to—his voice rising from his esophagus.

"No. Cyrus Price overdosed because of a drug interaction, not because of a quantity," he says. "OxyContin alone did not cause his death."

Today I learned something about the human brain: When a realization blooms, it's nothing like a flower. Instead, it blasts into being like an explosion. It plunders and pillages the environment around it and inevitably leaves a gaping hole of shock in its wake.

IT TOOK ME ALMOST FIFTEEN MINUTES TO FINALLY CALL 911, BUT IT took less than ten minutes for the police to get to my house. I guess a dead body and a murder confession will do that. I was standing in the living room, staring out the bay window, when the cruisers flew up the driveway, lights flashing and sirens echoing. In the past, when I'd thought about Cyrus and police, I'd always pictured him in handcuffs. I unlocked the front door, then went back downstairs to be with my brother.

There was no knocking, no doorbells. Once they were inside, it took only a minute for officers to fill the first floor, and then the basement. Unsure of what to do, I crouched down behind the couch and waited. Maybe if I was quiet, they'd come in and take Cyrus away without seeing me at all. Maybe they'd be more concerned with the body and less concerned with the pale girl hiding in the corner, the one who gave her brother the murder weapon in the first place.

They saw Cyrus before they saw me. Two paramedics ran toward his body, calling out directions to anyone who would listen. It was hardly a moment later, though, when two officers noticed me. By the look on their faces, I was something they'd never been able to catch before. I guess criminals don't usually stay at the scene of the crime and wait for law enforcement.

Once they had me on the ground, I saw Cyrus being covered with a white sheet and I was filled with an inexplicable sense of satisfaction. Like our childhood "Rabbit Hole," it was a barrier to block out the storm. All of a sudden, I was pulled up to standing. Something scratched my knees and ankles.

"Put your hands against the wall," a female cop said gruffly.

I spread my fingers wide against the drywall and closed my eyes. Arms wrapped themselves around my body and patted me down. It was a reverse hug, the opposite of a warm embrace.

"Got any weapons on you?" the officer asked me.

I shook my head and tried not to wince as the strange hands dove into the pockets of my jeans. It was a whole other kind of robbery. They came out empty-handed and still managed to steal something.

This was the beginning of my new life full of "firsts."

First time being handcuffed.

First ride in a cop car.

First time I started squinting, trying to blur out reality and blink back tears. I was always a multitasker.

Everything you've seen on TV about interrogation rooms is pretty accurate, except for the lighting. They always look so dark on cop shows; in reality, they're lit up with the same fluorescent lights they've got at Walmart. They make everyone look bloodless.

The man sitting across from me was a detective. Actually, a *Detective*—like, a label that came before his given name. A title more important than his identity. When we arrived at the precinct, he rushed me into this tiny room and left me alone, stewing in brightness and regret. When he returned hours later, he started to grill me in a way that could only be described as clichéd.

"It didn't take us long to figure it out." Detective is holding my prescription bottle in one hand. He keeps turning it upside down and right side up, letting the little pills rattle like some kind of tuneless musical instrument.

I'd seen enough *Law & Order* to know that I didn't have to answer anything yet.

"I want a lawyer," I said for the millionth time.

"They're sending someone from the public defender's office. Until then, it's just you and me."

He stood up and started to pace the room. I sunk back into my thoughts, trying to drown out the sound of the soles of his shoes scraping the floor. I let memories flow through me like water—the farm, the school, the hospital. The settings from my life flashed in my mind like one of those old seventies viewfinder toys. I started to squint again until the room grew hazy.

"A search of your house revealed some pretty interesting things, Ms. Price. Tampered MRI films with the name changed. A shoe box of cash in your closet. And a bottle of pills you got from over state lines. Not to mention the dead body in your basement. So, tell me, CeCe, how long have you been your brother's dealer?"

I bit down hard on the inside of my cheek and he shook his head.

"We found your prescription next to your dead brother and we've got at least two witnesses who say you've been dealing pills for months."

I let my lashes sink; they were a curtain call. I was not responsible for an encore. There would be no standing ovation.

And then the door opened.

"I'm Jennifer Reinhart," a petite woman with dark, would-be-curly-if-it-weren't-so-frizzy hair said to Detective, her voice kind of brusque. "I'm from the public defender's office. Can I have a moment with my client, please?"

Jennifer wasn't what I was expecting, but it didn't matter. She shuffled through some papers and I watched her hands move like tiny birds, floating and flying between files. I wondered what it felt like to be that kind of busy, to feel like you had a goal that was reachable—a goal you could meet on your own.

"Cecelia?" she asked. Her face was a mask of professionalism. I wondered: If I threw something at it, would it shatter?

"I'm Jennifer," she repeated, as though I hadn't been here when she said it the first time. I nodded and she pushed a sheet of paper across the table for me to read.

"I've been assigned to your case. This paper details the current terms of your arrest and what charges are being filed against you. Do you understand what it says?"

I looked at the charges, listed in order by statute. I read it. I nodded. Detective wasn't bluffing. But this was a list so unlike groceries, I felt that it shouldn't be in list form at all. I imagined something like a telegram—the word *STOP* separating the accusations, trying to undo them again and again.

Jennifer continued talking, but this time her words faded in and out as though we had a bad connection. As if I were driving through a tunnel with no hope of resurfacing.

Some words I heard were: *hearing, bail, officer, Cyrus, psychological assessment, holding cell, placement, murder, Piedmont, behavioral therapy.*

The ones that echoed were: *Cyrus. Cyrus. Cyrus. Murder. Murder. Murder.*

"How long have you been your brother's drug dealer?" Detective had asked.

"Were you your brother's drug dealer?" Jennifer was asking.

Here's what I knew for sure: There was no place for me to go. There was no place left that wasn't ruined, and the only avenues available to me now had bars on the doors.

I took a deep breath. I squinted again. Off in the distance

I watched my future fade like some kind of dream. Like a mirage I never had a chance of reaching.

"I gave him the pills," I said. "It's my fault. He's dead because of me."

County lockup. Yeah. It's as bad as it sounds.

The last time I'd stayed awake for twenty-four hours was when Natalie and I stood in line all night long for concert tickets to our favorite boy band. It had been September and unbearably muggy. Everyone had tents and sleeping bags, but no one really used them. One guy brought a grill and served hot dogs. We all sang a lot.

This was a whole different kind of vigil.

I didn't *choose* not to sleep. I *couldn't* sleep. The factors that prevented it were internal and external. Even my need for sleep battled against itself. On one hand, I just wanted to fall into oblivion and numb out some of this horror. On the other hand, I was absolutely terrified of what could happen to me in this cell while I wasn't awake.

There were two other women with me. Both were drunk. Neither was friendly. One of them was a prostitute who'd been picked up for soliciting. When they locked the cell door behind her, she spit in the officer's face. Which is when I realized what the worst job ever was.

The other woman in the cell kept crying and talking about "Benji," which I thought was her son, but could have been her dog. None of us were communicating with one another, but we were all communicating outward in our own way. The woman crying, the prostitute spitting, my staring at the ceiling—I can practically hear the words. *Let me out*, our eyes say. *You don't understand. It's not what you think. I can explain.*

But, really, I can't. Explain, that is. Or get out. The white-blue glow of the lights has a faint, high-pitched buzzing emanating around me, and I let it envelop my body like a cocoon of sound.

I know I fell asleep because it was morning when someone walked into the cell and boxed my ears. I sat straight up on the bench and was almost nose to nose with a female officer who looked weirdly like Grandma Jeanie, my dad's mom.

"Up and at 'em, sunshine," she rasped, her breath warm and syrupy, like the air at an IHOP. "You've got a visitor."

The glass between the living and the incarcerated is thick enough that it can't really be considered transparent. I mean, I realize I can see Dad sitting there on the other side of the window, his ear pressed to the old-fashioned telephone receiver, but it's almost as though he's a different color or tone or version of himself. And not paler, which is what you'd expect. Instead, he looks full and reddened. Swollen, I guess. I sit in front of him and pick up the phone on my side.

The silence is stereotypically deafening. Or, more accurately, it makes me wish I were deaf.

"Why, Cecelia?"

When you're in jail, be it temporary or long-term, I think there should be a limit on the intensity of the types of questions you are required to answer. I look at the mottled countertop between us. His side is a little bluer.

"Why what, Dad?"

The thick, resinous mix of pain and shame is practically oozing out of him.

"How could you do this, CeCe?"

What? I forced myself to look up at him. His eyes, blue and practically rheumy with the echoes of tears, were as shattered as eyes could be.

"Dad—I—I never meant for this to happen. I thought . . . I thought Cyrus was clean."

"Cyrus WAS clean!" His words took aim and launched right at my face. I was suddenly grateful for the glass.

"Cyrus worked so hard to get over his addiction. You of all people should know that. And you just—you just threw it away. You threw *him* away. Like trash."

My hurt condensed and frothed and I thought about rabies—about dogs that involuntarily foam at the mouth. I narrowed my eyes.

"I didn't throw anything away. Cyrus threw himself away. And you know what, Dad? You threw him away long before that."

"Bullshit." Dad's voice rose to a roar and I felt somewhat chastened at the sound. His broken, raw cry reminded me of all the ways I've tried not to disappoint him and all the ways I failed. I looked down at my hands.

"I can't . . . I don't know what to say, Dad. I screwed up. But I couldn't control Cyrus. No one knows that better than you."

I wanted to ask him what I was supposed to do now. I wanted to know our next step. In the past, whenever there was a problem, we'd always come to some sort of consensus about how to move forward. There was always a game plan or a company line or a workable approach.

Today, there was nothing but blame. The ones who are blamed don't get to move forward. Not with other people, anyway.

"They assigned me a public defender," I told him, because I wasn't sure what else to say. Dad sort of nodded, then stared through the glass at my new orange ensemble. I wanted to make a joke about looking good in bright colors. I wanted to say anything that could possibly make him not hate me.

"Please don't hate me" is what I finally came up with.

He didn't say anything for a long time. We both sat there, holding our obsolete phone receivers. Mine had a sticky texture on the side of the handle, as though someone had put tape on there twenty years ago and someone else just decided to peel it off.

In jail, there's a whole list of things you don't get—privacy, decision-making privileges, a balanced diet—but they never say how much you *do* get. Like this, now, this moment I have fingering the nubby glue residue left behind and having the time to ponder its origins. There is nothing, nothing in jail if not time. Endless, empty time. Time that multiplies and breathes and gets bigger. Time that's like an equation without a solution.

Finally, Dad said, "I'm glad they're getting you a lawyer."

He kicked a leg out to loosen the cuffs of his pants. I couldn't see his legs, but I knew that's what he was doing. It's a trademark move.

"Thanks."

He was getting ready to stand up, then he looked right at me.

"I don't hate you, Cecelia. I love you in a way I can't possibly describe."

And my heart blew up and open, the Hiroshima of major organs. It was the last time I believed there was a light at the end of this tunnel.

"I love you, too, Dad—" I began. But he wasn't finished. And I hadn't yet gotten my Nagasaki.

"But no matter what"—he looked around at the painted cinder blocks and the partitions and the nothing—"I know you are here for a reason. This is where you belong now."

He swallowed.

"I'm just glad your mother isn't here to witness this."

Direct hit. The impact is immediate and brutal.

After that, I saw things happen, but I couldn't hear them. I knew he hung up the receiver with a clatter and when he pushed back in his chair, it scraped the floor. I knew his boots' rubber soles squeaked on the tile and that the door clicked shut when he left.

Other stuff happened, too—things no one could see or hear. But I felt them. I felt them like something that was physical and painful—they knocked the wind out of me and made me gasp. As the world fell apart around me, my will to live slipped through the cracks in the tiles on the floor. My heart forgot its own name. Likewise, my name forgot its own heart. They passed each other in my body like strangers. Then something deep in my body began to crack.

24

IN MY HOLDING CELL, I MADE A LIST OF THINGS I KNEW FOR SURE.
It's something my mom taught me to do when I got nervous
or scared. Usually, she meant it as a test-taking strategy. If
I got stuck on short-answer questions, Mom said I should
picture them as multiple choice.

"Write down your options first," she suggested. "Then
you can choose the right answer from the wrong ones."

It never worked all that well, but I didn't tell her that. I never
liked to look at Mom's ideas as flawed, particularly after she
died. When you have a dead parent, you want to believe that
all their theories are insightful or true or important.

But sometimes Mom was wrong.

Like when she would tell me to wear a jacket or I'd get
sick—because I never wore a jacket and I never got sick.

Like when she said that we'd all be okay after she was
gone.

My list of things I knew for sure was short. It didn't really feel like a list so much as a pair.

When I squinted, the bars of the cell faded into something blurry and solid that could almost pass for a wall.

My brother died yesterday.

Other than that, things seemed pretty uncertain.

My lawyer, Jennifer, didn't blend in with the bars and the cement and the mint-green paint foreshadowing my future. Her taupe suit and over-powdered face made her look like a giant tongue depressor. The guard buzzed open the barred gate and pulled my arms behind my back with something less than a light touch. He half forced me out of my cell and down the hallway until we reached a sparsely furnished room with two chairs and a small square table.

"Good morning, Cecelia," Jennifer said, setting her briefcase down on the cleanest patch of floor. "How are you feeling today?"

"Shitty," I answered. Better to be honest than polite. "And it's CeCe, not Cecelia."

"Okay. CeCe."

Jennifer picked the briefcase back up and laid it on the table. When she snapped it open, it almost sounded like someone cocking a trigger. Both of my cell mates from the night before had moved on to the Land of the Drunk Tank; had they been here, I wondered if they would have ducked.

"I've spoken with the DA and I've managed to convince him to let you out of lockup," Jennifer was saying. I jerked back, a little dumbfounded.

"Seriously?"

"Seriously." She smiled, then pulled out a stapled packet of papers. "We'll be transferring you over to Piedmont's Behavioral Therapy program this afternoon."

Ah. So that's the catch.

"Great. I should probably start sharpening the end of my toothbrush now."

Jennifer ignored me, scanning the papers and avoiding eye contact with me. What a novel strategy—someone should make this chick a spy or something.

"The Behavioral Therapy wing at Piedmont Juvenile Facility is a revolutionary program," Jennifer said. I could tell she'd given this spiel before, which made me either furious or nervous as hell.

"Sounds an awful lot like jail to me."

She crossed her arms and stared at me before speaking again.

"Behavioral Therapy, or BT for short, isn't jail. It's like rehab. You can keep your clothes, you get a bedroom, you aren't locked up. There's a common area. You have access to all kinds of stuff that's contraband in prison. It's almost like college, if you think about it."

I don't think Jennifer meant to hurt me, but hearing her compare a psych unit to college was like getting punched in the stomach. College used to be a goal and a dream. Now it's more than improbable; it's *unattainable.*

"Getting you into the program wasn't easy, CeCe," she said, lowering her voice. "With these kind of charges, it's very rare that the judge lets anyone out of county at all."

"So what makes me so special, then?"

Jennifer gave me a tight, closed-lip smile. "You're a minor. You have a history of trauma in your life. You don't have any prior convictions. Believe it or not, you're at an advantage compared to many others."

It had been a long time since I'd been at an advantage. I guess I shouldn't have been surprised. Really, at this point, there was nowhere to go but up.

We all have preconceived notions of places like Piedmont. The razor wire, the extra-tall chain-link fencing, the somber expression of the officers as they wave you through the gates—they all supported my theory about this place. It was a place for trouble and the troubled. It was like that Eagles song Dad likes so much—you can check out anytime you like, but you can never leave.

And that's what I decided to do—I checked out. I squinted through the passenger's-side window the entire drive there, allowing the world around me to blur like Monet was in charge of all my realities. Everything was a version of itself, but not itself. Just like me. Just like Cyrus.

Getting inside Piedmont Juvenile Correctional Facility was a multiple-step process, and all those steps were humiliating. Jennifer waited in the other room while a female officer had me strip down to my underwear. She searched my clothes, and then my body; worst of all, she held my arms out away from my sides so I couldn't cover myself. The modesty-bordering-on-embarrassment I'd always felt about my body was the first thing they took away at Piedmont.

I was surrounded by stacks of folded gray jumpsuits, but the officer let me put my jeans and T-shirt back on. When we met Jennifer out in the hallway, her eyes betrayed the pity I didn't want her to feel.

"It's fine," I muttered. "I'm fine."

At the entrance to the Behavioral Therapy wing, a wiry man with graying blond hair and annoyingly sympathetic eyes stood waiting. When my eyes met his, he reached out a hand and I forced myself not to recoil.

"You must be Cecelia? I'm Dr. Barnes."

I nodded. "CeCe."

I shook his hand and tried to ignore the waxy texture of his skin. His handshake was limp and that made me like him even less. Still, he seemed kind to me. You could see it in his face, which made me wonder if he was really genuine or full of shit. Everyone is judging everyone else from just below their skin. Under our human shields, we're all just human.

Dr. Barnes unlocked the door behind him and led us inside a dimly lit hallway. At the end of it, two women in hospital scrubs were waiting.

"CeCe, this is Molly and Carla. They run the floor from noon to midnight."

The short one, Molly, smiled at me. Her hair matched her eyes, or vice versa. Carla had a tight ponytail and sharp eyes. When she tried to meet my gaze, I looked down at my hands.

"Welcome, CeCe," Molly said. Her voice was husky and low. "Let's go ahead and take your bio-pic, okay?"

"My what?"

"Your bio-pic—it's a picture that hangs outside your room."

I literally couldn't think of anything worse than getting my picture taken. What could I possibly want to capture right now? What would I want to remember about this moment and this place and this life?

But when the old-school Polaroid camera was directed right at me, I couldn't help myself. I smiled. It was like a reflex; all of it had an aching familiarity.

"You're right on time for a group session, CeCe," Dr. Barnes said, still smiling.

I felt the panic-turned-bile begin to churn in my stomach. Molly and Carla were moving folding chairs into a semi-circle. I tried to take deep breaths. It was like the first day of school—nausea and nervousness took over my body like some kind of cancer.

People started coming into the room and I sat at one end of the semicircle. Most of them were my age, give or take a few years. There were fewer girls than boys. Once everyone was seated, Barnes sat in a wheeled desk chair and slid over toward the group.

"Okay, folks. Let's begin—Serenity Prayer first."

The voices in unison were like thunder, but the far away kind. The kind that can't be a threat until it gets close to you.

God, grant me the serenity
to accept the things I cannot change;
courage to change the things I can;
and wisdom to know the difference.

Dr. Barnes began with introductions.

"Everyone, this is CeCe. She'll be with us for the next few months. How about we go around the circle and introduce ourselves?"

I'd always been good with names and faces. Because I'd started squinting and blurring my vision, though, it was going to be impossible to keep track of them. I just watched and nodded as the others identified themselves for my bene-fit. One of the girls—I think her name ended in a "y"—kept looking at me. She was Indian or Egyptian or something, and her face was so beautiful, it almost hurt to think about what she'd done to get here.

Barnes ran group therapy like some kind of soft-spoken, really nice drill sergeant. People answered questions. They participated. When they hesitated, he pushed them gently. When they got defensive, he redirected their attention. He was the Dalai Lama of therapeutic intervention.

When he got to me, I tried to convince myself that I could be honest—that I could tell my story, the abbreviated ver-sion, and feel some kind of release. But there was something about the way they all waited to hear my truth—like they were eager for it. Like if I told them what I'd done, they could somehow feel better about themselves.

So instead I said, "I'm not ready."

Barnes cocked his head. "You don't have to say anything you don't want to tonight, CeCe. But you might feel better if you do."

I didn't know what to say. I opened my mouth, then closed it. Someone to my left cleared his throat. When I looked over, my vision cleared and my eyelashes parted like curtains.

"I have a revelation."

His voice was dark in all the ways a voice can be dark. I was captivated, pulled magnetically by something inside me. I looked around to see if others were drawn, like me, to this boy with the voice like danger. He sounded like Lucas in ways that made me ache.

"What's your revelation, Tucker?" Barnes asked, then looked at me. "We encourage our patients to recognize important moments and epiphanies as 'revelations.'"

"Right." I looked at Tucker, who was looking at me. Something sunk down and settled in the pit of my stomach. It landed next to all my self-loathing and the tears that I wouldn't let fall.

I didn't hear Tucker's revelation. Before he began, Carla was behind me, touching my shoulder and motioning me to follow her. There was a strange ringing in my ears as I rose from my chair. Her lips moved, but I couldn't hear anything at first. She was taking me through a hallway, then into an office. When the ringing inexplicably ebbed, I heard her say "evaluation." A few moments later, I heard "urinalysis."

When she said, "We have to make sure you're clean," I couldn't help but bark out a laugh. Irony is difficult to understand unless you're living it. Sometimes it's a catch-22 or a paradox. Other times it's impossible to label.

I'd done so many things in one day that I never thought I'd do: I slept in a cell, I got strip-searched, and I talked to my father through glass far stronger than either of our faltering hearts. Sometimes we start living lives we never expected to live. Other times we pick up where one life left off. In the end, it's not about where you came from, but where you're going.

JUNE

PRESENT DAY

25

WHEN THE JUDGE REENTERS AFTER THE RECESS, THE COURTROOM becomes something other than quiet, something like a motionless ocean: all that potential, all that energy, frozen in place. I think about fish in the winter—do they freeze with the water, then come back to life in the spring?

I notice for the first time that Jennifer has my hand in hers and she's squeezing hard, like she expects it to release an elixir of positivity.

The words come from Judge Collins like a force beyond nature. They fade in and out by order of intensity—the stronger they are, the clearer they get.

". . . facing very serious charges . . ."

". . . one of the youngest defendants in my courtroom . . ."

". . . distribution of narcotics . . ."

". . . falsifying medical records . . ."

And then, worst of all:

"I'd like to speak to Ms. Price in my chambers. *Without* counsel present."

It's the first full sentence I've heard. I look up into the judge's solemn face and try to read his eyes. What goes on in judge's chambers? Is it better or worse than the purgatory out here?

Moments later, Jennifer leads me out into the hall. I watch the overhead light travel across the tile floor—a splash of brightness I can't quite catch up to. I'm perpetually running after the reflection.

This time, we head into the ladies' room and Jennifer lets me go to the bathroom. Afterward, when I'm washing my hands, I watch her in the mirror. I'm not much of a gambler, but my lawyer must be, because she took a huge gamble on me. When Cy and I got older, Dad tried to teach us about poker. I never got past the "face" part—I spent every hand of every game watching my brother's eyes and brows and the flare of his nostrils, trying to see what part of him was lying.

"Are you worried about me going in there by myself?" I ask her.

She shrugs. "It's a pretty standard request in situations like this with defendants like you."

"Defendants like me?"

She clears her throat. "This young. With charges this serious."

"Right."

But Jennifer doesn't seem overly concerned about the judge wanting to see me in private, or about the potential guilty verdict hanging over me, even though its imaginary sparks singe my hair and earlobes and eyelashes. We move from the bathroom to the crowded hall, but before someone can speak to me, Jennifer whisks me in through a side door.

The room is like a library for lawyers—huge volumes with the names and numbers of laws and ordinances I've never even heard of. While we wait, I think about logistics. Like, would it be possible to follow all those laws to the letter—to spend your life never jaywalking and never rolling through a stop sign?

Ten minutes pass. Then fifteen. At twenty-one minutes, the bailiff enters the room.

"The judge would like to address you in his quarters," he says to me.

Jennifer looks over at me. Her eyes say, *Are you going to be okay?* and mine say, *I'm fine. I can handle it.*

My eyes lie. It's the only part of a poker face I've ever perfected.

The bailiff takes me out a different door, and we seemingly start weaving through the inner bowels of the courthouse. I think about the time I visited Natalie at work last year—she was a cashier at a girly accessories store in the mall, which specialized in fluorescent plastic jewelry. When her break came, she took me through the depressing, messy back room of the store and out into a cinder-block-lined hallway that was sort of like a school and sort of like a jail. Mostly, it just felt buried—cool and damp and utterly empty.

This was like that, but not. It was behind the scenes, but it was also dry and uncomfortably warm, like sun on wool or jeans right out of the dryer, when the snap sears your belly button and the legs feel like vises made of rug burn. We stop in front of a nondescript door. The bailiff knocks, a sharp staccato shock to my system. A voice says to come in and the bailiff opens the door.

Just inside the room, the judge sits behind a desk, which, like the bench in the courtroom, is something solid still dividing us. Now, though, he looks a lot smaller. Not weaker, but at my level, a little more human.

"Ms. Price."

It's not a question or anything. Just my name. I blink, then nod.

"I've asked to see you because I'd like to talk to you about the medical examiner's findings."

"Okay," I say, not sure if I should be responding. I nod again, just in case.

The judge turns his chair and puts two fingers against his lips, like he's thinking or smoking an imaginary cigarette.

"There's also someone else who'd like to discuss those findings with you, Cecelia," he says, then gestures past me to the back corner of the room.

I close my eyes, thinking it might be Mason, then take a breath. I want to bolster myself up with the air we're all using. I want my share before he starts spouting off and taking more than is fair.

But it isn't the prosecutor.

It's my dad.

And that's when my knees buckle.

Seeing my dad is the last thing I expected. That goes without saying. A surge of emotions spouts off into the stratosphere of my frontal lobe. I try to sort through them as I examine his face. He looks inexplicably older since I saw him three months ago through that thick glass window at the county jail.

For a second, we just stare at each other. Then the judge's manners flare up.

"Cecelia, would you like to sit?"

He gestures to a wingback chair that's sort of next to, but sort of facing, my father. It's the world's most awkward furniture position. Who sits like this?

But I sit down, because it's what I'm supposed to do. Following the rules has become easier since my time in BT. I perch at the edge and wait.

"CeCe."

Dad's voice is dry and crackly, as though it might burst into flames. I force myself to look at him again and then, with every fiber in my being, I force my lips to bend up into a smile.

"Hey, Dad."

We're stuck here now. The words he could have said before we got to court—words he could have shared at Dr. Barnes's family sessions or with Jennifer or with Trina—those words are a waste. They're no longer needed. He can't offer anything but a window facing backward, a rearview mirror reflecting an enormous, irrevocable disaster.

"Mr. Price," the judge says, his voice soft, "I'm sure you will agree with me that the medical examiner had some very interesting things to report about your son and the medications he was taking."

Dad clears his throat. "Yes. I—er—the other pills caused a problem. Problems."

"Right. Without them, I believe that your son might still be here today."

Despite the gentleness of the words, they slice through the two remaining Price family members like something sharp and icy cold.

But Dad sits still. Really still. He listens as the judge and his robes and degrees and unfortunate receding hairline practically croon "Coulda Shoulda Wouldas." How the quantity of drugs in Cyrus's bloodstream was from a single incident—the fatal choice made in one afternoon. How my mistakes were mine and were legitimate and deserved to be addressed. How you can't go back in time. How there is no such thing as retribution without victims. How life goes on.

"CeCe," Dad tries again. "I want—I want to tell you something."

I blink hard. "Okay."

"I want . . ." He runs a hand over his head, the gray hair thinner than I remember. "I want you to know that I'm still a father."

He stops and I wait, confused.

"That I've lost a child, but I haven't lost both of them. And that I'm still your dad."

This could be a moment with some kind of heart-wrenching reunion embrace. But it isn't. It's my dad telling me something I know in my head. It's my dad telling me something my heart had almost forgotten. Between the two of them, I'm never sure anymore who to trust.

"Ms. Reinhart tells me you've made a lot of great progress at the Behavioral Therapy program, Cecelia." The judge looks at me encouragingly, so I nod because I know he wants me to.

"Um, yeah. It's been good, I think. I do a lot of group therapy and stuff like that. Dr. Barnes is really supportive."

"Do you like it there?"

My brows furrow involuntarily. It's not a question I'd ever asked myself. I hadn't liked something—really *liked* it—in a really long time. But the truth was simple.

"Yes. I do—I do like it there. I think . . ." I swallow, looking at my hands and then at my dad. "I think it kept me from doing anything worse after—after Cyrus. I mean . . . I mean, to myself. Worse to myself."

"Dr. Barnes is an exceptional psychiatrist," the judge says, nodding, "and I'm certain you are getting excellent care."

He turns to my dad now, gesturing to me.

"Mr. Price, this may come as a surprise to you, but I believe that healing is always possible, in any situation. It may not be a permanent 'fix' or a solution, but it can be a bettering of one's life."

He stands up and comes out from behind the desk to perch on the front of it. I'm suddenly transported to a principal's office and, for a minute, Dad and I are two students in conflict.

"Cecelia, it was important to me that, before I handed down my ruling, I had a chance to see you interact with your father. If nothing else, I need to know that you are willing to work at your relationship," the judge continues. Out of the corner of my eye, I see Dad trying desperately not to pick at his hangnails.

"I believe there is something left here to save," the judge continues, "but it will take time. It will take hard, hard work. Frankly, too many mistakes have occurred *around* your relationship as father and daughter. I'd like to see you find a center again, a place where your wife and son, Mr. Price, and your mother and brother, Ms. Price, can still exist. A place that will radiate from the love the two of you share. If nothing else, I believe in that love."

I'm baffled. So is Dad. We're still dumbfounded when the bailiff comes back and motions for me to stand up.

"Dad?"

I'm halfway out the door when I decide to say something true. I clear my throat.

"I love you. And—and I'm sorry."

My father has the best kind of eyes. They are eyes that

can look directly through you when they're angry or busy or exhausted. They are the kind of eyes that would literally "pierce" or "dart" if that were supported by the laws of physics. And when they are aimed right at you, like they're aimed at me now, you can physically feel them—a direct hit.

But he saw nothing and no one else when he said, "I love you, too, Cecelia. And I promise you—no matter what, no one is sorrier than me."

I consider that—consider whether it's possible that my father really feels the heavy, isolating realization that he didn't help, that he only hurt. That he couldn't save my mother or my brother or me. That he wasn't merely a victim.

And I decide that maybe the word *sorry* is the wrong one. That maybe what he really means is that he was wrong. That he knows he was wrong. And, for now, that's enough.

Back in the courtroom, Jennifer looks at me, then clears her throat.

"CeCe," she says quietly, "you need to stand up."

I don't want to stand up. I want to sit here and gaze off into space, letting everything blur and fade until I see nothing by my mother's smile, nothing but Tucker's reassuring gaze as it scans my face and settles on my eyes.

But when Jennifer shuffles a little closer to me, I check back into my body. Then everything goes quiet and the world is watching me again.

Then the world is watching the Honorable Judge Randolph Collins.

"I've given this an inordinate amount of consideration," the judge begins. He places his hands on the bench in front of him, palms up. Like he's asking for something.

"Cyrus Price was a victim—and so was everyone else in his life. In fact, according to key testimony by more than one reliable witness, it seems as though Cyrus Price was sometimes the catalyst who caused the problem. Sometimes our victims are also our criminals. Sometimes there is no clear-cut happy ending.

"I can't bring Cyrus Price back to life. I can't go back in time and stop him from taking narcotic medication that was, clearly, responsible for his downward spiral. More than that, I can't change biology. And that's what this is, correct? Biology—the makeup of the people involved, the interactions and reactions of their bodies?"

He looks at me and the expression in his eyes is the one I hate most—pity. It's the one that tells me I'm not going home tonight.

"Dr. Carolyn Schafer is a chemistry teacher at the school where Cyrus and Cecelia Price attended."

I swallow hard. I haven't let myself think about people who might actually still care about me on the outside. Hearing that name reminds me of how much I've been trying to forget.

"Dr. Schafer, in a written statement to me, extolled the virtues and skill and drive of Cecelia Price. Dr. Schafer called her"—he fumbles with a paper on the bench, lifts it up, then peers at the writing—"she called her a 'born leader with the determination to be successful and the heart to help the people around her at the same time.'"

I can feel the color rising up into my cheeks. It gets hotter and brighter when the judge pins me with his stare.

"Is that true?" he demands. I blink, then look uncertainly at Jennifer. She nods slowly.

"I—I'm not sure what you mean, sir," I say. He shakes his head.

"Can you help others? Can you improve the lives of the people around you?"

I can feel the tears piling like Tetris tiles behind my eyes. I swallow and shake my head.

"I don't know, sir. I'm sorry—I'd like to think I could help others and make people happy. I—I just don't know."

He narrows his eyes, then jabs a finger at Dr. Schafer's letter.

"Did she recommend you for a fellowship at college?"

I nod. "Yes, sir."

"Did you plan on attending Edenton University in the fall?"

"Yes, sir."

"What were you going to major in?"

Were. Not *are.*

"I—chemistry, I think."

"And who told you that you could do that? Who believed in you?"

My head is starting to spin, then subsequently ache. I know that Jennifer is unsure of what's going on, too, because she keeps shifting from one foot to another. Neither of us knows what to do here except to tell the truth, the whole truth, and nothing but the truth.

"My mom," I finally say. "My mom told me I could do anything. That I could be anything."

I look at my hands. I look at Jennifer's shoes. I look at Bruce Mason, then past him, out at the rows of benches. There aren't a lot of people who stuck around to hear the verdict. No Jason. No Lucas. No teammates or coaches or next-door neighbors. In fact, the whole back row is empty, save one person.

My father, sitting on the defense side. *My* side.

"I'm ready to hand down my verdict," the judge said.

26

I DON'T USUALLY DREAM, BUT LAST NIGHT WAS DIFFERENT. MAYBE it's because I'm back at BT. Maybe it's because there's more room in my mind for something like imagination. All I know is that, last night, I dreamed that Jennifer and Trina were twin sisters. They couldn't bear to live apart, so one moved across the country to be with the other. Then they moved again to be closer to me.

Now they're both standing in my room. Besides yesterday in court, it's the first time the three of us have been in the same place at the same time.

"We can appeal the sentence," Jennifer says quietly. "All the charges were dropped, save the distribution charge. An acquittal was the *only* acceptable course of action."

Trina nods in agreement. They are standing side by side, equally certain of what they believe. Each of them, so sure about me. I smile.

"Thank you, both of you, for everything you've done."

"I don't understand why you don't want to fight this, CeCe," Trina says. "You don't deserve another nine months in supervised treatment. You've already served your time here. There are plenty of outpatient programs I can recommend to the judge."

Trina looks frustrated. I change the subject.

"Since Dr. Schafer had me exempted from my final exams, the school sent me my diploma. Dr. Barnes enrolled me in your psych course in the fall. And I'm taking two more classes, too—Freshman Comp and Bio—but those are online."

Jennifer shakes her head. "You should be in college. *Real* college. You shouldn't be stuck here."

"You don't have to be *at* college to be *in* college," I say firmly.

"You don't get it. This is a sentence—a judgment. You'll have to carry this with you. It isn't fair, CeCe. Not when you're an innocent person."

I want to laugh at that. I'm many things, but I'm not innocent.

"Besides," I say, "it's nine months. It could be worse."

"What about your dad?" Jennifer asks.

I sort of shrug and fold a sweatshirt.

"I don't know."

"Has he come to see you yet?"

"No." I look down. "We talked after the sentencing and he said he'd come when he could."

Jennifer looks at me and shakes her head. "People are still going to think it's your fault that your brother is dead."

I look out my shoe-box-sized window of reinforced glass. The sky is white and overcast, like someone took a cloud and spread it thin over the world. I close my eyes.

"I know the truth."

Jennifer shakes her head.

"I've never left someone here who wasn't supposed to be here."

I want to chuckle about that. "It's about time you felt that way."

"You ready?"

I look up to see Tucker leaning on the doorjamb of my room. I grin at him and, just like that, we're wearing matching smiles. It feels glorious.

"Yeah—just about." I close my therapy journal and tuck the pen into the spiral's twisting metal binding. Barnes gave the "all-clear" for me to have writing utensils unsupervised, which feels sort of like a victory and a lot like a gift. I hugged him yesterday when I got back from court, and I think his heart might have stopped for a second, he was so shocked. I was kind of shocked, too, if you want to know the truth.

Trina and Jennifer both hug me now, too, and promise to come back to see me next week. Something tells me they actually will—and something tells me that I can't wait until they do.

Today's group therapy topic is role models. Cam looks a

little smug when Barnes announces it—apparently the theme was her idea. I roll my eyes at Tucker, who just shrugs.

"Role models," Cam says, her arms spread wide, "are people you admire, people who you feel are examples of what you yourself desire to be. So, today, we're going to talk about how role models have played a part in your life."

Dr. Barnes smiles at Cam, then looks at the rest of the group. "So, who would like to start today?"

I glance around, then slowly raise my hand. At least half of the eyebrows in the semicircle pop up in surprise.

"Cecelia," Dr. Barnes says, nodding at me encouragingly. "Please—tell us about a role model in your life."

I clear my throat, then cross my arms over my chest. It's a defensive move and I know it, but I feel like I need a little bit of armor on if I'm going to open myself up.

"My brother," I say. My voice is sort of scratchy and I cough to clear it. "My older brother, Cyrus, has always been my role model—ever since we were really little."

Cam nods, then leans forward to rest her elbows on her knees.

"Can you think of a memory with Cyrus where you were looking up to him? Where you wanted to be just like him?"

I force myself not to snarl at her, not to say "no" and clam up the way my body wants me to. Despite everything that's happened in the last several months, or maybe because of it, I know that keeping quiet isn't going to do anything but hurt me. Keeping quiet—keeping secrets—well, the things

291

I carried silently ended up making me want to speak more than anything else.

"Cy and I—well, we fought a lot when we were little. I mean, not when we were *really* small, but when we were both in elementary school."

I smile, thinking of how I'd followed him around like a puppy, wanting to be part of his secret clubs and soccer teams and never understanding why he wouldn't let me.

"But there were a few things we did together with just each other—no friends or parents or teammates. And when it came to Queen's 'Bohemian Rhapsody,' Cyrus and I were totally on the same page. I don't know what it was about that song. We just loved it. We'd perform it like we were actually out onstage.

"I wanted to be just like my big brother—and he let me copy him. He would lead and he'd let me follow in a way he usually didn't—at least not at that time."

I drag air into my lungs, wait a few beats, then exhale. Talking has never felt so physical. Or so necessary.

"We had a tradition—we'd always sing the last lyric the exact same way. And it felt . . . good. It felt like we were sharing something important."

I look down at my lap, then up at the faces around me. Aarti is grinning at me and I smile back at her. Barnes and Cam are both wearing the same expression directed toward me—pride mixed with something else. Something like wonder.

"What was the lyric?" Tucker asks softly.

I blink over at him. He's got both hands cupped on his thighs, palms up as though he's ready to receive something. I can't believe I've managed to find this beautiful boy in a place so full of damaged souls. I can't believe I've been this lucky.

"Any way the wind blows," I answer softly.

His mouth kicks up on one side.

"That's a great lyric."

I nod.

"Yeah. It really is."

As the focus shifts away from me, I try not to watch Tucker—his face, his hands, the parts of his body that inexplicably seem to draw me in. Instead, I watch Aaron as he talks about a recent visit with his mother and sister—about how difficult it was to look them in the eye and say all the words he'd been saying to us for weeks. Words like *I fucked up* and *I'm ashamed* and *I'm sorry*. For the first time in group therapy, I'm feeling less zoned out and more tuned in. For the first time, I'm actually feeling empathy.

When Barnes dismisses us, Tucker and I walk close enough together that our hands brush periodically. It's probably obvious, but the guard behind us doesn't say anything. At the end of the hall, I duck my head into the common room, then motion for Tucker to follow.

"You wanna play checkers?"

He quirks an eyebrow at me. "Seriously?"

"Yes, seriously. I love checkers. My mom and I used to play all the time when I was little."

Tucker heaves a sort of patronizing sigh, but I know he doesn't really mind. We sit on opposite sides of the small square table by the window and I start setting up the board.

"You don't talk about your mom a lot," he says. I glance up at him and he's watching my hands as I sort through the red and black plastic pieces.

"What do you want to know?"

He's quiet for a second and I hand him a stack of red discs. "How did she die?"

I exhale. "Cancer. Breast cancer. She'd had it before I was born, but it came back when I was eleven. By then it had metastasized in her liver."

"That must have been hard."

I swallow. "Yeah. It was hard. It still is hard."

We fall silent then and I glance out the window. I try not to close up and bolt from the room. All I want to do is run. All I ever want to do is run. And I can't do that anymore. I don't *want* to do that anymore. I want to let him in.

"Did she look like you?"

I glance back at Tucker then. His eyes, with their chocolaty centers, feel more and more like a gift I couldn't have possibly expected. I think of Mom's smile and her sharpened green gaze. I think of her laugh and the way it was more musical than music. I think of everything I've tried to forget.

"She was beautiful," I say quietly.

Tucker reaches out to take my hand. "Then she must have looked like you."

I can't help but smile at that, then sort of shrug.

"She gave me all the best parts of myself." I glance around the room, then look back at Tucker. I know he sees the tears in my eyes and, for once, I don't care. "And I'm going to spend the rest of my life proving it."

Tonight, when I'm alone, I sit down on my bed and face the wall. I have three pictures taped there now. One is of my mom holding a newborn me at the hospital. The second is the Polaroid of Tucker. The last one is a snapshot of me and Cyrus. I think he's eight or so, which would make me six or seven. We're both grinning at the camera; I'm missing a few teeth and Cy's got a cut near his right eyebrow. I remember he got it falling out of a tree at our grandparents' house. A branch had barely missed his eye. By the time the picture was taken, though, he'd gotten over it. That's something I'd always admired about my brother, my role model. He could forget being hurt in favor of being happy.

So, I'm attempting to take a page from my brother's book, attempting to be happy as I'm starting to feel things again—things I haven't felt in longer than I can remember. Things like potential for the college classes I'm taking with Trina. Things like kinship with Aarti and the desire to write Natalie a letter—something I probably should have done a long time ago.

And things like romance. Like the need to be in someone else's arms. Tucker told me Barnes pulled him aside while I was at court and gave him a long lecture about romantic fraternization and rule-breaking and code violation. At the end of it, though, he'd patted his shoulder and said, "Be good to her." Which I guess is the closest thing Tucker and I are going to get to his blessing.

Now I open up my composition book to the page where I'd left my pen tucked inside. Last night, I wrote a poem—my first one ever. I sort of hope it isn't my last. Science and math always seemed to be my strengths. Now I'm not so sure.

I'm beginning to think there could be a place for me in a world that's less brain and more heart.

CANOE

By Cecelia Price

In this life, I've found
we have to be in pairs for balance—

two oars, two life preservers,
one person on each end.

When we row,
it's for the sake of moving.

When we have to jump,
we take a deep breath,

close our eyes
and count to three.

RESOURCES

Drug addictions have tentacles—they twist and turn and wrap around people, making victims of the family members and loved ones on its periphery. If you or someone you know is struggling with the far-reaching effects of addiction, please do not hesitate to contact a local support group or hospital in your area.

You can also visit the following:

Center on Addiction and the Family (COAF)
Toll-free: (888) 286-5027
www.phoenixhouse.org/family/center-on-addiction-and-the-family

Partnership for a Drug-Free America
Toll-free: (855) 378-4373
www.drugfree.org

AUTHOR'S NOTE

We all remember certain days best.

For me, it was one snowy Christmas Eve, when I looked at my strung-out, almost-unrecognizable brother and thought, *Maybe it would be better if he just overdosed and ended it. Then we wouldn't have to do this anymore.*

That was a really horrible moment. When you live in a family invaded by addiction, there are a lot of really horrible moments.

But, unlike Cyrus, my brother is still with us. He has human struggles like the rest of our family, but he has triumphed over a kind of evil that most people will never have to face. As I write this, he's recently reached his fourth year of sobriety. I am proud of him in a way I can't possibly explain in words.

My brother isn't just the hero of his story. He's the hero of *my* story.

It took my brother's sobriety to heal our relationship, just like it took his sobriety for me to write this book. It also took a lot of time and tears and reliving terrible memories. I had to ask my brother questions I didn't want to know the answers to. And, most of all, I had to forgive him. And to forgive myself.

If I could go back in time, I would wish I'd had more empathy as my brother struggled through his addiction. I wish that I'd understood better. In some ways, writing this book has allowed me to leave my anger and my pain behind, to shed the emotions I'd carried for so long. My family is better for what we've gone through. Yes, we are still in recovery. But every day is something like a miracle, something we never really thought we'd get back.

And I wholeheartedly wish that for everyone who knows this struggle—the parents, the children, the siblings, and the addicts themselves—I hope all of you will find what I've found: miracles and empathy and your own personal hero as we all take things one day at a time.

When writing this book, the single most important thing to me was authenticity. In order to create and maintain this authenticity, I tapped into an assortment of sources to capture the varied nuances of families in crisis due to drug addiction. Among those sources were the A&E Network's *Intervention*; *Unguarded: The Chris Herren Story*, by ESPN Films; Current TV's Vanguard series, including *OxyContin Express*, *Gateway to Heroin*, and *Facing the Dragon*; the books *Beautiful Boy*, by

David Sheff, and *Tweak*, by Nic Sheff; the movie *Winter's Bone*; and Lisa Ling's investigation into heroin abuse for *Our America* on OWN.

In addition, the music of the Offspring, Fuel, P!nk, and many others played a key role in my process. I owe these artists a debt of gratitude for writing the kind of songs and creating the kind of music you write books to. Similarly, a handful of excellent, well-crafted novels were my "go-to" tools to help both write and structure this text, most notably *Teach Me*, by R. A. Nelson; *Liar*, by Justine Larbalestier; *Speak*, by Laurie Halse Anderson; *Clean*, by Amy Reed; *Please Ignore Vera Dietz*, by A. S. King; and Sara Zarr's *Story of a Girl*. Also, everything Barbara Kingsolver has ever written. Maybe even her grocery lists.

Lastly, I originally wrote CeCe's poem, "Canoe," for my good friend Ken Robidoux, and a different form of the poem was first published in *Potion* magazine in 2004.

ACKNOWLEDGMENTS

I'm indebted to so very many people.

My agent, Suzie Townsend, whose enthusiasm for this book and my career has brought me here. She understood CeCe from the moment she met her and was willing to be her champion—and mine. Likewise, Joanna Volpe, Kathleen Ortiz, Jaida Temperly, Danielle Barthel, Pouya Shahbazian, Jessica Dallow, Jackie Lindert, David Caccavo, Mackenzie Brady, and everyone at New Leaf Literary have been so welcoming. Thank you for inviting me into this wonderful agency that you've created. It's nice to call it home.

Karen Chaplin is a tremendous editor and her influence is indelible in this book. She was able to push me further and rein me in—it's the best kind of dance you can perform with your editor and I'm beyond grateful. Likewise, I need to thank everyone at Harper Teen, including my cover designers, Erin Fitzsimmons and Kate Engbring; my production editor, Bethany Reis, and copyeditor Daniel Seidel; and Kimberly VandeWater, Olivia Russo, and the rest of marketing, publicity, and sales. Your support has been astounding.

I wrote a lot of words before I met poet Michael Waters, but he's the one who taught me how to write them well. I am indebted to him, as well as to Jim Harms and Mary Ann Samyn. Taking poetry workshops was the best thing to happen to my prose. Likewise, my beta readers—Dahlia Adler, Chelsea Pitcher, and Rachele Alpine—are as much to thank for the coherence of this book as anyone. Their support and kindness have been phenomenal. Without ever meeting in person, I've found three people I trust implicitly with my work.

I am incredibly "lucky" to call myself a Lucky 13. These 2013 debut authors have been friends, confidants, venting outlets, creative muses, and so much more. I owe them all a huge thank-you for their support and words of encouragement, especially Justina Ireland, Karen Akins, and Ellen Oh.

My fellow Binder Mods—Jess, Hebah, Tess, Sharon, and Dahlia—are the best daily sounding boards and cheerleaders with whom I share so much through the magic of Facebook messenger. Thank you, ladies, for always being so willing to listen or commiserate or send stickers of Pusheens. You're the best.

A handful of close friends and family members have been nothing if not supportive, and I owe them a debt of gratitude, especially Matt Fiore, Ali Lazorchak, Katie Wheeler,

Carly Keene, Lauren Martin, Ken Robidoux, Kaite Hillenbrand, the Nichols family, and Danny O'Brien.

I owe Josh Stultz a thank-you of epic proportions: he continues to be my attentive audience, my immovable rock, my willing chauffer, my shoulder to cry on, my photographer, my therapist, my boyfriend, my best friend, and my biggest fan. He keeps me sane and he makes me brave, and I completely love him for it.

My parents are more than just supportive—they were willing to allow me the creative and emotional freedom to explore our struggles as a family in order to write this book. Thank you, Mom and Dad, for being pillars of grace and the strongest people I know.

My son, Max. Darling boy, regardless of where my imagination takes me or where my characters run to, every highway leads me back to you. I love you big much.

Most of all, this book would not exist in any form had it not been for my brother's brave battle with addiction and his commitment to sobriety. I don't even know how to say thank you to him, but I'm so very glad he's still alive to hear me say it. In all ways, this book is for him.

JOIN THE

Epic Reads

COMMUNITY

THE ULTIMATE YA DESTINATION

◄ DISCOVER ►
your next favorite read

◄ MEET ►
new authors to love

◄ WIN ►
free books

◄ SHARE ►
infographics, playlists, quizzes, and more

◄ WATCH ►
the latest videos

◄ TUNE IN ►
to Tea Time with Team Epic Reads

     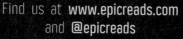